THE BEST OF
Mr Walker

THE BEST OF
Mr Walker

A Collection of
Max Walker's Favourite Stories

HAMLYN

HAMLYN

Published 1992 by Hamlyn Australia,
an imprint of the Octopus Publishing Group,
a division of Reed International Books Australia Pty Ltd
22 Salmon Street, Port Melbourne, Victoria 3207

Designed by Rob Alston
Illustrated by WEG
Typeset in Bookman by Magenta Publishing
Printed in Australia by Magenta Press

National Library of Australia
    cataloguing-in-publications data:

Max Walker, The Best of
A Collection of Max Walker's Favourite Stories.

ISBN 0 947334 51 3

Introduction

We live today in an information society where technology regularly bombards each and every one of us. I believe, as a consequence, we are losing the common art of communicating – talking to one another and telling stories.

When I was a small boy nothing would excite me more than spending hours with my grandparents listening to them describe how life used to be . . . it truly was a wonderful investment of time – the interaction of young and old.

One of the most powerful tools of communication is humour. The ability to laugh at oneself and life's many sticky predicaments, is a valuable asset.

I have discovered writing to be a therapeutic distraction. Many a long night spent pondering alone with my trusty fountain pen, searching for the right sequence of words to unlock the laugh.

I actually became a writer by default. Very early in my television career it became apparent that few script writers were able to consistently capture my turn of phrase. So as a self-imposed discipline I began penning a weekly page for the *Australasian Post*. Over the course of two years 104 articles were completed.

A selection of the best anecdotes formed *How to Hypnotise Chooks* – a title which took much time to sell to the publisher. Incredibly it proved to be an enormous success. The positive verbal and written feedback encouraged me to write more.

How to Tame Lions, *How to Kiss a Crocodile* and *How to Puzzle a Python* followed in quick succession.

A warped Tasmanian sense of humour has certainly helped the flow of tales.

. . . I trust this collection of my favourite stories brings more than a chuckle or two and thanks again to everyone who supported my literary efforts with the past four titles. Words are not sufficient to express my gratitude.

Max

To my wife, Kerry, who is everything a man could wish for and our beautiful baby daughter, Alexandra. Together they provide much love and laughter in my life . . . a reason to smile every day.

Contents

CHAPTER ONE

Growing Pains at the Empire

**The more my stick of chalk came to the tip of its beak,
the more cross-eyed it became.**

Learning to Hypnotise Chooks

"HE WAS HAVING A LOT OF TROUBLE TRYING TO STAY ON THE PERCH"

When it comes to eating it would be fair to say I'm not too bad on the old fang.

But after eating chicken for dinner at nine out of every ten speaking engagements for the last decade – I'm about up to my adam's apple on "chook".

Don't get me wrong I still appreciate the odd Chicken Kiev but I am now in the ideal position to understand how former Australian vice-captain and opening batsman Keith Stackpole built up such a strong dislike for eating chicken while in the Caribbean during the 1973 cricket tour of the West Indies.

During that tour we ate chicken, or should I say very, very wild water fowl morning, noon and night, with the odd variation being curried goat, fried rice and twenty-three different varieties of blow flies.

Actually the color of the chicken meat served up to us varied from white, as it should be, to a sickly looking brown, to a greyish hue and camouflaged with a different type and colour of gravy at each meal. My goodness, many of those water birds were tough, too!

At one evening sitting in Guyana I can vividly remember Dougie Walters attacking a very brownish "drumstick" with a serrated-edged knife – it literally ricocheted off the flesh and bounced back towards him. He traded his chicken dish for something a little more palatable and definitely easier to eat – tomato soup!

I appear to have been plagued by these feathered "friends" all my life – and I suppose the odd first ball "duck" too! Even as a kid, they used to cause more than their fair share of trouble!

I think I was about fourteen years old at the time, on a Saturday the week before Easter. Halfway through the afternoon Dad was pulling beer in the bar of the Tasmanian pub he owned when this character came in. He walked straight up to the old man and asked him if he'd care to buy half a dozen "fresh" chooks.

"How much?" asked Dad. Five bob was the reply.

"Are you sure they're fresh?" Dad followed up, with more than a passing amount of interest. In those days five bob was a pretty good price for fresh poultry.

The chap immediately produced a flour sack on the bar counter and proffered the birds for inspection. They were fresh, right enough. In fact they were barely cold.

The hotel proprietor examined each one critically, hefting them to test their weight, pinching their tails for plumpness, and flexing their breastbones to gauge their age. Each apparently passed this professional judgment satisfactorily because Dad made a counter offer.

"Give you four and sixpence," he said.

"Make it four and ninepence."

"Done," said my old man, who went to the till, counted out one pound, eight shillings and sixpence, gave it to the bloke (who immediately bought half a dozen bottles and left) and took the chooks through to the kitchen and gave them to Elvie the cook.

Shortly afterwards a couple of customers came back from the toilet with a most unusual complaint. "Max," they said to Dad, "you'd better get out the back – your toilets are blocked."

When we went out to investigate, a quite astounding sight greeted us. The place was covered in entrails, heads and feathers from wall to wall. It didn't take much figuring out to realise that the recently departed poultry purveyor had killed, cleaned and plucked the beasts in the gents.

This prompted Dad to make a hasty visit to the kitchen and warn the cook that perhaps she should take a little extra care when washing the birds.

All of this was bad enough – I was given the job of cleaning up the mess – but the punchline came at about six o'clock next morning when the yardman banged on Dad's door.

"Hey, Max," he said, "you'd better get down to the chook yard. Six of yer best layers are missing."

My father was about the only person who didn't enjoy Easter dinner!

After replacing the six missing hens I used one of the new ones for an unusual experiment – I'd read somewhere that chooks were very easy to hypnotise . . . so I followed the instructions very closely. The hard part was catching one. When I entered the fowl yard I was viewed as an unwelcome intruder! Nevertheless, I soon snatched a black one from behind, grabbed it by the legs and immediately turned the unlucky bird over and placed it on its back.

As suggested, I began to drag a piece of chalk across the abrasive concrete path surface which was now supporting the upturned chook's head.

The closer my stick of chalk came to the tip of its beak the more cross-eyed it became until finally the chalk stopped hard up against the bewildered bird's head. Success, one hypnotised fowl.

I stood back a pace to admire my effort in rendering the laying bird motionless when Paddy my pedigree boxer dog swooped on the poor unfortunate thing. And, with barely the bright red crown showing from the corner of the dog's mouth, my pet made off with my subject.

Unfortunately for the squawking chook it took me several minutes to track my dog down . . . there he was, glint in his eye, feathers hanging out of his mouth like a red indian chief's head-dress!

Paddy had himself and the chook jammed into a tight little space hard up against the back fence and between the fowl-house. Yes, my fine feathered friend had been plucked from the eyeballs down to the nape of its neck, and it wasn't liking it either. Well, you couldn't blame it.

To this day I still don't know how to snap a chook out from under its hypnotic spell. My friendly canine pet had achieved that end for me without even knowing it. It really was a pathetic sight to see this strange, half-strangled red neck stagger across the fowl yard to rejoin his mates.

At that stage he was having a lot of trouble staying on the perch, so, the obvious happened! He ended up on the meal table of the Walker household that night.

As for the dog, well . . . he'd got a taste for the feathered variety.

Even without drawing any blood the beautifully proportioned four legged animal enjoyed what he did.

This first encounter perhaps was the reason for several future escapades by Paddy, the chooks' friend. After all, they are such a playful breed of dog . . . the more reaction to their playing, the more they want to play. Our cook could vouch for that every time she put out the rubbish!

The last straw came about twelve months later when the neighbouring veterinary surgeon lobbed in the hotel foyer demanding to see Dad.

"Your dog's just killed fourteen of my chooks . . . and what are you going to do about it?" he said rather gruffly.

Dad said, "It couldn't be our dog because he's in our back yard . . . anyway he wouldn't do that sort of thing!" I knew better – he was my dog!

"You want proof?" demanded the red faced vet. "Yes," answered my old man rather smugly.

Well you should have seen it! There he was, my beautiful tan boxer dog being dragged bodily through the front door of the pub by his silver studded collar, head at forty-five degrees to the vertical but looking ever so pleased with himself. The tell-tale signs were sticking to the saliva dribbling from his mouth. He must have had fifty feathers stuffed in his choppers!

Paddy had climbed the metal fire escape stairs and up a 30 degree inclined corrugated iron roof to the ridge.

The dog must have dug in his toe-nails on the way down the other side . . . then crashed into the box guttering and parapet wall. After recovering from the slide he probably plucked up enough courage to leap five metres into the adjoining yard full of hens – with catastrophic results.

My dad had to buy fourteen fully feathered squawking hens and unfortunately Paddy, my mate, was found guilty and received "life" on a country property.

Every day a new adventure!

Rations for an Old Digger

"A BIT OF MUD AND CLAY ADDED FLAVOUR"

Growing up at my dad's Empire Hotel in North Hobart, Tasmania, a good beer drinking pub, I was able to witness firsthand a lot of crazy, memorable characters – some will stay etched in my mind forever.

Perhaps the most unforgettable was Eck Sonners – a very different man whether listening to him talk or watching him go about his daily chores.

Eck had a problem with his sight. I think it would be fair to say that his glasses were every bit as thick as the base of a coca cola bottle. When you peered at his eyes through those large lenses it looked a lot like a double serving of oysters kilpatrick – there was only a blur of grey blue colour on the white background. I can't imagine what it looked like from Eck's side!

He was an incredible guy, and as a young boy I used to love him because he was so friendly. A gentle bloke from a very religious family and also one of the best pick and shovel men my old man, Big Max, ever had. Boy, did Eck know how to dig a trench. He really had a passion for it . . . beautiful clean cut edges, no fill or rubble fell back into the bottom and the walls were always vertical – a real artist with the long handle.

Eck used to take his lunch to work on the building sites, and what extraordinary meals they proved to be. He wouldn't eat bread unless it was at least a week old and covered in mould. The pick 'n' shovel maestro also had a taste for steak that had turned green!

Ol' Eck enjoyed nothing more than chucking a slimy slab of raw beef on top of his dirty old shovel – a covering of mud and clay added 'flavour' – put the recipe skilfully into the coals of the site fire and then whack it onto a slice of stale bread complete with healthy, furry growth on the outside. Eck would really chomp into the sandwich, delighting his taste buds with every bite. Often I could see his false teeth pop out half an inch further than they ought to . . . only to be sucked back in at the critical point.

Everyone would stare at him, swallow in reaction, feeling a combination of disgust and disbelief. How could anyone possibly put that much dirt and mould into his mouth? Old Eck used to wash it down with the contents of an old billy. Three or four spins above his head to consolidate the brew, and down the hatch, tea leaves and all. Beautiful! Five star dining.

After a dirty day's digging in the trenches, Eck would make a regular dash to my dad's hotel on the corner of Burnett and Elizabeth Streets to whet his whistle and have a welcome yarn to some of the other loyal clientele.

The wharfies would come in and often drink us out of beer – Tango Ford and his sons were very regular – like clockwork. We used to have some women drinkers, too. Women were not allowed by law to drink in the main bar. Instead they would quench their thirst in the mixed bar – the 'Snake Pit'. Decor consisted of a basic green fleck laminex and chrome trimmed setting of table and chairs. On every table was a plastic ashtray – spartan to say the least. Drink, smoke and talk.

In those days, when I was about eleven years old, women could buy a Seppelts Solero Sherry for twenty cents. Some of the ladies, sadly, were every bit as devoted to the demon drink as the permanent gents – still seated on the same bar stool twelve hours after arriving . . . at 10 p.m. closing. And when the doors re-opened next day they were again waiting to place an unsteady hand on their first for the day.

Eck used to park his bum on a particular stool each night. The drink would always be the same . . . a sort of ritual.

"Give me a whisky . . . a straight whisky with a wee dash of milk!" he'd confirm. His sweaty hat rested on the bar to the right of his drink – a short stretch away. Below his left elbow on the black vinyl tiled floor, surrounded by cigarette butts, was his trusty old gladstone bag – limp from years of rough 'n' tough service.

I will never forget one dreadful night that was catastrophic for old Eck. He slowly walked out the pub door, and went to cross the road to buy a feed of fish and chips. The night was clear . . . about seven o'clock.

The traffic at the intersection was usually heavy at this hour. A large set of traffic lights and a pedestrian crossing were the only obstacles between Eck and his meal. But the worst happened. Eck, who couldn't see too far in front of himself at the best of times, ambled halfway across and was knocked over by a speeding car.

From inside the hotel the screeching sound of rubber on bitumen was followed by a sickening thud of metal against body, then the tinkle of shattered glass.

Within seconds the total occupants of the front bar were anxious onlookers to the accident. Without asking the question, our friend couldn't be at fault . . . after all, what are mates for?

He was a very tough nail our Eck and built like a gnarled old oak tree. Fortunately the labourer was still in one piece – far from down and out for the count. His precious glasses were shattered on the road like a broken soft drink bottle. His vision was distorted but he also discovered his beloved old pipe was snapped in half. He began to see red!

It didn't matter that the car's headlights were smashed or that Eck had blood streaming from a gash in his shoulder and another wound down the side of his jaw. He gave the driver the most almighty 'serve' you could ever expect to hear. Not because he ran into him but because his trusty pipe had been broken!

But after a close inspection it proved to be nothing another whisky without the milk, and the right application of glue wouldn't fix.

The hotel's cook, dear old Elvie, a lovely lady, took Eck under her protective wing. She'd do just about anything for Eck, including leaving a meal for him when he wanted. It was far safer than crossing the busy road to the fish and chip shop!

Elvie used to feed me too – well, force feed was probably closer to it. She made me eat all those dreadful vegetables – cauliflower, cabbage, swedes, brussel sprouts, spinach. But I can't really complain, I've grown into a healthy big lad. My sister and I used to enjoy a terrific breakfast and the tupperware 'special' for school – cut lunch and a piece of fruit. Not too flash when every other kid was sinking his teeth into a meat pie and sauce or a sticky bun. In hindsight I can't thank Elvie enough for monitoring my intake. How big would I be had she not?

She didn't have to be nearly as selective when appealing to Eck's taste buds.

Another evening it was pretty much business as normal at the Empire Hotel. Eck had a few scotches, a cup of milk and then reckoned it was about time he tackled his feed. The hour was late, about 9.30, and Elvie had by this stage gone home well and truly. But the pub was not shut yet, so my dad suggested to Eck, "You better slip out back for a bite, Eck, or otherwise you are going to miss out tonight."

Away he trotted, out of the smoke-filled bar down the corridor, through the grey swing door and into the kitchen. In the kitchen was a typical huge industrial stove which contained eight different hotplates, and there were lots of pots and pans everywhere, several full, some empty.

If it was late, Eck always found his food plate balanced on a pot of boiling water with a saucepan lid placed on top. That would keep it warm until he was ready to eat and I suppose many people still do the same these days, if a microwave isn't handy.

Sometime later he lobbed back into the crowded bar to sink one for the footpath. He reckoned it was the best feed he'd ever had in his life, "Gee Max," he said, "Elvie's gone to a lot of trouble, she left me a lot more food than what she normally does. Maybe you haven't got too many in the house tonight, but gee it was one hell of a feed." So a happy Eck went home with a full tummy.

At 6.30 the next morning, Elvie came in as usual. Before she cooked breakfast for anyone, she used to always take the scraps down to the fowl yard out back. Into the chooks she'd chuck all the scraps – bones, tea leaves, soggy pieces of bread, half eaten spuds, blobs of custard – you name it, the chooks would love it.

All had been collected the night before in Elvie's slops container – a large black boiler – which she had left on top of the stove. The oversize boiler was there all right . . . but there was absolutely nothing in it. Clean as a whistle.

Sure enough, eggs, steak and chips – the meal Elvie had left for Eck – was still sitting on top of the other pot, cold and untouched, with the lid seated on top of it.

Later, that morning the poor old chooks were having heaps of trouble trying to peck into a piece of dried out steak, eggs like leather soles and withered chips resembling strands of frayed rope . . .

I guess Eck left me with his home-spun philosophy that evening – everything doesn't necessarily have to be neat 'n' tidy, proper and conventional to be good. Eck, you're special.

A Pain in the Rear End

"MAYBE HE JUST LIKED OUR DUNNY"

Living in a pub during my early adolescent years brought me face-to-face with many great characters.

One of the more colourful identities who would regularly pay us a visit was a large tram conductor – I'm not sure of his name! Not that I ever spoke to him – all I did was stare!

Just like clockwork, almost to the minute every day at about 10.15 a.m. this giant of a man, dressed in his plain, navy blue tramways uniform would sneak in through the Burnett Street entrance to the pub – hoping nobody would spot him as he urgently raced down the corridor to the gents' toilet and relief!

His constitution must have been like clockwork too – at the same time, at the same place, every day of the working week! Or maybe he merely appreciated our dunny – we'll never know!

The potential Tasmanian sumo wrestler used to time his waddle beautifully, despite not being blessed with much natural pace. Off he'd scamper as soon as the driver had stopped the tram! The driver then 'clocked on' at the green tramway key clock, fixed to an ageing telegraph post, not far from the traffic lights at the corner of Elizabeth and Burnett Streets, diagonally across from the red brick building known to all affectionately as the Empire! A good beer drinking hotel.

Generally, this stopover used to last between two or three red light changes . . . the break also gave his driver a chance to have a quiet smoke!

Looking back, the catastrophic events of one visit were very funny to everyone present at the watering hole at the time except for our overweight, lead-footed clippy!

It wasn't No. 1's he wanted to do, it definitely was No. 2's – some belly ache, eh? All twenty-five stone of him rumbling . . . the mind boggles! Probably two or three pies inside that stomach without even teethmarks on them. He was a ginormous man!

Well, it just so happened our desperate hulk of a man was similar to the late Howard Hughes – a cleanliness freak! Worried about catching something off the toilet seat and all that silly rot.

It was a silly consideration anyway because the sparkling white porcelain bowls didn't have a timber seat and plastic wasn't invented then! There were too many vandals around and the odd, eccentric alcoholic who thought they'd make a good picture frame. So my dad Big Max cut his costs and left his clientele to put up with an occasional cold bottom during the winter months.

Observing and accepting this fact, our regular trammie somehow used to climb successfully on top of the bowl to avoid contamination and engaged in the 'kangaroo' style squat. The fragile porcelain fixture was supporting his entire body weight because both feet are on either side of the pan. But that's not the end of the story.

Unfortunately for him that day, the porcelain bowl could stand no further strain and shattered during proceedings with disastrous effects . . . I heard the poor man's awful scream in the kitchen. By the time I rushed to the WC to see what was happening, he'd courageously staggered out to the well-patronised main bar.

He'd waddled out to the packed main bar.

There he stood – his blue trousers crumpled around his thick, hairy ankles. Blood was streaming down his right hamstring from a nasty deep gash in his buttocks. The injured colossus wasn't a pretty sight and I was standing behind him! It took a doctor and twenty-three stitches to stem the flow.

All the time he stood there, he shouted profanities about Big Max and his bloody toilets.

The 'fallen hero' of Hobart's trams was going to sue my dad for having faulty fittings in his toilets and causing grievous bodily harm.

Some months later, the case did go before the courts of Hobart . . . the judge had this to say in his summation of the unfortunate incident, "In my view it was an unnatural technique for a normal action. Had the victim had both feet on the ground at the time of the accident, he may have had a case, but he didn't! Case dismissed!"

I suppose you can be unlucky.

Funny how after that the tram never used to stay long at the tramway clock on the corner of Burnett and Elizabeth Streets, North Hobart. After the grief it caused, the conductor must have spent weeks getting over the injury, with his right cheek buried in a tractor inner tube . . . well, it wouldn't fit in a car tube, would it?

One of my other favourite characters was a poor nameless soul who lived on sweet sherry. He had a face that had done a million miles, heavy lines etched deep into his leathery skin, in fact, his mouth was like a torn pocket.

Above his bushy eyebrows was a beautifully polished bald head with a horseshoe shaped layer of hair softening the shape of his XXOS ears. Those large ears were something else. They looked for all the world like a huge set of amplifiers and not much got past them either!

He had been banned from the premises more often than bartenders could remember. Yet, he still continued to drink at the Empire. Always in a stupor, his survival prompted an amusing albeit predictable performance from staff and drinkers. As he was ushered from one bar, he would take to the street, and immediately enter another doorway. Five steps forward and three steps back . . . it was a struggle, but he always succeeded in getting to the next bar.

After being ejected from all three hotel bars in quick succession, our mate headed for the main entrance – office, dining and accommodation area. Unfortunately he was confronted by Big Max . . . immediately his bloodshot eyeballs stood out like a new range of billiard balls. Both feet left the ground simultaneously, searching for traction as he was grabbed by the scruff of the neck.

Before Big Max could boot him up the backside and out the door he asked the ultimate question: "How many more bloody hotels in Hobart do you own, Max?"

Sordid Saga of the Money Box

"SHE LEAPT NAKED FROM THE BED, SWEARING LIKE A WHARFIE"

For a young man barely past the age of puberty, a hotel was probably not the ideal place in which to be brought up. Nevertheless, it did provide me with a wonderful street education.

At the age of fourteen, I believed I truly was a man of the world after witnessing the arrest of Francey-Ann, a prostitute with flaming red hair, who was known as much for her fits of rage as for the services offered at unexceptional rates.

My adventure began when my sister Lexie reported that her money box and beloved Beatles record collection had been stolen. The police were called promptly and officers immediately made a search of the twelve accommodation rooms at the hotel.

They were hardly surprised to find the goods in a room occupied – that is when schedules dictated – by Francey-Ann.

At the time of the police raid, she was in bed with a very drunk Chinese sailor. The lady was very upset by the intrusion and in the most colourful language possible told police officers, hotel staff and yours truly that these accusations were a very serious slur on her impeccable character.

My vantage point through all this was the narrow crack in the slightly ajar door.

Offended by the barrage of laughter her remarks had drawn, she became enraged. Swearing like a wharfie, she leapt naked from the bed and threw her stiletto-heeled shoes at the nearest police officer.

As policemen queued for the right to make the necessary rugby tackle, she made for the window.

The police then thwarted her get-away bid and while two burly officers held her by the ankles to make sure she did not complete a dive from the second storey window, the tiny sailor slowly dressed in silence and exited quietly.

Francey-Ann was charged with possession of stolen goods, prostitution, resisting arrest and a few other offences, while her amorous client returned to the docks.

For many weeks, I was the toast of the school yard as my friends and others gathered to hear my version of how Francy-Ann was apprehended. I might add that with each hearing I used artistic

Swearing like a wharfie, she leapt naked from the bed.

licence and added what might be termed embellishments – for my dad once told me: "Son, never muck up a good story for the facts."

The pub provided me with the opportunity to hear and tell many a yarn. Not all were as titillating as FA, but nevertheless, it was this early environment which encouraged me to share my experiences – some seamy, but many humorous.

Next door to our hotel was the oil-caked premises of Frank Hammond Pty Ltd, Trucking Services. The company carried many consignments of 44-gallon drums, and often had drums, both full and empty, stored at the bottom of the yard. On one unusually hot day the metal drums expanded, the bungs leaked and tar oozed out under the fence into the fowl yard at the back of the Empire Hotel.

When Elvie, the cook, went to feed our fowls at about five o'clock, she found some of them stuck and the tar beginning to set hard. My old man immediately assured Elvie and myself that everything was under control and that the situation could be remedied easily.

He strode confidently into the fowl yard and put both hands under one of the fowls and vigorously pulled it from its fixing. Believe me, the technique was crude, but very effective, except that its feet and drumsticks stayed anchored in the black tar.

Not easily deterred, the Master Builder produced a chisel from his tool box and as delicately as possible chipped around the feet of another stunned hen, leaving it with two solid black squares of tar stuck to its claws – like licorice.

That worked, too, except that it could not fly and kept slipping off the perch. The final result was that this hen and a few of her mates died of fatigue four days later.

A witness to all this was a great pal of mine, Paddy, the pet boxer dog. Unfortunately, I did not have the same control over him as I occasionally had with a cricket ball.

Paddy was well-known to the drinkers at the establishment and was the nemesis of postmen, policemen on the beat, women in expensive hose and children intent on stealing empty soft drink bottles from the bottom of the back yard.

To the acute embarrassment of Big Max, Paddy's name was on file at the Tasmanian Tourist Bureau.

A most incredible happening led to him being regarded as an impediment to local tourism.

As a kid, I enjoyed many hours playing cricket with reprobates, who spent most of their waking hours at the hotel. I would lure them into batting or bowling as they went to and from the gents' lavatory at the back of the building.

One such time, a drunk managed to straight drive me through the open window of one of the accommodation bedrooms. The ball bounced off the window sill, landing on the lap of an unsuspecting guest resting on a bed. Paddy, who was trained to retrieve cricket and tennis balls, scrambled up the metal fire escape stairs on to the roof and from the window ledge leapt on to the guest's rib cage to recover the ball. And he was successful.

The incident must have frightened ten years off our resident's life.

The indignant visitor promptly contacted the Tasmanian Tourist Bureau, asked for alternative accommodation and implored officers not to send any more guests to the Empire as there was a mad adolescent armed with a cricket ball and a wild dog loose in the grounds.

On another occasion my dad had to call on his carpentry skills as a result of Paddy's appetite.

The sight of raw steak being beaten by the kitchen staff so over-whelmed the dog that he crashed through the window, showering glass and pinning Elvie, resplendent in her white pinafore, to the floor.

In a gesture of apology, he licked the cook's face before chewing the tassels of her well-worn slippers and making off with the meat. Too shrewd, my mate.

Dying for a Laugh

"THE FIRST YEAR BOYS USED TO GET PUT IN THE COFFIN"

Recently I was reading a newspaper and the headline stated, "Mourners sent home as coffin jammed in grave." The article reminded me of a couple of stories my dad – Max Walker senior – used to often tell. As always he embellished the truth to make them even more interesting . . . well, as interesting as a story about coffins can get, without being offensive to someone.

You see, a young man was learning his trade as a carpenter and joiner under the watchful eye of one Mr Tom Lipscombe, one of the largest and most successful builders in Hobart of the time. One of his company's lesser contracts was to supply local funeral parlours with all of their coffins, depending on the demand.

In those days the basic coffin was constructed from the now precious timber, Huon pine, about 1¼ inches (32 mm) thick. The shoulders were bent with a saw-cut and glued while the bottom was made from banana cases and a sheet of waterproof sisal paper – much better than today's supermarket version!

Once enough of these sombre capsules were completed they'd be piled onto a lorry about six high by ten coffins long, and then delivered to the undertaker.

I believe on one occasion Mr Lipscombe's company ran foul of the health department because the naked truck load of coffins was not covered from public view by a tarpaulin – how terrible! Once you're dead you're dead, and all the germs or contamination in the world aren't going to make an ounce of difference. But if you're alive . . . well, that's a different matter as I'll describe.

As is the case with most apprentices, there is always an initiation ceremony – the first year boys used to get "planted" in a coffin, and the lid nailed down.

One day while the boss was out, a startled young man named Timothy underwent the ordeal. He seemed to fit snugly into the unlined coffin, according to my old man. The lid was then tightly nailed down amidst some very abusive language – I couldn't blame him!

After approximately half an hour of carrying the poor guy around the workshop on timber studs, mocking pall bearers and mourners, the boss unexpectedly arrived back at work to see this weird ritual going on.

"What are you blokes doing there?" he said.

"Picking it up to see if it's balanced sir!" came the reply in unison.

"Where's Timothy?" asked Mr Lipscombe. "Gone to lunch, sir!" the mischievous wood workers shouted, in order to muffle Tim's protestations.

No sooner had the boss man disappeared down the stairs than the coffin was placed on the dirty timber floor of the carpenter's workshop to continue the initiation. Heaps of shavings and blocks were quickly shovelled on to it as if falling dirt was filling up a grave-site.

Meanwhile my "father-to-be" began reciting the last rites on the poor fellow: " . . . On the green hills far away . . . may he rest in peace . . . for thine is the Kingdom, the power and the glory, for ever and ever, Amen. God rest his soul!"

Again another stifled shout for help! Timothy had now been in the coffin for almost 1½ hours – poor lad!!!

Finally the bullies let the terrified apprentice out of the coffin . . . it was like a jack in a box. He leapt out of the pine masterpiece and raced down the stairs screaming about a lot of mad crazy fellows upstairs and adamant he would definitely not be coming back!

My old man confided it did take a long time before he came back to work.

Then there was a real funeral – a dear friend of my dad's.

As the four impeccably dressed pall bearers carried the beautifully polished, ornate coffin from the church to the waiting hearse, the bottom half of the coffin sub-stratum pulled away from the upper coffin . . . remember, today these bases are only made of a compacted fibreboard and fixed by staples to the upper section of the box.

Two of the quick thinking pall bearers shoved the dead man's legs and coffin base back to where it ought to have been – saving an awkward situation, but the solution was only temporary.

On the walk from the hearse to the cut in the ground at the cemetery, the other half of the sub-strata opened up. Nevertheless the funeral proceeded, placing the coffin over the burial site in the usual manner.

Worse was to come. As the ledges were removed and the coffin lowered into the badly dug grave, it jammed, so the ropes were loosened from the under-side of the coffin.

The priest suggested to one of the grave-diggers that maybe a gentle tap on the offending coffin corner would work. As you can imagine the results were nothing short of catastrophic.

The grave-digger feared the lid might move and open up but no one could have predicted the body falling out the bottom and resting on the grave floor.

It was a terrible ordeal for the mourners to witness and embarrassing for the priest who promptly told everyone to leave the area while some very hasty repairs were done and the poor fellow resurrected back into the coffin.

Needless to say more research and modern technology are needed in coffin construction! I only hope when I visit the great MCG in the sky that the silly so-and-so making my coffin gets enough staples into the sub strata. Because by then I could be a big lad – well I'm a big bloke now, but wait 'til I finish growing!

Maybe I should put my architectural skills to work and design a decent coffin with a damp-proof concrete slab floor and cedar-lined internal walls and a solar-panelled lid. The mind boggles.

Rest in peace.

Pointing in the Right Direction

"BAZZA MACKENZIE WOULD HAVE BEEN PROUD OF HIM"

I can vaguely remember the night. It was New Year's Eve, 1962. A few months earlier I had celebrated my fourteenth birthday with a few school mates – the strongest drink in sight that night was Coca Cola. How, in the course of just three months, things can change, eh?

Being a young man of inquiring mind, and also the son of a hotel proprietor meant that a glass of beer and I weren't exactly strangers. In fact, it was not unusual for my old man to allow me the taste of an odd beer or two. His theory was he might as well give it to me himself rather than hear of his boy acquiring the amber fluid by devious means. And that was fair enough!

But he took his philosophy a step further amidst those New Year's Eve celebrations at our hotel – the Empire Hotel, Elizabeth Street, North Hobart. My dad had decided to deter my liking for the front bar's standard line – a 7 oz with a head please!

His efforts proved to be fairly successful as I recall. After about sixteen glasses of beer which I had been unknowingly encouraged to consume, it was my opinion I'd had enough. So had my thirteen-year-old cousin Michael, who had also unwittingly become a victim!

It had already been a big night for all concerned, especially the Empire Darts Club players who were enjoying the contents of a free keg of Cascade. Supper consisted of a huge feed of fish and chips from George's Fish Supply. Michael and I had placed the order and delivered the goods, much to the delight of the beer-swilling crowd.

My father, "Big Max", threatened us with a fate worse than death if we didn't drink another two glasses of beer. A difficult task too, because I could feel the water line inside my body around the gum line on my bottom teeth – and that is full!

No sooner had my younger cousin emptied his final 7 oz glass, than Big Max who, by the way stood about 6'3" and weighed seventeen stone at least, picked the little fellow up in both hands, raising him above his head.

It only took about three revolutions, like a helicopter blade cutting the air, for this exercise to take effect. Michael landed at the base of the staircase leading to the house guests' rooms. He took one step, and threw the entire contents of his tummy on to the eighth step of the floral carpeted stair with all his heart and soul. Bazza MacKenzie would have been proud of him!

I really did feel crook. Someone suggested I ought to go to bed – I agreed. The only problem being that the moment my head touched the pillow, the walls started spinning and the ceiling closed in on me! Some smarty said, "Why don't you turn him over? That'll fix him!"

It did, because moments later I too became very ill – and those hotel room hand basins only hold so much, don't they?

My lesson had been learned the hard way – my dad had succeeded.

Four years later, the time following my Matriculation exams, gave me an appropriate excuse to sample the fire water again but I was still to be convinced of its merits!

By January, 1967, my sporting career had taken me to Melbourne to play Australian Rules football with the Melbourne Football Club. This also enabled me to pursue my cricket ambitions with the Melbourne Cricket Club and to study architecture at the Royal Melbourne Institute of Technology.

In those days I aspired to be a Test batsman but my efforts in my district cricket debut were not sensational. No wicket for 45 runs off five overs was the result in my first match and a duck first ball with the bat.

But when I took five wickets in just my second outing in district cricket it seemed a fair enough reason to 'break out' again. My drinking partner for the night was team-mate, Peter Smith, the son of legendary Melbourne Football Club coach, the late Norman Smith. Norm was the man who would coach me in my first VFL game of football against North Melbourne.

As I was new in Melbourne, Peter Smith invited me to stay over at his place, especially since the game in question was played just up the road from his parents' house at Pascoe Vale.

Peter and I arrived home around midnight in less than a fantastic state. How we drove between the two brick posts into the neat driveway still amazes me.

Now the Smith family was a very close-knit family. Whilst I wobbled from left to right in the coach's bedroom doorway, Pete attempted to kiss his mum goodnight. The result was . . . Peter landed on top of a sleeping Norm on the other side of the bed and caught him a nasty blow to the groin with his knee . . . what a way to be woken up, eh?

At this stage the atmosphere in the house was electric. It really isn't much fun when you're in a strange house with nowhere to go.

Marj, Pete's mum, was really paying out on him, when she turned to me and said, "You boys have been drinking, haven't you?" I replied honestly saying, "Yes, just a little." I didn't sleep much that night – maybe I felt guilty?

Daylight arrived all too soon. This time it was Norm who was paying out on Peter – he was in tears as he left the house through the back door.

What does a bloke do when his mate's in trouble – you try to help. So I followed my mate to the door when I heard Norm say, "Pull up a chair son."

I was frozen because I had heard some of those vivid stories of Norm Smith verbally ripping strips of flesh from many of his senior players in the privacy of the property steward's room at the MCG. I too had seen grown men leave that room with wet eyes and emotionally shaken by the words of the red-haired coach.

As I pulled up the chair my eyes focused on the red and white fleck laminex table top. Marj was doing the washing up – you wouldn't reckon a woman doing a small amount of washing up could make so much noise.

The next twenty minutes or so were quite revealing. My future senior coach described my obligations to the Melbourne Football

Club, himself, my parents and most of all, myself. At this stage I had not attended any pre-season practice for the MFC – that was to begin in late January.

We eye-balled each other for the first time that morning. He set about philosophising about the pros and cons of drinking so clearly, that as I look back on my entire sporting career, both football and cricket, this was the most important moment of my life. It was at this point that I decided not to have another drink.

His parting words on the subject were, "We will not discuss this topic again, you're big enough and ugly enough to make up your own mind."

I knew he meant it too – then he challenged me to a game of tennis. At fifty plus years of age, yes, Norm Smith proved too hot for me to handle. Down I went 6-1, 6-1, 6-0 even at that age the man was a fierce competitor.

Time passed rapidly during the next couple of years for me as new challenges appeared almost daily. My life's commitment was now to being successful at VFL football, cricket and also as a student of architecture.

Not many challenges were more difficult than the rejection almost daily of the great Aussie invitation "D'ya wanna beer, mate?" There was continual pressure by my peer group to "Go for it" as they'd say or, "Don't be weak." Believe me it took a lot of strength to say, no and mean it.

Things may have changed a lot these days and even towards the end of my cricket career I might have indulged in just one or two. Ask any of my friends at Bay 13 or fine leg at the MCG or any other ground for that matter.

When I accepted a spectator's drink, I was accepting them and their mates. It would immediately open up a line of communication. There probably is no better way to have a chat over a drink whether it be in a bar or at the cricket.

I've made some great friends on the other side of the fence. Late in the day, under the hot burning sun, they can come in pretty handy. At some grounds you can almost nominate your drink. BUT a word of warning: make sure YOU pull the top off the can, because boys will be boys and they will get up to some terrible tricks if you let them.

I suppose the moral of the story is, if you want to be successful at anything, you must first assess the cost and just how badly you want to be successful. Unfortunately you can't be one of the boys every night of the week and a talented athlete on weekends – the scales will never balance.

Fortunately for me I ran into Norm Smith at the right time of my life – I thank him very much for pointing me in the right direction.

*Really it wasn't even a challenge. I pretended to be helpful by
. . . picking up a piece of wayward chalk.*

Reading, 'Riting and the Cuts

"HER AIM WAS PERFECT,
WHACK! WHACK! WHACK!"

Can you remember getting the cuts at school? Gee, I certainly can. Those were the days when a classroom consisted of a rectangular-shaped room, with a blackboard at the front. No open-planned study areas, calculators, television monitors or computers.

Chalk and the blackboard were used for instruction. Reading, 'Riting and 'Rithmetic – the 3Rs.

Discipline was basic too! If you did the wrong thing then you got into trouble. For a minor misdemeanor the teacher in charge got to dish out the punishment, but for a serious offence it was a rendezvous with the headmaster.

I doubt if anyone could pass through a decent education system without getting into strife sooner or later.

In my case it was pretty often I guess, but then again I have never professed to be an angel . . .

My first taste of the cane was delivered by a dottery, little old lady named "Old Ma Hughes". She must have been ninety at the time.

In many ways she was an unforgettable character . . . deep lines of experience were etched into her face. Dangling from her witch-like chin were five or six strands of silver hair – the subject of much sarcastic back-chatting from her students.

I'd run foul of the old lady because ego got the better of me. Stupidly I accepted a challenge to place one or two 'stink bombs' in the old lady's hair, while she was writing on the blackboard.

Stink bombs, as we called them, were created from biting the tiny seeds from one of Tasmania's native flowers and depositing a fair lathering of saliva on the gaping flesh. The result was a vulgar lingering rotten-egg smell.

Really the dare wasn't even a challenge. I pretended to be helpful by creeping up behind the skinny and fragile little teacher, picking up a piece of wayward chalk from the bare timber floor boards. Quick as a flash I placed the "bomb" in her hairnet, before handing over the chalk.

It was a great laugh for a while . . . until she could stand the odour no more! In fact she discreetly asked if anyone was having trouble with flatulence, but nobody understood what the strange word meant.

The back row of the classroom of which I was a member, couldn't help themselves, and burst into loud laughter. At the same time the teacher's pet, named Annette (butter wouldn't melt in her mouth), dobbed us in . . . me in particular.

Well, time for the cane. The little old lady was blue in the face after standing on a stool to reach the old faithful willowy piece of branch hidden carefully on top of the stained hardwood cupboard, near the stage. To say the teacher was upset would have been an understatement.

"Hand out, Walker!" she shouted.

She then launched herself off the 300 mm high platform with all her might . . . her aim was perfect. Whack! Whack! Whack! Whack! Four of the best in quick succession. There was a stunned silence in the classroom as I struggled to hold back my feelings.

I didn't plant stink bombs in her hair ever again.

But I did put a frog in Annette's ink well. The frog jumped out of the well and on to the horrid little girl's transcription book. I received four more cuts for my troubles.

I was quite a lad with the marbles early on too – a real dead-eye dick!

I always carried several pockets full of marbles with me at school – they eventually became my undoing.

It just seemed natural to want to continually play with them but the familiar noise of marbles bouncing on the floorboards irritated Old Ma Hughes – with the expected result.

I don't know what it was but I seemed to be attracted to that frightening piece of equipment that lived on top of the storage cupboard in Old Ma Hughes' classroom.

Before my fourth year was completed I managed to feel the biting pain of that big stick a few more times . . . yes, fourth grade was a bad year for yours truly!

I even got caught nicking out of the classroom fifteen minutes before school finished, so I could arrive at football practice early. I was given several hundred lines to write as punishment and missed football practice altogether!

By the time I was in grade six, I pretty much knew what to expect, if I managed to find myself on the wrong side of a teacher.

The major question was . . . whether to risk placing an exercise book into the bum of your trousers, just in case the headmaster demanded, "bend over son"?

Also there was the myth about rubbing orange peel on the palms of one's hands. The intention being that the orange-skin moisture would make the cane slide quickly off an outstretched hand. It doesn't work.

Then, there was always the rigid hand versus the limp fingered approach – both of these hurt a lot!

But not as much as having the back of your hand placed on the desktop . . . then whack! That was the worst – similar to getting your hand stapled to a bench top with a hydraulic press!

A few of the masters or teachers I met under these difficult circumstances, had a definite sadistic streak in their nature – they never used to aim at the numb and calloused upturned hand! Much more painful was a direct hit to the knuckle area at the base of the thumb.

One of these discipline sticks even had a name – 'Excalibur' was one, like the mythological sword of King Arthur. It belonged to Mr Wilfred Asten, deputy headmaster of the Friends' School in Hobart. My chance meeting with Excalibur was as usual self-inflicted and deserved.

My only crime really was to be a good hooker of the short-pitched delivery at cricket practice . . . high over the fence adjoining our cricket practice nets and into the apple orchard next door.

When you're a growing boy there's nothing quite like a free feed of fresh apples from a nearby orchard, is there?

The problem for me was that I'd hit the ball, so therefore I had to go and fetch it. Foolishly, I took my time getting back – and the owner of the property sprung me. Teeth deeply sunk into a beautiful ripe Jonathan, juice trickling from the corners of my mouth, I couldn't have been happier. Until, I saw a very irritable old man (the owner) coming after me with a broom handle.

I managed to scale the paling fence without copping too many prods and bruises . . . but much verbal abuse was being poured at me. So I replied in kind.

The ageing orchardist reported me to the headmaster, and his deputy had me standing outside his office door quick smart before the school bell rang at nine o'clock next morning.

Yes, I was guilty, but dead set unlucky – we'd been pinching those apples for years! Why now? The time was very near for this Apple Isle boy to meet Excalibur . . . I had heard so much about the dimensions of this magnificent piece of cane, and I didn't fancy the scenario at all! Nor the resulting hurt.

Soon Mr Asten explained how I'd crossed the thin white line which separates RIGHT from WRONG. Then he introduced me to his friend of much reputation – Excalibur.

My life seemed to race past my eyes at a million miles an hour, as I stemmed back a well of tears. I'd never even imagined pain of this magnitude before. Head down, sorrowfully, I dawdled in the dim, smelly, highly polished corridor and on to the ablution block to check out the damage and dry off the pain expressing itself in front of my eye-balls. I didn't need the other kids to spot me like this. They'd call me a sheila if I cried.

Nothing wrong with crying after six of the best deliveries I've ever faced in my life . . . including those from the West Indians.

Too hot to handle.

CHAPTER TWO

How to Kiss a Crocodile

How to Kiss a Crocodile

"I WAS THE ONLY ONE OF OUR EXPEDITION PARTY TO HAVE INSURANCE AGAINST BEING EATEN BY A CROCODILE"

The more I think about it the more I ask the question. What was a fully grown Tasmanian, with a reasonable amount of common-sense, doing cruising around a crocodile infested billabong at 9.30 at night . . . ?

To make matters worse, I was in an aluminium vessel, barely better than an upturned VW car bonnet that used a sick lawnmower engine for propulsion! Gee, it could have easily been my last good-bye. "See ya later alligator" or "See ya in a while crocodile."

This death-defying, extraordinary event happened in September, 1988.

Yours truly, "Wide World of Sports" producer, John Murray, our very talented camera man, Phil Hanna, and his assistant, Brad King, were invited to cover the 1988 Barramundi Classic, one of Australia's most unique game fishing tournaments.

Here was a great opportunity to step aboard the big bird in the sky and head off for some sunshine in the Northern Territory. Definitely too good to miss after a nippy Melbourne winter!

The event was to be contested along part of the meandering Mary River system some 300 kilometres south west of Darwin. Our accommodation for the stay was at a place called, appropriately, the Wildman River Safari Lodge situated on the Wildman River – part of the waterway. This austere cluster of metal deck, louvre windows, concrete block and flywire screen structures was not exactly Sydney's Regent Hotel, but then again what could we expect hundreds of kilometres from nowhere!

Our task was to capture on video the week long competition for Channel Nine's "Wide World of Sports" programme. The concept being to tell the story through the eyes of a fisherman.

Now the best way to understand what goes on is to have a go. As honorary commodore of the two-man teams in thirty boats, I did. And in doing so I almost lived up to my Tooheys 2.2 commercial reputation as the world's worst fisherman! In fact, between the four of us we travelled 28,000 kilometres and caught only one fish in five days. I guess that fish had a right to feel unlucky – he was in the wrong part of the river at the wrong time!

Whilst that "hook-up", "tag", and "release" sequence of vision was an important part of our footage, the chance to shoot images of crocodiles in their natural habitat, under spotlight at night, was what made the Barra' Classic a memorable one for all concerned. None of us could have predicted the drama that would unfold during our adventure in the balmy darkness under a vivid Milky Way.

Our nocturnal expedition consisted of two craft and was co-ordinated by the rangers of the Northern Territory Fisheries Department. Don't get the idea for a moment that it was a hair-brained idea spawned by a wish to emulate the antics of Mick Dundee of *Crocodile Dundee* fame. No way! We had a serious task.

We'd heard about the notorious rogue saurian named "Sweetheart", only the day before. She wasn't too fussy about eating humans or fragile tin can boats like ours. The story came from the manager of the Safari Lodge, Ray Alright, after a comforting, belly-warming port or three in the early a.m.

A man of much experience, integrity and never one to exaggerate the truth, he willingly divulged that Sweetheart had snapped the bum out of his dinghy . . . and didn't even chew the stem of the outboard motor before gulping the lot down! Now that's what's called a cast iron constitution! And clearly the tale suggested a very large mouth.

Sweetheart was then quite a local identity, although she was to be caught by the rangers a few months later and moved to a reserve. A quick glance at the visitors' book made this point. Mick Dundee's cousin in comedy, Daryl Somers, the host of the top rating TV show "Hey Hey It's Saturday", had lobbed at the lodge a few weeks earlier and had added his experiences to the Sweetheart legend. His personal note of warning in the visitor's book was both blunt and colourful. There was no way we could avoid reading what Daz said. All I can say is thanks a lot, mate! You certainly put the wind up and out of me and my team.

That fateful night, I was assigned a seat in the middle of the tiny lead "vessel" . . . and I use that term loosely. Honestly, it was barely three metres long and sat very, very low in the water. The precarious level of the plimsoll line had a fair bit to do with the bulk of my four minders, all strong, rugged angler types.

Will, an intrepid bare-handed croc catcher, hung continuously like a question mark over the bow with bulging eyeballs scanning the shiny, moonlit lily pads for those telltale eyes of "old scaly".

Standing up beside Will was our human lantern, holding a car-battery powered spotlight. He had the worst job in the crew. Apart from being our navigator he also became the easy target of thousands of mosquitoes. This had to be the ultimate test for a can of Aerogard!

There were so many mossies around that everytime he opened his mouth, which wasn't often, his tonsils became speckled with tiny insects. I knew he was breathing mostly through his nose, because so was I. Even with my ample hooter, it got clogged up very quickly.

The only respite from being eaten alive by the biting squadron was to turn off the light, but then we'd be in the dark . . . and I definitely didn't want to be left in the dark! Not here! I was nearly seven years old before I could go to sleep with the light out. The only thing we planned to turn off was the outboard motor that barked painfully in our eardrums. Then we experienced an eerie feeling as we drifted, the light stabbing silently ahead of us.

The other two crew members of our "Boat One" had their bums firmly planted on the rear seat. One had a hand on the tiller and an ear to what his mate was saying. In between the odd nervous cigarette, they both looked a bit toey. I think they were more concerned about appearing on national television for the first time than coming face to face with a rogue croc.

I was the bloke who ought to have been nervous. No way known was I prepared for what was about to happen when Will zeroed in on the first crocodile for the night. From my "safe" seat, all I could see was the end of a scaly tail threshing about to one side of the dinghy.

Will confidently shouted with the voice of experience as he struggled: "No, he's too big!" Immediately he let go of his target! Away the startled croc bolted like a frightened goldfish. I reckon this one that got away was every bit as long as the boat, and most of that consisted of a powerful tail! Nevertheless, with any croc there's still plenty of room for a full set of teeth.

The theory is to stun them with the glare of the spotlight. Then grab them firmly around the mouth so they can't snap their powerful jaws. But the trick here is to ensure that you can actually *get* your hands around the bugger's mouth – one slight miscalculation and you're always going to be a little short when counting the fingers on each hand! I'm told that while their jaws can close with great tenacity, the opening muscles are much weaker.

At night, with the aid of a spotlight, it's very easy to judge how big these scaly monsters are . . . by the distance between their eyes, which light up like shimmering, pale pink marbles.

What a profile – nostrils, eyes and ears all above the water line enabling the creature to breathe, see and hear whilst the majority of its body is hidden. The huge flattened tail makes up about half its body length. This is also a massive weapon. The back legs have webbed feet, which are useful in climbing muddy banks. The jagged teeth offer a firm grip on struggling prey.

These snapping jaws and surprisingly fast reactions give our awesome Australian "salties" numerous teatime snacks along the water's edge. They are also very territorial and when pressed for space between the river bank and a dinghy, can become quite explosive. It's really frightening when what looks like a floating log suddenly erupts into action right before your eyes. It leaves a big, gaping hole in the water – that's how fast they dive.

It should be mentioned that anything a large crocodile sees in the water or on the land . . . or even in a boat, is regarded as good, so their diet ranges from insects to kangaroos, cattle or people! What a comforting thought.

Anyway, there were no flies on my mate Will. The next time our boat got into the action, there was definitely no mistake. "Clunk", just like a giant handcuff snapped around the croc's mouth . . . and barely a ripple on the billabong. "Extraordinary," Phil said ecstatically from the camera boat following. "Beautiful stuff," he confided.

His boat was slightly larger than ours with a flat bottom and rails of tubular pipe. The shape made it ideal for setting up the camera tripod and viewing over the side. Seven people were comfortably piled aboard this second boat, and not all related to "Wide World of Sports". Chris Makepiece, the tournament director, was overseeing proceedings, along with Bob and Kathy Dennis, the husband and wife fishing team from Fort Smith, Arkansas. Would you believe Kathy was six months pregnant at the time!

Sitting back with a firm grip on the throttle was a true blue Territorian. A philosophical character who, in passing, mentioned how "the crocodile that can be seen is not a worry, it's the one you can't see, because he's a hunter!" All terrific information to have on board in the black of night, knowing that crocs mostly feed then and have splendid night-time vision.

For the moment though, we were floating around aimlessly in their back yard. Maybe they had already eaten. I hoped so. A conservative estimate was that about 160 of these ancient reptiles, with a lineage of 200 million years, live in this small part of the river system, known affectionately as the "Home Billabong".

Since 1972 these cunning, deadly creatures have been a protected species and the number of attacks on both man and boats have increased dramatically in the Northern Territory. In Darwin harbour alone, 250 crocs are pulled out of the area by water police every year. Needless to say there are many more still enjoying their "harbour freedom'.

So, why would anyone want to catch one with their bare hands at 9.30 at night? Well, it seemed like a good idea at the time!

Some four hours earlier in the light of day, over a dust-settling beer, the idea was floated to capture one, a little one too . . . maybe 1.5 metres in length. I reckoned I could handle a little bloke like that!

Our man with the hands of steel didn't let us down this night. A "classic catch", if ever I've seen one. I couldn't believe my eyes . . . bare handed! As soon as Will landed our new television star, a loop of string was slipped around the bottom jaw of the tentatively snapping, prehistoric reptile. Quick as a flash, a second loop was wrapped under and over the upper jaw, not unlike the methods used by our early Aborigines in securing their prey.

Now I thought that was about it for the night. Mission accomplished. But without the hint of a warning the captive croc was flung, head first, straight at me! I'm not too proud to say it: I was scared stiff! Years of patrolling the third man and fine leg boundary fences of the world was of absolutely no use to me now, in my moment of desperation. This was a catch I had to take.

The stunned, dripping wet denizen hit me firmly about ribcage high . . . The sort of pass Mal Meninga would be proud of – four sets of toe nails, two above and two below the nipples, gripping my chest as if there was no tomorrow. The cameras just happened to be rolling, and my ungainly catch of this poor, gagged creature was captured on video tape forever. What a set up!

I didn't say a word. I instinctively eyeballed the camera lens and for the first time in my life I was speechless. Nothing came out – until the baby monster began to kick and thresh its tail around. That's when the odd expletive slipped out . . . couldn't help it. Could you blame me? Hardly a word able to be transmitted on national TV.

Then my little mate began uttering a guttural sound through his clenched jaws. It got louder and seemed to start from halfway down his flaying tail! The look on both man and monster summed up our relationship – we were definitely not going to be lifelong buddies. I was told to cover his eyes, it would make him calmer. Strangely enough, it proved good advice. But which hand?

Meanwhile everyone around me, in the two boats, was in a state of hysterical laughter . . . That was OK, I don't mind a joke, and obviously it was great footage. It must have seemed very funny at the time, me speechless for a change . . . and the croc with a gob full of string!

While I struggled with the protesting croc until we reached dry land, I also made a mental note: their day of reckoning will come, and I'll get my laugh . . . at their expense! Time was on my side. No-one could have reckoned on most of them getting theirs less than half an hour later.

Well before that drama unfolded I had thought out a plan of action. Back on land I would try and hypnotise my crocodile friend. I couldn't wait! I'd read that it was possible to hypnotise a crocodile (if you're game) by gently tickling its white underbelly. After that, I fig-

ured I would slip quietly back to the lodge and tent city for some dev-
ilish fun. I just had to wait a while.

With my "catch" held firm we calmly motored back along the billabong towards the ever popular watering hole which despite the late
hour, was still supporting many anglers who were declaring some of
the day's biggest lies. Isn't it amazing what a beer or two can do for
the length of the "one that got away"?

I was trying to imagine what sort of reaction our overdue appearance would receive! I planned to call for some "helpers" to unwind
the string and free the imaginary hook from "junior's" mouth – that
would sober up a few of the aquatic bar hounds – and then I'd claim
extra points for having hooked up a catch far in excess of the longest
"barra" so far tagged, at 83 cm. So much for the plan. Even the best
laid plans sometimes don't turn out.

The mental story-board looked great, except there I was, both
arms well and truly occupied. One hand was stuck firmly over those
large, dreamy "come to me (I'm gonna eat ya)" eyes, and the other
bunch of fives supported my friend's soft, white "handbag" underbelly. How was I going to take control of the situation and make it
happen? Not easily!

All I want to do was get this King of the Territory's waterways back
to shore. Had it been Mick Dundee, I'm sure he'd have asked for a
stuffed one to be thrown at him and with at least three rehearsals!
This croc was for real and the action was "live".

Yours truly urged the throttle to be tweaked to "full on", not so
much to get a move on, but to conceal my pounding heart. It was
sounding like an Apache war drum thumping out its message . . .
ke-boom, ke-boom, ke-boom.

We'd scuttled off into the darkness leaving the camera crew in the
shadow boat to shoot the final scene before they could call it a
"wrap" . . . and follow us back to the shore. This was to be the scene
where my rather kitch black Akubra, complete with plastic crocodile
teeth band, was floating away among the water lillies!

The explanation of what transpired over the next half an hour
came from the survivors! I didn't have to fill in too many gaps with
my fertile imagination because even I couldn't have scripted events
any better by tampering with the truth in this hilarious situation.

Dedicated camera man Phil and his tall, bronzed, fair dinkum
Aussie lifesaver type assistant Brad, didn't think it was good enough
to shoot the "deadman's" hat scene from their usual position. Their
creative energy was now flowing freely. No, they wanted the $150 per
head ringside seats on the rails, right up the front, where they could
almost touch the camera lens on the soggy rim of my floating hat. So
too did the other five spectators. Shouts of, "Maxie, Maxie, Maxie . . .
where are you?" punctuated the outback tranquillity.

So, there they were, the "magnificent seven", all crammed up one end of the aluminium tray. Standing room only! The boat acted like a child's see-saw – one end up and the other down.

Now you don't have to be Albert Einstein to work out the result. The working platform took only a few seconds to be swamped and capsize amidst scenes and sounds of chaos and fear.

Territorian Timmy, the most experienced sailor aboard kept shouting with embarrassment, "Bullshit – I've never sunk a ship in my life!" It was especially embarrassing to him, as they were stationary on a millpond-flat river! "No one is ever going to believe me!" he said as the water lapped around his bare knees.

To most people the unknown is darkness and danger! To big Brad – it was definitely crocodile infested water! Earlier in the day, he wouldn't even plunge his hand in the water to paddle the dinghy into a better line of view for the camera. Now fearing for his life, he was heading to the bottom, wearing his gurgling headphones and still rigged up to the VCR. The unit's "standby" light was still glowing red 30 centimetres underwater! The sock on the boom microphone accepted water with the capacity of a sponge and sank like a grey soggy loaf of bread stuck on the end of a metal skewer.

When the water started filling the dinghy, Phil quickly realised that they were all at the point of no return. He didn't intend to sink to the bottom accompanied by his heavy video camera. Time to look after number one. "Bye bye, camera," he waved as camera and cameraman hit the drink simultaneously, but separately.

Everyone understood there were plenty of crocodiles lurking around. It's a pity that Australia's Olympic swimming team had already been selected two weeks earlier . . . especially as the 50 metre dash had been reinstated as a gold medal event at Seoul. In this crisis there was every potential for a world record swim – fully clothed! Either that or all seven would be walking on water without divine intervention. Left or right, the equation for safety equated a 50 metre swim.

Chris was at the helm when the dinghy capsized and couldn't understand why it happened! "All I know is that for some reason a large amount of water came in over the front and next thing we were in the water," he said later. "The only thing I'd been able to put it down to was a wave of some description or a croc swirl."

Let's eliminate the first . . . you can't catch a wave on a millpond, can you? But we had seen plenty of big 'uns (crocodiles) earlier in the night . . . capable of leaving a gaping hole in the surface when they dive.

Chris was more worried than the rest as he prepared to go down with the ship. Unfortunately, he knew exactly what might be lurking beneath the lily pads. His biggest worry was not JUNIOR'S family and friends but one of the plentiful, three metre-long "King Browns" – which rate as one of the world's deadliest aquatic snakes. Maybe it was better that the sinking happened at night – they couldn't see a snake or a croc swimming towards them!

Spare a thought for Kathy, the expectant mother. She had been checking a few facts about crocodiles the night before. "I kept thinking about what I read," she recalled. "It was kind of scary because it all happened so quickly. I hit the water and someone landed right on top of me! I was pushed under and it was a struggle to get back to the surface with the weight of my clothes and shoes."

Husband Bob reckoned he didn't have time to worry about the crocs because he was only concerned about his wife. "It was probably a more traumatic experience because she is pregnant," he drawled.

What the American couple didn't realise was that this time of the year is the mating season for Territory crocodiles. That's when they are at their most dangerous! They become frisky, their appetites increase with the build up in heat and males are on the lookout for a shapely female tail. A lot like humans aren't they?

However, I was later assured by Territory Conservation Commission croc expert, Bryan Walsh, that crocodiles are not the ogres they are made out to be.

"They are pretty wary animals really," he said. "They would have been more reticent about approaching a group in the water than if each person had swum to shore alone."

Now he tells us! That numbing piece of information didn't help our seven survivors as they clung terrified to the top of their upturned boat. Fortunately an airpocket had righted the punt-like boat in a matter of seconds and within reach of everybody. Its hull was barely out of the water. Nevertheless there was still enough support for each person to clamber on top . . . and keep them bobbing above the glistening lily pads.

John and his unfortunate companions endured ten spine-chilling minutes riding on that unstable raft. You can bet they were all thinking exactly the same thought . . . "A CROCODILE'S GONNA GET ME!" "THE ONLY GOOD CROC IS A DEAD ONE!" But none would admit their fear.

Here they were, sitting ducks, like a smorgasbord on a suspended tin tray. Take your pick, crocs . . . feed from either side tonight!

As his life flashed before his eyes in the gloom, our intrepid producer remembered the previous night's discussion about crocodiles especially enjoying a feed of dog or two. Clean out of luck Johnny – not a dog to be found anywhere on board or overboard!

We were told that Aborigines used to put a dog into the water ahead of them if they had plans to cross a river! Crocs just loved to zero in on a splashing, bite-sized canine morsel!

Now this was a huge worry for Johnny. He wouldn't mind me telling you he is not the greatest swimmer in Victoria. And can you believe it, the only stroke he knew was . . . the DOG PADDLE!

After a few minutes the air began escaping from under the rocking hull. Water started washing over it, and legs began dipping deeper into the crocodile and snake-infested, black, stagnant water. Ideal crocodile bait! It must have looked a very appetising sight from below.

Every time someone sneezed, the vessel would rock awkwardly. So collectively they sat in a primitive monkey pose, holding their ankles and hoping our boat might soon return and discover where they had got to. No such luck, we were long gone and there was not another living soul around at that time of night.

At one point, Phil actually slipped off the slimy hull. He went completely under and came back up again with an almighty splash similar to a crocodile swirl. There followed a violent lurching movement and for a moment no-one knew whether or not Phil was being attacked. It frightened the living daylights out of all of them.

With their life-supporting platform almost completely submerged, it was Chris who made the decision to swim to safety. Thankfully everyone remained calm as Chris uttered a few reassuring baby white lies through a tight smile and clenched teeth. "It's OK. Crocs don't feed at night!"

Chris organised his survivors into an orderly group. Everyone was now in the water and probably not aware that crocodiles are attracted to vibrations in the water more so than noises. And when they are lurking in the water, eye balls and snout protruding above the surface, you know then that they are ready to feed!

From all reports there was plenty of initial thrashing around in the water and it was getting murkier. It had absolutely nothing to do with the algae or marine life! Talk about tight clingy underpants.

Timmy was doing his best to prevent everyone from panicking while Chris tried to inject a little humour into the tense occasion by asking the navigator where he obtained his licence to drive a boat . . . Amsterdam? No one laughed.

"Oh. Can everyone swim?" questioned the tournament director, accepting responsibility for the night's proceedings. "OK. Bunch up and slowly . . . we'll head for shore!" he explained.

Suddenly the full moon and stars had gone. The night had turned pitch black.

Last man into the water was Timmy, who was thrust clear as the boat had one final gasp and sank. Bubbles were all that remained.

He had wanted one last cigarette badly but couldn't find either the packet or his lighter. It didn't really matter, they were probably still wet from the earlier dunking.

The Arkansas couple were now coming to terms with the very real possibility of their off-spring being born three months premature, without a visa, on a lily pad, in a crocodile-infested swamp downunder. Don't laugh, it could have happened!

Kathy was reciting Hail Marys. Husband Robert was trying to turn back the clock and regretting bringing his wife along this time. If the crocs had their way, it would be the last time! While he cursed himself, he also crossed himself and treaded water at the same time. Quite a difficult routine by Robert. He may have received thunderous applause at Seoul in the new Olympic sport of synchronised swimming! This night the only feedback he received was a deafening silence, backed by a symphony of insects and bugs.

Brad realised his chances were one in seven of being snatched from the pack. That showed more intelligence and rat cunning than raw courage. He didn't miss a beat, his rhythm was perfect. Maybe his breathing was a bit fast . . . but that was because the big fella was trying to reposition himself into the safest position – middle of the line. That reduced the odds! And by his terrified reasoning they'd have to gobble up at least three of 'em before they could taste him.

Then the not so composed Brad observed a shooting star drop to the horizon. Immediately he made a wish: if there were any hungry crocs looking for a feed, please make them overlook me!

Johnny tried breast-stroke for the first time in his life to minimise the splashing that might make him croc supper. But he had sunk too low in the water and was taking in too much of that stuff that fish copulate in! Back to the good ol' dog paddle. Not a pretty sight but effective.

The natural reaction was to want to swim like hell for the unknown security of the river bank but commonsense prevailed. Slowly their heads bobbed up and down causing concentric ripples on the surface, just like frogs hopping onto a lily pad.

The boat was well underwater now. There was definitely no turning back. If ever they were going to be on the menu for a crocodile snack, it was tonight! All a hungry croc had to do was slowly open wide and they'd end up straight in its mouth. Snap – all over red rover! Then over and over and over . . . they call it the death roll.

Every second seemed like an eternity. Will we ever get there? Stroke by stroke, side by side, forty-nine metres, forty-eight metres . . .

Five minutes later the dark, shadowy masses of mangroves on the river bank loomed up and a new meaning was given to the word excited. The daring dash was over . . . they were able to feel the slushy bottom of the billabong and waddle towards the bank, hip deep in the shallows.

Here, they realised . . . this was even more risky than the swim because it was amongst these same mangroves that all the larger crocs were spotted earlier in the evening! Back came the fear and the chilling thought of: "When will my leg be chomped off!"

Actually their teeth are not suited to chewing. They either eat their prey whole, or shake the body vigorously until some flesh breaks away.

Timmy quickly took on the role of an Aboriginal tracker and led the way, looking for a safe path up the muddy river bank. Struggling to stay upright in the slush, he kept head butting trees, left, right and centre. Up to his ears in it, sometimes, he stumbled on through the thick tropical undergrowth. Persistence would pay off.

I suppose it is difficult to imagine what was exercising their minds so close to safety . . . a friendly lilly pond stalk wrapping itself ever so softly with a gentle caress around the inside of the thigh – a very sensitive part of the body!! Hitting a kneecap against a submerged branch, having a fish dart between your legs or even provide a nip to exposed flesh on the arm. Any of these happenings would be enough to momentarily numb the brain!

Timmy was the ideal man to see in the dark. He regularly ate witchetty grubs and his knack of finding fish by feeling the vibrations on the water surface was uncanny.

John was second in this anxious Indian file. Chris brought up the tail.

Suddenly Timmy came to a dead end, his khaki green stubbies and singlet dripping with water and mud. Maybe he'd lost his thongs?

The other six hadn't planned to stop and couldn't see in the dark. They kept charging on in desperate effort to get to dry land. In no time the fragile little "guide" was splattered firmly against an elderly tree trunk which was blocking his way . . . and in danger of being planted himself! Trees were all around them . . . so there was nowhere to go but BACK out into the croc-infested shallow water!

Oblivious to these goings on . . . my little sardine can had successfully made it back to the jetty. Happiness, and a "wrap", was knowing that we had fulfilled our objective of filming a night-time crocodile capture. It would certainly make the story much more interesting.

Let's head for a Tooheys 2.2. If we had been aware of the traumatic happenings in the eventide beyond, we probably would have traded our 2.2 cans for a straight whisky!

The jetty was an unsteady construction – floating on old and rusty 44 gallon drums – so I walked gingerly back along it with my "prize" capture still securely in hand. As I did, my mind flashed back to my only other encounter with one of these venerated creatures a few days earlier.

Dressed in full Mick Dundee attire – black Akubra hat with imitation crocodile teeth band, tan leather waistcoat, denim jeans, cowboy boots and a grin from earhole to earhole – I sucked in a first breath of Northern Territory air. It was like walking into a sauna, nevertheless I was dressed for anything. Little did I know that the greeting at the bottom of the Boeing's mobile staircase was going to be even hotter.

First, there was the presentation of an insurance policy against my getting eaten by crocodiles – to the value of $50,000! How much is a bloke worth – not much it seems! This was followed up by my first touch of LIVE crocodile skin – supplied by a local croc farmer.

The meeting was almost love at first sight! Especially, when I noticed that the four footer's razor sharp teeth were clenched tightly together, thanks to a neat ball of string tied carefully around the snout and a rubber band added just to make sure. You can never be too wary. Baby crocodiles do bite.

He or she (I don't know which and I wasn't about to turn it over to find out!) had eyes full of fire and vitality: golden circles with large black pupils.

After posing for several photographs and entertaining several television crews, we sadly parted company knowing we'd never set eyes on one another again. I thought that's the closest I'm going to get to one of these scaly babies. How wrong I was!!

Back to the real story.

Shortly after getting ashore my companions and I were all involved in jovial conversation. The "local" barramundi fishermen were talking about the reptiles and chuckling at many of their taller crocodile tales. While we sampled a light ale or two, the subject of hypnotising them cropped up. Suddenly, I was supposed to be the expert, BUT I declared, only where CHOOKS are concerned. Just a matter of placing the captive fowl on its back and drawing a chalk mark back towards its beak. Easy as one, two, three!

The line I was being served up by these thirsty Territorians was hard to swallow. It sounded as if they were trying to see how gullible I was. After all, it was crocodile territory and I didn't know too much about the subject.

Despite their cranking me up, I was beginning to get quite interested and excited at the prospect of sending one of these fellas into a trance.

Remember the part in the *Crocodile Dundee* movie when Mick Dundee "hypnotises" a water buffalo. A few days earlier I actually tried this, by pointing and rotating two fingers at a herd of water buffalo – from a safe distance of course. Didn't work! They kept putting their heads down in a show of strength and scraping the ground vigorously with one leg. Maybe I'd have better luck with a croc?

Anyway I was prepared to give it a go if they were . . . so everyone gathered around the headlights of the four-wheel drive that memorable night. Spotlight on sport.

You won't believe me, but I am telling the truth, the whole truth and not even a teeny weeny bit of exaggeration! I successfully upended my little scaly mate to reveal his shiny belly, but always keeping one hand tightly clasped around the jaws, just in case.

Before he could wiggle in protest I began stroking the soft creamy skin from below his belly right up to the chin. There was no doubt about the little fella enjoying the treatment. Any amount of tickling was definitely the order of the night.

Soon he/she was spreadeagled on his/her back, motionless, legs up and toes curled in – a bit like my drinking partner Dougie Walters after a night out on the town!

And just to prove how fair dinkum it was . . . I picked up my wonderfully relaxed patient and planted a great big kiss right on the end of the snout. There was no immediate reaction to an ugly bloke like myself tickling its sensitive flared nostrils with an overgrown moustache – and just as well!

My friend's lips, gums, teeth and string all felt pretty wet and cold to me – not that the contact was extended beyond a hundredth of a second. Yes, I'd actually kissed a crocodile . . . and had hypnotised it to boot!

And for all those interested (and I can't imagine who) . . . I'll talk you through HOW TO KISS A CROCODILE.

I performed the exercise again but for this second time I was dared to take off one of the pieces of string, seeing my mate was in a state of unconscious bliss and *not* likely to bite. Well, that was their opinion. I was the one who was going to get the love bite – they'd get the laugh!

I was feeling a knot in the stomach at this stage . . . it soon appeared just below my adam's apple!

Advice – don't kiss crocs without first hypnotising them. No matter what size, they all bite, particularly if approached with a view to amorous intentions like kissing.

The exercise was a whole lot better the second time around . . . not that I was gonna attempt anything stupid like putting my tongue in its mouth! But I did get to feel the razor sharp outer edge of several tightly clenched teeth . . .

I also tried to gaze deep into my friend's eyes as I took my grip a little lower behind the brow . . . no such luck. It was a bit like my mate, Lou Richards, who used to be on a "Sunday Edition", the lights were ON but there was no one home!

All over in a matter of seconds . . . and no crocodile tears when I put it down, just relief I expect after being man-handled so much. Then again, it was hypnotised!

Gee, it would take a lot of make-up, false eye lashes and lipstick to make this croc look half good. Nevertheless, I will always retain a tremendous affinity with crocodiles. I had kissed this one, the only way you could – slowly, gently and with a great deal of sensitivity. Call it awareness or confidence from knowing where the teeth are if you like. And I participated not realising that its brothers and sisters probably had different thoughts about our wet and soggy seven. Maybe they would get a gentle love bite on the neck?

Yes, it was definitely time for a celebratory drink, even in the absence of the camera boat. By the way, where was the rest of the party? No sign of a flood light on the billabong. The only sound was the non stop chatter of insects. No evidence of the monotonous drone of an outboard motor rising to challenge the insect choir. In fact, the silence was very worrying.

Meanwhile down at the river, our shipwrecked party was forced to back track in the warm, shallow water that is favoured by those sleeping, breathing logs.

The slow heart beat of cold-blooded crocodiles allows them to sleep underwater for hours (their heart rate can drop to one and a half beats a minute which reduces their consumption of oxygen), ready to grab any unsuspecting passerby that disturbs them, whereas the heart beats of our sopping wet heroes must have been 170 plus beats per minute!

This excursion through the crocodile sleeping quarters continued on . . . step by step they carefully placed their feet around large obstacles on the bank, over fallen trees and the chaotic root systems of the plentiful mangroves. Was that a dead tree we just jumped over, or was it a slumbering croc? And to think I was the only member of our expedition party to have insurance against being eaten by a crocodile.

They knew they were lucky to be alive, marooned on the edge of the billabong, looking like wet scarecrows and exchanging bear hugs in the moonlight; to stay together and press on through the slush and slime. It was important to keep moving, they figured. A moving target was harder to take and swallow!

The group was making slow progress as they headed back in the direction of the jetty, although on the wrong side of the river. It was just a matter of time, they had all agreed, before the other "tinnie" would come back, realising something had gone wrong, reacting to the absence.

The comment Brad added took the wind out of their sails "When the boat returns . . . won't it be terrific if they don't hear our screams for help and keep on going past us? After all, they didn't hear us before!"

No noise pollution law out here in the outback. The racket that the outboard motor made was enough to give a bloke a migraine. No wonder crocs kept clear of our boats!

Meanwhile back at the moorings half an hour had passed. Surely they had finished filming by now. Still no sign.

A search was mounted. Two rangers jumped aboard little boat ONE and returned to the area of our earlier filming. Before they got there they heard frantic shouts from the far bank, "HELP, HELP, HELP . . . !" It was a panting Phil and Chris who had decided to trample their way ahead of the rest of the stranded bunch in a desperate bid to find some assistance as soon as possible.

Only three at a time could be ferried back in our smaller mobile bath tub so the overseas tourists got priority. And they had been expecting a quiet time downunder with no telephones ringing and the chance to sit down with a good book. Now they'll be able to write one themselves!!

Who would get the number three berth? Pulling rank and claiming that he had a wife and baby to feed was our "Wide World of Sports" producer John, who quickly planted his bum on the seat – no discussion would be entered into over seat allocation as far as he was concerned!

The poor helmsman of the rescue vessel had a packet of cigarettes sticking out of his shirt pocket. The pocket was immediately attacked by our bedraggled friends – except Kathy – as therapy for frayed nerves. Even hubby Bob had a drag on a fag – a good effort for a bloke who has a disliking for the habit.

Two cigarettes later they were back on the jetty looking like drowned rats. The three of them received a mixed reception from yours truly, while the rescue team returned to pick up Phil, Brad, Tim and Chris.

I suppose I have spent too many of my days around guys such as Dougie Walters, Dennis Lillee, Gary Gilmour and Rodney Marsh. To say the least, they were a mischievous lot and each one a great practical joker.

I wasn't positive but I thought this might be another set-up. So I asked a leading question of John, "Where in the bloody hell have you been?"

"Where do you bloody reckon!" he snapped.

I couldn't help myself: "Gee, you picked a top night for a swim.

But couldn't you wait until you got back to the lodge? There're not so many crocodiles in that pool! And by the way . . . what's the water like? Wet?" His eyes half closed and he fired an evil look back at me.

"Don't you care that we could have been eaten alive out there?" asked John.

" 'Course I do mate . . . did you see any of those bucket-mouthed barra we missed today?"

Kathy could not stand my sarcastic barrage for another moment. "Slap that man's face!" she shouted to her husband.

Bob wasn't sure how to take my ribbing, neither was Johnny.

John suggested I feel his hair. "What for?" I said. "Anyone could have wet their hair!" It just looked and smelt too much like a set up.

"Well, what about my tee-shirt . . . and my trousers are soaked!" he gestured. "So too is Kathy's!" In fact hers had large peg marks.

"Nice try, mate. But you're not gonna get me that easily," I teased.

Kathy chipped in with a more serious scowl, "He's telling the truth. We could have all been killed or drowned!"

"How lucky are you . . . " I laughed, " . . . to come to Australia and swim in a beautiful river like this amongst some real live crocodiles! You'll be able to dine out on this story for the rest of your lives!"

Now pregnant women are not the best subjects to take the mickey out of. And by this stage I was inclined to think there was an element of truth in their story.

So I beckoned John to step over my croc (through all this, my hypnotised crocodile remained motionless, flat on his back on the bank . . . not a worry in the world) so that I could see his face in the dim interior light of our four wheel drive.

The producer was not a happy boy. He felt like kicking Junior in the guts but decided begrudgingly to stroke the little fella's tummy a couple of times.

By contrast, Phil – Mr Optimistic – was still full of beans and reasonably circumspect about the night's proceedings. He could have been a Vietnam veteran he was so together.

On the other hand, our audio man Brad had flat batteries. We couldn't get a sound out of him. Speechless.

We called a "Wide World of Sports" crisis meeting shortly afterwards. Consensus concluded that nothing could be done tonight. At first light we would attempt to salvage what equipment we could.

The most important item on our hit list was not the sophisticated portable camera and VCR but two $20.00 video tapes. Because the billabong is part of a fresh water system, the possibility of the video tapes still being OK was very good.

You see, no-one would believe us if we lobbed back at GTV 9 in Melbourne without a story. In television, if you haven't got pictures, you haven't got a story.

The tape in the camera was important because it had the night-time scenes on it, but equally as important was the fact that it also had footage of the afternoon spent at a place called Shady Camp.

I don't know why they called it Shady Camp because it was like a moonscape! Hardly a tree to be spotted anywhere. Crocodiles, however, loved this location along the sandy river banks and were in plentiful supply. We must have seen at least 100 crocodiles that afternoon, all in the space of about three or four kilometres.

Here, one of the major problems for rangers is attending to the 44 gallon drum rubbish tins placed near the boat ramps. It seems the larger crocs have a real fascination for these containers and consistently upend them to scavenge for food.

From 100 metres, the big boys looked enormous. Close-up they were absolutely terrifying! Several must have stretched the measuring tape to six metres . . . and a lot were three or four metres long.

Gee, there was a lot of lair in 'em too! They are very quick to show off what they're made of and how many teeth and tonsils they possess – plenty. As Phil said a couple of times, "Not a great place to water ski, this!"

No matter where we looked there was a gallery of them staring back at us. Now, that was a worry when you consider our tiny 3 metre long craft would have made a useful first bite for a couple of these playful predators.

Phil had captured some fantastic footage of sweeping tails and gaping crocs' yawns. And it was depressing to think his efforts may be lost in the mud up river.

Even after a pleasant midnight shower, thinking about the drama of the night made sleeping difficult. Everyone kept replaying on their "bio recorders" what might have happened – all embellished by a fertile imagination.

And as for the shower, this really was a unique experience. Shower late at night and beat the early morning rush was the theory. Only six showers serviced the ninety odd people present for the Barra Classic.

There is nothing quite like being in an open air shower cubicle in the middle of the night with fluorescent lighting attracting any creature that flies or crawls. There must have been thousands of tiny insects, moths and spiders that paid no entrance fee to witness big Max have a scrub. The majority of these uninvited spectators wanted to get close to the action too! Even the soap was speckled with little black dots that moved. Giant cockroaches flew out of the floorboards and crashed into walls and body alike.

First light saw an armada of three dinghies head off along the Wildman River. What a different place it was in the light of day. The river banks were alive with activity beyond the reeds and water lillies. Wild geese, magpies, ducks, and jabiru (big black birds with stork-like beaks and orange legs) fluttered and water buffalo frolicked. Overhead huge sea eagles glided like model aeroplanes on display.

The water was very still, the fresh aroma was invigorating. There was also anticipation in the air. Not knowing what we'd find made the hair on the back of my neck stand on end.

The night before, one of the rangers was thoughtful enough to place an empty beer can on a branch to mark the location where the magnificent seven cheated an ugly death.

Chris was in control of the lead boat. Talk about a glutton for punishment. On board with him was the cameraman who no longer had a camera – Phil.

As we rounded the river bend, and the scene of the previous night's mayhem, there right before our eyes was the ill-fated boat. It had surfaced and was floating still, bottom up. And what do you reckon was perched on top, basking in the morning sun light? Yes, you guessed it . . . he must have been about three metres long. We couldn't be sure how big this croc was because some of his tail was submerged. It was so nice of him to mind our belongings for us!

Looking on from the river bank where the camera boat crew had crawled ashore the previous night were a couple of big jabiru. They were abiding by the philosophy that we heard mentioned at the Wildman River Safari Lodge after we arrived at the nearby dirt airstrip amongst the wild brumbies. That was: "We don't swim in their river and they don't drink at our hotel!" Seemed pretty fair to me!

So the idea of actually diving to the silty bottom of the billabong and salvaging the mission equipment was just not on.

We needed some luck. Did the camera, tripod and VCR fall directly below where our crocodile sentinel was floating?

Our grappling pole and hook was not long enough . . . we were in need of a Red Adair.

Chris didn't let us down in Red's absence. He slipped the aluminium pole inside a long piece of PVC pipe to add a bit of length. Apart from being a bit too flexible, it was our best shot. No one volunteered to get wet!

Within minutes, success! First up was the porta-pak video cassette recorder which is about the size of small television. You little beauty . . . all of the previous night's filming was still loaded in the machine. We got the camera as well, still connected by cable to the recorder. No luck with the tripod or the second tape. We could only hope that the plastic case was water tight and like the upturned boat, the package would float to the surface – sometime. Perhaps it was under the boat and could be retrieved later when the boat was righted.

Watching the salvage operations from another dinghy was fisherman Bob from the USA. He captured everything on video for all back home to see. Now friends would have to believe the couples' tale of woe.

Lady luck must have smiled upon us because with much patient drying the first tape was OK. We found it very usable when we returned to Melbourne. A few days later, the second tape arrived! Chris and his fellow anglers had eventually found it floating intact. Not a crocodile tooth mark on it either, so obviously old scaly likes being on TV too! No colour correction necessary either.

Of course the plan for the trip north was to film a fishing story about the Barra Classic, using myself as a key contestant to explain what went on. Well I ended up doing a story on my three mates and their aquatic adventures – and a better yarn too.

The most difficult part of my tale was trying to interview the three survivors – Brad, Johnny and Phil. Talk about camera shy!

I thought I'd talk to them as a threesome, but no way. It was like trying to win Tattslotto . . . you gotta keep persisting and sooner or later your luck will change. In this case – never! Talk about hard work!

Brad couldn't stop himself from laughing when Phil rolled the camera and I asked him to explain the chain of events. I had to bite my bottom lip to stop laughing with him . . . otherwise we'd never have made a start.

John was different. He realised how important it was to have comments to validate the drama. His only problem was he couldn't speak properly! He couldn't even answer the first two questions without his voice breaking up because of nerves. It sure is a different story in front of the camera!

Finally what about fabulous Phil? Well, this exercise was Mission Impossible, because Phil had to do the filming. I offered, even begged him to let me operate the camera myself, if he would come out from behind his trusty old camera, and "star" in this story! No way.

The man with the creative eyes insisted he made a pledge when he got into camera operation that he was never going to become involved on the other side – and he's a man of his word.

The moral of this story is to take nothing for granted and live each moment for what it's worth – it may be your last. No crocodile tears please!!

Life in the Old 'Gator yet

"A DREADFUL LOOKING, SLIMY THING WITH A MOUTH FULL OF INCH-LONG TEETH"

It was during a fishing excursion down the Demerara River in Guyana that Doug Walters learned of Terry Jenner's phobias regarding crocodiles, piranha fish and the like.

As understandable as the aversion might be, it provided Walters with a chance to floor his room-mate and also (and much more importantly) his skipper, Ian Chappell.

I was lucky enough to be privy to the whole dastardly performance.

This was on the 1973 tour of the West Indies and at the end of the fourth Test match at Georgetown, Guyana, Doug said he'd like to go fishing. So he quickly organised someone to set up a day on the Demerara River – a tan, murky, muddy waterway.

The best way I could describe the boat is that it was "no more than a long dug out log".

The Geelong antique dealer and our opening batsman, Ian Redpath, was seated at the front or bow of the "log". And every little wave the floating log passed over sent Redders' Adam's apple crashing into the underside of his very angular jaw bone.

Naturally the centre position was occupied by Dougie himself and bringing up the rear was leg spinner Terry Jenner, from South Australia.

TJ, as he was known to his team-mates, just happened to have a can of beer in one hand, the other was dangling over the edge into the brown, muddy water.

Behind him stood an enormous Guyanese man who must have been six foot six inches tall and had muscles growing out of muscles. He was poling the log along and also acted as our guide for the day.

After a short while he shouted in Jenner's ear: "I wouldn't leave dem dere fingers in dat dere water mate!!!"

"Why?" asked TJ.

"Cause dem dere piranhas dey really love dat white meat man!!!"

Naturally, this caused Jenner's right hand to be yanked rather quickly out of the rapid-flowing river.

"I suppose you've got crocodiles and alligators over here too, mate?" questioned Jenner with a tone of sarcasm.

Silence reigned supreme for a moment, then the big black man spoke, "What do you think dąt is over dere – a block of flats?" Just as a 12-foot long greasy alligator opened up its jaws and yawned. Quick as a flash it slid through the mud at the water's edge and into the river.

At this stage the lads didn't want to fish any more – in fact they were beginning to sober up very smartly. Then, the huge black man with the well worn pole in his hand, shouted: "Look out boys. If those three hippopotamuses yawn and we crash into dem, we'ez dead. We really are!!!"

I need not say what happened. That gnarled hollow log headed straight back to shore and not one of the lines had been dampened.

Along the way, Dougie mentioned that he'd love a stuffed crocodile to take back home to Australia. He reckoned it would look tremendous sitting on top of his TV set – just below the three flying ducks – and fitted with a couple of cat's eye marbles for eyes. Dougie always did have his taste buds in his bum!!

He soon obtained one and christened it "Inshan", after the left-arm spin bowler from Trinidad named Inshan Ali . . . and was determined to have some fun before delivering it to the taxidermist.

The crocodile he had been given was about four foot long, a dreadful looking, slimy thing with a mouth full of inch-long teeth. Ideal for tearing food apart.

His room-mate, TJ, had had a truck load of rum and coke on the fateful night and was hooking yorkers when he finally came home.

The team was staying at a hotel in Georgetown rated as five star accommodation. Honestly, they were pretty dim stars.

About eleven o'clock that night, while TJ was out, Dougie short-sheeted his bed and in between the crisp white sheets was placed Inshan, the slippery, slimy crocodile.

As you can imagine, as soon as TJ eventually made it to bed, and I might add, not wearing a stitch of clothing, he sat bolt upright. Now the inside of the thigh is fairly sensitive and the deeper he slid into the bed the closer the teeth got to the action.

He had sobered up in seconds and was obviously terrified, Doug and I just happened to be in the wardrobe at the time.

TJ refused to sleep in the same room as Dougie Walters for the next two nights. Prank or no prank it really did shake the lad up badly.

The boy from Dungog had struck again!

Despite his succesful efforts on TJ, Doug's crowning glory was to get his captain at the time, Ian Chappell. It took him ten years to get him but he *really* nailed him with Inshan.

Chappelli and Walters had organised a game of golf at Royal Georgetown, Guyana. It is an unbelievable golf course – the caddies wear Dunlop rubbers, size 12, made in India, with enormous hammer head toes extending from each shoe.

The lurk is to pick up the golf ball between the big toe and the second toe, if it is positioned in a bad lie, then walk 50 metres down the fairway shouting, "Gee boss lovely lie right here", pointing to the end of their shoes.

Dougie knew that Chappelli would wear his favorite lucky golf clothes; those diabolical red and white checked trousers that he so often wore. There's no doubt they must have been a table cloth before they were stitched up.

Chappelli left the strides folded neatly over the back of a chair in his room and then went to breakfast – casually dressed in shorts. That was the moment Dougie had waited for. While his captain was at brekkie, Dougie grabbed the master key by bribing the girl at the front desk with a couple of tickets to the next cricket match, and gained access to the room.

He then carefully placed the limp crocodile with the large teeth into the crutch of the trousers and waited. Doug stood outside the room to urge Chappelli to hastily pull on his trousers. Walters was convulsed with laughter when the contact was made with Inshan, the cold crocodile skin.

Needless to say, Chappelli had screamed, jumped about and succeeded only in ripping the crutch out of his beloved golf pants. He fell to the floor entangled in a mass of shredded material as Inshan fell limp under the bed – tanglefooted team-mate!

All that could be seen was a magnificent set of crocodile teeth smiling from the floor at Chappelli's hairy legs.

Dougie couldn't believe his good fortune, although he lost a little of his enthusiasm when Chappelli suggested that it would be very unwise for him to sleep heavily in the near future.

He rather emphatically told Dougie: "I'll get you, somewhere, some place, at some time. It might not be this trip or even this year, but I promise I'll get you."

As it has turned out over a career spanning three decades the boy from Dungog has proved to have a more acute sense of humour, superior reflexes, less need for sleep and a certain rat cunning when it comes to getting a laugh at someone else's expense.

CHAPTER THREE

The Funny Side of a Sporting Career

**She couldn't help but notice the three
rapidly spreading blobs of blood in my mate's bowl.**

The Day of my First Kick

"DOWN I WENT LIKE A BAG OF WET CEMENT"

It is pretty natural for young fellas of eight years to spend most of their school days gazing out the classroom window. I was no exception. Like almost every boy in my grade, I wanted to be a VFL footballer and I also wanted to be a Test cricketer – as a batsman!

Now there is nothing wrong with dreaming. In fact, all man's greatest inventions and achievements have been a direct result of dreaming. Someone once said, "What can be conceived and believed in the mind can be achieved in reality." This philosophy remains the basis for all positive thinking.

I was too young at the time to realise that those wonderful childhood dreams were the building blocks of a process that was later to become second nature in my future sporting endeavours: all of these dreams were displayed on a big wide screen, rich in colour, full of familiar sounds like whistles, occasionally painful physical clashes and never too far away from the smell of linament!

At night, before dropping off to sleep, I would shut my eyes and visualise playing my first game of VFL football. In those days there were no video cassette recorders or computers. In fact, television wasn't introduced to Hobart until 1960, four years after the 1956 Olympic Games in Melbourne.

In these days of high technology, I still believe that the best computers in the world are not the big ones from IBM, Apple, Digital or Data General, but the ones between our ears. Each person is responsible for the pictures they see on their own screens. It's definitely your own fault if you compile bad images in your bio-computer.

Anyway, I used to imagine getting my first kick in VFL football somewhere near the members' wing on the MCG, in front of 70,000 screaming fans. The dream was always consistent. The struggle of gaining possession, then the kick!

The kick was the easy part – just a matter of putting the football, lace-upwards, gently to the ground. You see, drop kicks were my specialty, whereas today they are non-existent. A player would be dragged from the ground by his coach and fined $1000 for even attempting one.

This wasn't the case during my dreams in the Fifties. Nightly, I used to feel the bag of wind make perfect contact with my highly polished boot (my dad used to say, "Even if you can't play the game, at least look as if you can"). The resultant energy would propel the football spectacularly, end over end, some 65 metres onto the half-forward line where a team-mate would stand on an opponent's head to take "a screamer" – the mark of the day.

Then the members stand would rise as one to applaud the efforts. Dressed in their grey, gabardine overcoats and with cigar smoke creating a blue grey haze above their heads, they would continue to clap like mad. Gee, I used to enjoy getting that kick!

I must honestly say that almost a decade later, when I finally realised my schoolboy ambition of playing VFL football, my first kick didn't come so easily.

The year was 1967 when I made my debut in senior football for the Melbourne Football Club. With only seven games of the season remaining, I'd finally been given my chance against North Melbourne at the MCG.

I was the last player selected on Melbourne's supplementary list for the year and subsequently was given guernsey number 46. Yours truly was so skinny in those days (12 st 9 lbs or about – 79 kg) that the "4" started just under my left armpit and the "6" finished under my right. Embarrassingly, on the occasion of my first senior game, I ran down the race in a short-sleeved jumper – my "suntan" in the middle winter could be described as "polar bear white" and my elbows were like razor blades.

Halfback flanker Don Williams was playing his 200th game but I was so excited, I didn't know whether the team was lining up in ceremony for his 200th or for my first! I charged through the large red and blue banner and jogged a couple of laps to soak up the atmosphere. It was fantastic, just as I dreamed it would be . . . until moments before the start of the contest . . . There I was in the middle of the fabulous Melbourne Cricket Ground. The umpire held the ball aloft in one hand and drew the tiny, stainless steel container to his lips with the other.

It was then I noticed the ruckman standing opposite me in the blue and white vertical striped jumper – Noel Teasdale. A giant, barrel-chested man, almost 17 stone (108 kg). On his forehead he wore a leather patch which protected a metal plate inside his skull, the legacy of an old wound. To me the patch looked like it was holding his brains intact! I didn't relay that message to him at the time. He had a massive weight advantage. The umpire hadn't even bounced the ball, yet I was apprehensive!

Off went the siren, down went the ball and around went the pea in the whistle.

It should be understood that at eighteen years of age, Maxwell Henry Norman Walker was a willowy, high leaping young fella from the Apple Isle. With eyes firmly fixed on the ball, I charged at the centre circle and leapt high in the air for the knockout, so high in fact that a copper on the boundary line later tried to book me for "Loitering in the air". Unfortunately my leap wasn't high enough!

At precisely the same time as my hand made contact with the footy, Teasdale's huge frame crashed into mine with catastrophic results. He punched the ball about 40 metres towards his goal and sent number 46 for the Demons about 25 metres in the same direction.

There I was lying flat on my back and gasping in the middle of the MCG with not an ounce of wind in my lungs and wondering what in bloody hell had hit me. I opened my eyes and remember seeing some beautifully shaped cumulo-nimbus clouds floating overhead. It was then that I realised league football was not going to be easy.

Nothing in the world beats perseverance . . . so I persevered.

Five minutes of the quarter had elapsed when the ball went over the boundary line in front of the smokers' grandstand on the members wing for a throw-in. I then recalled what the legendary coach, Norm Smith, had told me before the game: "You're a big kid son, make them climb over you!"

So I took his advice. Immediately I used my edge in natural pace to gain front possie and knock the pill down to rover and captain Hassa Mann who had a baulk, a weave and bounce or two before dobbing a magnificent goal.

At this stage I thought to myself, "How long has this game been going on? You little beauty!" and headed back to the centre circle for the bounce-up. Teasdale jogged level with me and whispered bluntly, "If you get in front once more, I'll knock your so-and-so head right off your shoulder blades!" And I've cleaned that comment up for publication!!

Now, why should I take notice of this gorilla with the headgear? I'd heard similar comments from others and all to no avail. Without thinking too much more about his threat, I prepared to contest yet another boundary throw – still on the members wing.

No worries, front position came easily to me. I got my hand on the ball quickly to palm it down to Hassa, but then the unexpected happened. Whack! Right in the back of the neck. I pulled up only centimetres inside the white boundary line with my chin firmly implanted in the moist turf.

"Play on!" was the call by the umpire. "Gee, a bloke can be stiff," I thought, "No free kick." Remember too, I hadn't had my first kick yet! Still, I was prepared to give my ugly opponent the benefit of the doubt. How could anyone clobber his opposition ruckman that hard "on purpose", and get away with it?

Lady luck wasn't smiling on me at all, because the football had carried only 20 metres before rolling over the line and out of bounds!

Being a creative big man, I thought about the possiblity of still taking front position. But instead decided to nudge the ball out to nippy winger Stanley Alves at the back of the pack . . . it was a good idea and it would've been great! But little did I realise that "Teaser"had no time for creativity. This time he got me with a "coat hanger" (elbow) behind the left ear! Down I went like a bag of wet cement, church bells ringing inside my head. Seconds later the umpire nearly burst my right ear-drum by bending down blowing the whistle as loud as humanly possible, and pronouncing he was awarding me a free kick!

Like a flash, out came Sam Alica, the MFC runner. "Kick it, kick it . . . !" he demanded. Sammy must have thought I was Superman because my legs had buckled under me. I couldn't stand up until Sam's strong hands supported me under each armpit. A kick was still out of the question. Maybe a handball?

Suddenly, the experienced runner dug deep into his trouser pocket. Like most trainers who've been around a while, Sammy had a small packet of "smelling salts".

The lid was off the packet in a flash and under my nose it went. The smell was dreadful but did the job. My subsequent handball reached a Melbourne player effectively .

I was beginning to wonder whether or not I'd ever get a kick in VFL football.

But whilst recovering in the back pocket, my dream came true at the eleven minute mark of the first quarter. I attacked the ball as it cleared the halfback line. The elusive football was about to bounce about two metres in front of me. Which way would it bounce? Fortunately for me, it hit me fair and square on the left nipple! Here was my big chance!

There it was, safe in my possession. I held it at arm's length and looked . . . MATCH 11, Tom Sherrin, rawhide leather . . . made in Australia. The real thing! You bloody beauty!!!

Now for the kick . . . blue and white jumpers everywhere, not much time, unlike in the technicolour dream in the computer of my mind, this memorable first kick was a wobbly old flat punt which travelled approximately 35 metres.

Whatever it looked like didn't really matter. I'll remember that kick for the rest of my life, simply because it was my FIRST!!

And I was quickly beginning to realise that getting a kick in this great game, in such distinguished company, was not going to be easy.

Ninety-four VFL games later the time seemed right to stop. I'd been selected to play Test cricket against Pakistan in the second Test of the 1972-73 season.

And in the meantime, as a student of architecture at the Royal Melbourne Institute of Technology, I was to spend most of my holidays as a member of the maintenance staff at the MCG.

Looking back I reckon I painted at least 40,000 seats. Firstly we had to sand down the timber seating planks, then we applied the red-lead orange base coat, two coats of green and finally the more difficult task of stencilling on all the seat numbers.

My mentor in those days was a marvellous guy, Joe Kinnear, a top sportsman in his own right. But as the scoreboard operator he'd never missed a VFL game in forty years. Joe was a pretty hard man but had a great sense of humour, generally at my expense.

After I had displayed an unusual amount of ability with a paint brush in my first two weeks, Joe decided it was time for me to accept some responsibility – a sort of promotion, more like an elevation actually.

Joe had delegated me the task of painting two flag poles on the Members' Stand roof.

White was about the colour of my face as I craned my neck to view those two lonely flagpoles, perched 150 ft above, on the corners of the old corrugated iron roof. It appeared the only thing supporting the base of the poles was the guttering at the front edge of the roof.

Nevertheless, equal to the task, I soon found myself brush in pocket, paint tin in hand and ladder between myself and the pole, peering over the edge of the roof to the sound of laughter below.

It was Joe explaining to an audience of groundsmen and maintenance staff what a precarious position I now happened to be in – and that he had no real intention of me painting the poles!

Over a period of many years Joe and I became great friends. The Melbourne Cricket Club acknowledged his service with life membership.

We talked often of cricket and football, especially during the first class cricket matches held at the MCG. Then our job allocation changed to operating the old three storey high scoreboard – the Jack Fingleton Scoreboard now occupying a new site at the Manuka Oval in Canberra.

The Long Room is perhaps the best place in the ground to view a game from. It is a very historic space, steeped in nostalgia and choked in tradition.

History expresses itself in all forms within this room as does a certain code of ethics – and not just for sportsmen.

After playing a hard game of Aussie rules for the Melbourne reserves it was suggested that several of us younger players should watch the senior game from the Long Room.

We arrived dressed in MFC blazer; tie and grey trousers, as was the club policy, at the end of the first quarter. To my delight I found three vacant seats on a huge brown leather couch positioned directly in front of the glass viewing area.

Not to miss an opportunity like this, I sat down quickly as did my two team-mates. After a short stay, my left ankle was tapped very formally with a cane walking stick extending from the hand of a very stooped old gentleman. He must have been ninety.

He explained in a rather croaky voice that I was in his seat and he had been occupying the same place or close to it for many, many years.

Embarrassed, my mates and I left rather sheepishly to later find out that the seating on that couch was traditionally for only the oldest members of the MCC.

As one member died, they all moved up by one place to their left. I had obviously occupied the oldest club member's seat!

Memories easily come flooding back again . . . like painting the seats in the "outer" below the old Southern Stand. It had been a long hot day under the Melbourne sun.

The time was about 3 p.m. and I hadn't had much rest. I explained to my boss, Joe, that I had a bad bellyache and nature needed to take its course.

Joe suggested the ladies' toilets beneath the ageing grandstand would be the quickest, and that seemed OK as it was only a weekday afternoon, and no-one much around.

Seconds later I was seated in one of the cubicles in the women's conveniences.

I looked around the walls, deep in thought . . . the graffiti was unreal!

The silence was broken by the sound of footsteps coming towards my door. I immediately extended my foot to the base of the door in nervous fashion – no hardware on the door.

I breathed a sigh of relief as the adjoining door slammed shut. But how was I going to escape? How long would I have to sit there?

In those days, the toilet paper holders were fixed to the column between two doors. I tried to imagine, what happens if I stretch my hand out the door at the same time as the lady next door . . . fortunately the scenario didn't eventuate and I completed the "paper-work".

Then bolted as fast as I could, holding back my nervous laughter until I was safely outside.

I couldn't wait to tell Joe and the others painters what had happened . . . they laughed a lot.

Then, Dave, one of Joe's offsiders arrived on the scene ten minutes later with a story about disturbing a woman in the ladies' toilets below the Southern grandstand! What a woman!!

Today a new 160 million dollar structure using the latest architectural technology has replaced the tired old stand, but memories of the "outer" will linger with me forever.

Going Crackers over a Meal

"IT WAS A MATTER OF PUSHING ONWARD, EVER ONWARD"

Three huge drops of blood made an interesting abstract pattern as they splashed quietly into the bowl of cream of chicken soup!

My team-mate, Peter "Crackers" Keenan, had managed to get his nose broken earlier in the afternoon, while playing football – it was a bitter brawling encounter between our team, Melbourne, and Essendon.

Judging by the swelling and the exaggerated kink in Crackers' more than ample nose, Essendon not only won the match, but they also won the fight!

Nevertheless, our weekly after-match ritual of getting together was now well underway – win, lose or draw, it was always good for team spirit and morale.

Honestly, Crackers Keenan is not a handsome man. In fact I'm sure his head was chiselled out of granite – now his busted beak didn't help the image.

Sitting opposite the huge, macho ruckman was the wife of one of Melbourne's most respected businessmen.

The businessman's blue Rolls-Royce was parked outside the restaurant and his other half was dressed in splendor – blue-rinse hairdo, bright red lipstick, enormous diamond sparklers hanging from each ear-lobe and several dead foxes draped across her pale shoulders.

The beautifully manicured lady couldn't help but notice the three rapidly expanding blobs of blood in my mate's bowl!

But cool as an ice-cube, the big fella looked up, straight across the table, took a deep breath through his partly blocked nose – to stem the flow of blood without having to use his handkerchief – then confidently plunged his silver spoon deep into the heart of his soup.

At the same time the elegant lady's cheeks became ashen-grey. Yes, she'd guessed it, Crackers was going to eat it – blood and all. How could he? There he was Peter Pious Paul Keenan, fresh from the famous Catholic college at Kilmore – Assumption – dressed in a "closing down" sale, purple polyester suit, pink shirt, wide Paisley tie matching his even wider lapels, white socks and an outrageous pair of black pointy-toed shoes. It was clear to see our man was right at the forefront of early Seventies fashion, even though he was sitting on his taste buds.

Within seconds he'd swallowed his first spoonful of blood-stained soup, with much disgust all round – it really was a sickening sight.

His "friend" across the soup bowl, waited only three more spoonfuls before leaving the party . . . but as Crackers said, "Where's she gone, the night's only just begun?"

But so too had the meal . . . although not much more was eaten by anybody after the starter from Crackers!

Funny how every minute detail of some meals seem to become etched into one's mind.

When I first came to Melbourne from Hobart as a teenager to play VFL footy and study architecture at the Royal Melbourne Institute of Technology, I must admit some of my own home-cooked meals were pretty ordinary . . . something I bet many students can relate to.

Not much money, not much time and no expertise in the art of cooking – if it didn't come in a can, I was in trouble. I even had trouble boiling water.

One night the kitchen cupboard was bare – all that remained was a box of spaghetti; it had been there for nearly six months and I just wasn't sure how to cook it. But no guts no glory . . . I had a go!

Into the saucepan full of boiling water went the long, slender splinters of spaghetti, several breaking off, and the rest bending in the heated water. Soon the strands were limp and white as spaghetti should look.

Now it was ready to eat . . . the mouth watered at the thought of spaghetti bolognaise. One minor problem though – what about the meat sauce?

I'd completely forgotten and time was moving on . . . only one thing to do – go for the Heinz Big Red tomato sauce.

It certainly lacked meat, but I loved tomato sauce anyway, so everything was fine!

Although cold, bottled sauce on steaming, over-cooked spaghetti wasn't the norm, the serving tasted fine to me . . . well, after all that effort, I wasn't about to turn around and criticise my own creation.

I sat down to a pretty bland old meal, but I got through it . . . even had some leftovers in the simmering pot.

So why not have some sweets, like macaroni, I thought, and I did!

It was merely a matter of cutting up the remaining, rubbery strands of spaghetti into tiny lengths, adding some sugar for sweetness and topping it off with a scoop of vanilla ice cream. The taste at best, was different.

When I think back to those formative years as a student, I wonder how I ever got through . . . but as for ALL goal-oriented young people it was a matter of pushing onward, ever onward, no matter what the circumstances were.

A very good friend of mine through the RMIT days, Dal Wild, had accommodation in a trendy terrace house he shared with four other students – three guys and a girl.

Dal's room was a wonderfully arty expression of the man at the time. He used a British flag as a bedspread.

Light for the room came from a lonely filament globe trapped in a sawn-off champagne bottle. His drafting desk (a secondhand door), was neatly supported on concrete building blocks. The desk was beneath an elevated bed built of "recovered" timber from a nearby demolition site. The only access to his almighty place of slumber was up a rope ladder. I can only say that Dal had many a hair raising climb up the primitive stairs after a big night on the red wine.

Still, it was a great meeting place for the spontaneous exchange of ideas . . . we had many a feed of fish and chips on the old pine table out the back.

But one day we arrived home unexpectedly to find one of his flatmates cooking – an Asian student named Jonathan. He was preparing a very different meal.

Much to our horror, he had Dal's pet goldfish out of the glass bowl and into the frying pan. It was such a pathetic sight – these two tiny little fish, no more than one inch long, sizzling away in a great big black frying pan.

If we hadn't been so angry I suppose we would have offered him some of our chips, because there was no way known the two sardine-like pieces of fish would have made a meal.

For Jonathan that experience was sadly the beginning of the end. The writing was on the wall. He went completely off the rails and had a nervous breakdown – too much pressure to succeed from his parents back home.

But before he left, he chased Susie, the only female lodger, out of the shower, naked, and into the street, brandishing a very large, super sharp carving knife.

Jonathan also asked Dal a most difficult question late one night . . . The handwritten piece of paper was given to my mate as they sat down to meditate and drink a cup of tea.

"I can hear two hands clapping. What does one hand clapping sound like?"

He promptly took back the paper, set fire to it . . . submerged it in his tea cup and drank the brew.

Any answers?

So much for being a student. It takes all kinds, but it sure was a fascinating period of my life.

A Thirst for the Game

"THEY DON'T EVEN STORE THE BEER CLOSE TO THE FRIDGE"

I'd be lying if I said that members of Australia's Test cricket team didn't have a drink at some stage during their career. I used to . . . and most of the current fellas don't mind the odd ale or two. No harm in that. It helps prevent dehydration in the heat of the day!

After all, when you're a deep fine leg and third man "specialist" like myself, having to cope with all that area from deep fine leg way around to forward of square leg, would drive you to drink! Apart from that, having to win the game with both the bat and the ball in a one-day limited over match, puts a bloke under pressure too – and you wonder why a fella's nearly grey! I've also had to meet the Queen a couple of times during my Test career. Now let me tell you . . . that would also drive a modest young man like myself to drink.

There was one such night in the north of England in 1975 when some of our Test heroes were having a quiet one that we will never forget. The local watering hole had a beaut, intimate atmosphere – low ceilings, dim lighting, great for a social night out.

Those terrors of the 1975 Ashes tour – West Australians Dennis Lillee and Rodney Marsh – were there having a quiet sip from their Whitbread "pint" mugs, between bets of course.

I should tell you that in England you're in no danger at all of getting a cold beer . . . well, in those days we weren't . . . because they didn't even store the beer close to the fridge, let alone inside it. So there they were – Rodney and Dennis, pint mugs in hand, with tons of ice blocks melting as quickly as they could get them into the warm beer.

Down went the pints – one, two, three, four, five. About half an hour later, nature took its course. That fabled drinker, Rodney Marsh, was the first to signal to the little Pommie barman. "Hey pal, whereabouts is the GENTS?" he demanded. Bacchus chuckled at the directions shouted across the bar: "Down the corridor, over the dirt track, come to the green saw-tooth door . . . and that's it!"

"Bloody beauty, we're away . . . " Rodney says, as he sways to his feet, relief near at hand. Five steps forward and three back, the little fat fella waddled out of the bar, bounced off the wall of the corridor and across the dirt track until he spied a green saw-tooth door.

"Aaah!" Very few sensations in the world go close to that when you're under pressure, do they? Sensational!

About fifteen minutes and a few more pints later Lillee realised his little drinking partner still hadn't returned. Must have fallen in, the fast bowler chuckled. So across the bar . . . down the corridor . . . over the dirt track – not much quicker or straighter than Marshie had managed – marched Dennis. He came to the same green saw-tooth door and barked his arrival.

"Hey, Bacchus! Bacchus, what's happened? You fallen in or something?"

A pained reply came under door. "No, but every time I go to stand up some bugger grabs me by the 'Niagaras'."

Fearing his little mate was in real trouble, Lillee kicked the door open.

One look at the scene inside and Dennis doubled up in laughter. "You silly bugger, you're sitting on the mop bucket!"

Most of the pain was facial!

A Swig the Skipper didn't see

"THE MAJORITY OF THE MOB BEHIND ME STOOD UP AND CHEERED"

One of my favorite cricket stories occurred during my first trip overseas with the Australian team. This was the 1973 official tour of the Caribbean. Our first stop was Kingston, Jamaica, where we played a handful of games.

As the door of our B.W.I.A. jet opened wide we were greeted with a blast of hot, humid air similar to opening a sauna bath door. Maybe we were lucky because the locals reckoned B.W.I.A. stands for "best wishes if you arrive!" It was worth thinking about though, eh? Some of the small aeroplanes were very old and decrepid.

I wondered how a bloke like myself could stand up all day and bowl medium-fast anything in this sort of oppressive humidity – believe me it wasn't easy. I thought, gee, I might even hallucinate if I become dehydrated.

It was during this early stage of the trip that I made the decision to make as many friends as I could through the ten feet high barbed wire fences which were obviously built to keep the players inside the playing area for the entire duration of the game! Maybe I could con a drink. It didn't take too long for this theory to prove successful.

The first few wickets that I took whilst in Jamaica were very satisfying but also somewhat unsettling. Every time I returned to my permanent fielding position at deep fine leg I would be greeted with shouts of "Walker, you bad man, Walker!" It was easy to see they weren't smiling when they said that. When they did, and that wasn't often, it looked like a piano keyboard set in a large mouth. Too often those smiling mouths were closed . . . fortunately things changed as the tour progressed and the calypso singing spectators quickly warmed to the tourists. As one local said, "The cricket's real good man!"

Australia played Jamaica at the Sabina Park Cricket Ground before the first Test match. As usual it had been a very long, hot day and I was approaching my twenty-fifth over – I needed a drink, I really did.

My prayers were answered under a cloudless sky that afternoon. The perspiration was leaking from my body like a dripping tap – not one part of my cricket attire was dry. Yes, at last I'd won a friend . . . no, not the one that offered me his wife if I took another wicket, but a different guy. He screamed "Wokko, ya wanna drink of my rum?" It was a deep and bellowing voice. I attempted to explain to him that if the fellow at first slip with the baggy green cap on his head, Ian Chappell, saw me drinking his rum, I would never play cricket for Australia again. His reply was, "Ee won't see ya man!" But in my opinion 10 foot high barbed wire fences didn't create a big enough shadow for cover.

And with that remark, the big black man turned to his mate in the back row of the bamboo grandstand. He let out a piercing whistle to catch his friend's attention. Immediately a huge black umbrella was relayed overhead to my new pal in the front row. His name was George.

Before I knew it the umbrella had been thrust through the fence and opened to a diameter of about six foot. I thought to myself, "There is no way known anyone will be able to spot me having a drink now."

Through the fence came a dirty, grotty, green bottle of home made rum. I looked carefully at the neck of the bottle – it was not too flash! Keith Miller well may have been the last Aussie to drink from it.

Then all the possibilities ran across my mind. I could just have a little sip straight from the bottle not exactly safe. Maybe if I just dipped my finger in the top of the rum bottle it would be OK. Finally I said, "Bugger it, I'll go for the whole catastrophe!" And I did. With the black umbrella for protection, I squatted down on my haunches, and raised the dirty receptacle to my parched lips.

The homemade brew must have been about 500 per cent proof – bloody unreal! I could feel the warm liquid sting as it passed my cracked lips on its rapid journey to my stomach. It was a strange burning, searing sensation. A heart burn even a Quickeze wouldn't have cured! My Aussie cap almost jumped off the top of my head – this was good stuff, "oh yeah, oh yeah!"

West Indian crowds really react when something tickles their fancy. The majority of the mob behind me stood up and cheered. Some of their very colourful hats and caps were thrown high in the air above their heads. How they got them back, I really don't know.

Now with all this noise, first slip, second slip, cover, mid-off, mid-on and even Rod Marsh, the wicketkeeper, spun round to see what was happening. I had already handed back the brew to George, who was attempting to dismantle his mate's very large black brolly, but not without a lot of trouble. From where I stood, it was very difficult to tell the difference between some bent umbrella spokes and the barbed wire fence itself.

I slowly walked away from the crowd as though nothing had happened, although I was coughing from the sting of the rum.

The skipper saw nothing and had nothing to say. I had been successful in partaking of some liquid refreshment and believe me the drink did the job.

Two overs later, when I was fielding again in front of my friends in the primitive bamboo stand, things began to happen.

I stood and gazed at that simple structure, which was definitely overloaded by 50 per cent and contemplated: "What chance of this grandstand being designed and built in Melbourne, Victoria? None."

A batsman named Maurice Foster had hit a lofted hook shot behind square leg. The ball hung in the air for a long time. With all the pace I didn't possess, I managed to get close enough to attempt a diving right-handed catch. Without exaggerating, I must have run 40 metres around the boundary line to pull off the catch – it was magnificent. I even rolled over an extra couple of times, after coming to ground heavily, so as to make the effort look even more spectacular.

The masses erupted yet again as I came to my feet, brushing the orange dust from my trousers. Every second bloke in the stand swayed to his right as if to mimic the catch. The noise was incredible as my catch was being described over and over again by the cricket enthusiasts. There was no huge electronic scoreboard here to replay the dismissal, only the memory.

I felt obliged to acknowledge the crowd. Obviously it was not my natural pace and ability that enabled me to take the ball safely – it had to be the home-made rum I'd been given! So I began furiously rubbing my hand around in a circular movement over my stomach to show the effects of the jungle juice. Again the crowd roared in acceptance.

At this stage I had my back to the centre wicket area and began really playing up to the rowdy, colourful spectators. I was enjoying myself when a deathly SILENCE came across the entire ground. I must have been the only person at the ground who didn't realise that it had been called a NO-BALL, and the batsmen had just completed three runs. You can imagine my embarrassment, I wished the earth would swallow me up.

Glutton for Punishment

"HE ONCE ATE FOURTEEN MEAT PIES AND NINETEEN SAVELOYS – WITHOUT SAUCE"

It was hard to believe that anyone could possibly stuff at least a dozen fresh prawns into their mouth all at once! But I saw the incident with my own eyes . . . in the person of a fragile, little old lady dressed in a black and white pom-pom hat, black and white cardigan and black knitted dress.

And to top off her outfit she was wearing a pair of blue and white runners with no socks – hardly dressed to kill, eh?

Nevertheless, she was very intent on winning the prawn eating competition that I'd somehow got myself involved in.

My primary reason for being in Gladstone, Queensland, during Easter 1986 was for a single wicket contest, and certainly not to make a glutton of myself in public.

There I was, along with seven other hungry characters, standing around an old timber trestle. In front of each of us was placed a huge plastic bag of medium-sized prawns . . . the pile must have been a foot high. That's a lot of prawns, so the first prize of 40 kilos of fresh prawns was the last thing I needed!

Each contestant was poised, forearms tensed ready for a standing start, especially the tiny old lady with the big appetite and wrinkled face opposite me.

The atmosphere was electric, the starter's gun punctured the air and was followed by the sickening sound of prawn munchers! There really is no other sound quite like the simultaneous crunching of prawn shells! Although, one of the contestants decided to shell them and stockpile until there was a sufficient number to cram into his mouth for one huge gulp – not a pretty sight!

The pace was hectic – both skill and technique were necessary to keep up with the leaders. A muscular, tattooed dude and the little old lady were neck and neck – or should I say mouthful and mouthful.

The man with the tattoos on his arm was a "peel and stockpiler" . . . three easy actions. Head off, tail off, then shell the rest.

On the other hand, the skinny little woman with the rubbery face had very little class . . . in they went, heads, tails and whatever else, sometimes twelve at a time. Incredible.

My stomach squirmed as she continually chomped away like a pelican swallowing a huge fish. Never once did that tell-tale lump in her throat surface as a painful expression. Her eyes remained fixed on the diminishing pile of pink prawns.

I had barely made in-roads into my quota of prawns when the contest was all over. A muscle-bound sailor standing opposite me signalled he had finished by raising his right hand above his head. He half-smiled through clenched teeth, saliva and prawn shell dribbling from the corner of his mouth. It was easy to see he'd made a complete guts of himself.

Just seconds later a shout of relief as the black and white lady punched the sky like Rocky's grandmother.

She was very outspoken at the result, claiming victory was hers, on the grounds that she had eaten the shell and heads whereas the other guy hadn't. The final result stood, but she didn't leave empty handed – the organisers gave her 20 kilos for a very courageous effort!

Meanwhile cricketers Glenn Trimble, Peter Clifford and myself performed like novices and were still eating prawns out of a plastic bag an hour later.

My heart and stomach weren't really in this episode, but don't get me wrong I used to be pretty good on the tooth! So too was my dad!

He once ate fourteen meat pies and nineteen saveloys, without sauce, to win a local football pie-night eating competition, in Tasmania. In fact, he won by three savs, after his main rival had failed to keep his tally intact – I'm told he left the changerooms in search of fresh air, in a big hurry and looked a trifle green around the gills when he came back.

My only success at over-indulging came to me quite by chance during the 1973 Australian cricket tour of the Caribbean.

We'd spent a few weeks in Guyana and apart from the cricket, it was a pretty depressing place to be. Everywhere we looked poverty confronted us. So too did the politics of the country.

On top of all this the food wasn't too flash either. A steady diet of chicken ranging in colour from white to green was consistently fed to us. So too was the alternative – curried goat, fried rice and twenty-five different varieties of blowflies, some of 'em big buggers too.

But, much to our relief, our next venue was the beautiful island paradise of Tobago. Now here food was not a problem, nothing was a problem.

We couldn't believe the range . . . this was the ideal venue for an eating competition.

Jeff Hammond, the South Australian fast bowler with a build like a walking coat-hanger, reckoned he was a better 'fang-man' than me. I accepted the challenge with a great deal of pleasure and confidence.

By sheer coincidence the evening meal on our first night in Tobago was a smorgasbord – you beauty! The spread was virtually 10 square metres piled high with every food conceivable – salads, hot dishes, cold meats and a magnificent assortment of sweets, which I love.

After bulldozing through two plates each containing two corn on the cobs, two huge slices of beef, two potatoes wrapped in silver foil with a few peas, we tackled the cold collations with a great deal of vigor.

Almost an hour of absolutely identical eating had passed when I suggested we tackle the sweets, my strong point!

The two bowlers began by downing three pastry tarts and three colourful jellies. I must admit I was beginning to feel the pinch as my belly was stretched to the limit!

Next the tall black waiter tempted the two of us with the largest banana splits I've ever seen. He said, "Compliments of the chef." The word had spread to the kitchen that we were nearing the business end of the meal.

Each banana must have been 30 cm (12 inches) long, enclosing three scoops of ice-cream and with strawberry topping and nuts . . . absolutely delicious. My rival with the reputation was beginning to struggle – I could see it in his eyes.

I don't know how but I emptied my plate of fruit and ice-cream . . . then applied some old-fashioned gamesmanship. I grabbed another six jellies and placed them on the table in front of Jeff.

His reaction was predictable – almost physically sick as he accepted the offer of a drink. Coffee was the medium-pacer's choice, mine was lemon tea.

I said, "Three more jellies each mate then we'll get fair dinkum!" The strategy worked.

The coffee swilled around in his mouth and refused to dive down to the depths of his stomach. The level remained constant, at about gum-level, as he tried to combine a smile and a burp. I polished off one lone jelly and the contender conceded . . . I was definitely bluffing. One more jelly and my game would have been over and out.

How the Windies Unwind

"THE MIGHTY ATHLETES FROM THE CARIBBEAN CRUISED AMONGST THE LADIES"

Every story teller has the ability to embellish and it is this tampering with the truth that often is the difference between a yarn worth listening to and one that really ought never be uttered.

Sport and the subsequent characters always provide abundant subject matter and more often than not they remain unaware that their names have been used for the sake of a laugh.

This is possibly the case with one of my favourite cricketing stories and it involves two of the heroes of World Series Cricket – Viv Richards and Joel Garner.

Playing cricket against either man at night under lights had its problems and it had nothing to do with the nipple pink gear they used to wear.

In fact, merely playing the game at night presents problems for the players of both teams . . . all a bit of a gamble.

You don't know when to eat, whether the captain will decide to bat or bowl, should I have a bite before play at noon – maybe we'll bowl second – I should leave it until tea time around 6.00 p.m. Amongst all this uncertainty there remains the final QUESTION – what do we do after the game, when the lights go out?

Let me tell you. A player can't stroll out of the Sydney Cricket Ground at half past ten and expect to be asleep by 11.15 p.m., all neatly tucked away in the hotel cot. Everyone needs to "unwind" a little. At that hour, there's still plenty of adrenalin surging through the body, maybe the heartbeat is pounding out a heavy tune after a close finish.

Australians, being the committed sportsmen they always have been, will hurry back to the hotel where the team stays and most probably relax over a cappuccino (maybe I am exaggerating a bit here but forgive me) and hamburger.

On the other hand the "Calypso Kids" will be more interested in a party . . . any party! And in every city on the touring calendar involving a West Indian team, there will inevitably be "the party". If not these players set one up themselves . . . and I don't think I'm giving away any secrets when I say that Australian women love going to parties where the Windies hang out! Just a cool breeze blowin' through the body all the time, ma'am.

For example, after a day/night clash at the SCG in the late Seventies, the typical invitation to "party" predictably arrived in the form of a folded piece of paper via the twelfth man. He's the guy who had spent the entire evening scrutinising the state of play outside the fence – up periscope. The ball bearings in the neck of Bernard Julien were working overtime scanning the grandstands for potential party goers of the female kind.

The unanimous team decision after a comfortable limited over win was: "YES, we'll be in it!"

The venue was North Sydney, over the Harbour Bridge and turn left. Inside it was standing room only . . . wall to wall women and a hyperactive, winning team – the chemistry was ideal, the music very up tempo and a truck load of rum 'n' coca cola to quench the thirst on a balmy night.

The mighty athletes from the Caribbean cruised amongst the ladies flashing a smile and ignoring the men. Tonight was not the scene to replay the game over and over again – better things to do.

The Master Blaster, Viv Richards, was playing the old bull . . . he didn't have a sign above the gate, but he might as well have, saying: I am available.

Desmond Haynes, one of the happiest cricketers ever to pull on a pad, had more moves than Warwick Capper when he spearheaded the Sydney Swans forward line many, many seasons back. And you couldn't forget the human clothes peg – Joel Garner. The big fella had a wonderful vantage point, head and shoulders above the crush . . . and an easy swig of his drink.

The hours danced by and the level in the various varieties of bottles drained steadily . . . but all good parties come to an end. It was 3.00 a.m.

The captain of the side, Clive Lloyd, a charismatic gentleman, used his authority to maintain discipline: "Right boys, that's it, back to the pub!"

And to a man they responded . . . even if one or two didn't want to leave immediately!

Into their white BMW courtesy cars and away they drove towards the giant coathanger that spans Sydney Harbour.

The first vehicle to depart contained Viv and Joel. Obviously the "big bird" wasn't driving, his 200 cm frame wouldn't fold under the steering wheel – Viv was in control.

Joel had left in a hurry and was feeling the pressure. The giant fast bowler was desperate for a "you 'n' me" – legs crossed, arms crossed and maybe even his fingers. But all the crossing in the world wasn't going to relieve the agony of a bursting bladder.

Just before the halfway mark of the bridge the passenger shouted: "Stop the car man . . . stop the car!!" and his mate knew he meant what he said.

So out they stepped . . . it was so dark, nobody could see them . . . and just as well.

Like two large silhouettes they stood at the balcony of Australia's famous landmark admiring the reflections of the moonlight on the water below. To their right were the lights of Luna Park, the sound of a lone ferry dominated the moment – their needs were still pressing.

First to address the problem was Joel . . . beginning to smile: "Gee, the water's cold tonight Viv?" he confessed.

And with the recoil of an elephant gun, the world's finest wielder of a willow replied: " . . . AND it's not that deep either, is it Bird?"

This yarn can only work whilst chatting about West Indians. Use an Australian cricketer and I'm certain the punchline would fall very short of its mark . . . what could you expect from the rest of us mere mortals! A drop in the ocean.

CHAPTER FOUR

Tell us Another one Mr Walker

*Everyone fell about laughing
as I strained to concentrate on my line.*

Giving 'em Plenty of Lip

"HE BARELY KNEW WHICH END OF A CRICKET BAT TO PICK UP"

On March 14, 1923, when the doctor delivered Louis Thomas Charles Richards, they tell me it only took one smack on his bare bottom and a quick flip upside down to get that cute little mouth to make a noise!

And ever since that day, Louie has been making a lot of noise! Hundreds of thousands of people from Cape York, Queensland, to Broome in the West have become fans of this lovable little fella from the back streets of Collingwood where even the corrugated iron rooftops are painted black and white. Yes Lou Richards epitomised the miner's cottage and chimney stack tradition that made the Collingwood Football Club famous.

These days Louie is a very successful television personality and businessman. He's immaculately dressed, thanks to his lovely wife Edna (Lou wouldn't admit it but the whisper is . . . she even selects his underpants! C'mon Lou who does wear the pants in your house?) and sports a very distinguished shock of silver hair (often referred to as the grey flannel hairpiece). But it wasn't always easy! In those rough and ready days of the Forties and Fifties there were no fashion garments, tailored clothing or Christian Dior undies, only a set of overalls and a gladstone bag.

Australian Rules football was his game and boy, could the little bloke play. He kicked off his career in 1941, just a couple of drop kicks away from home. He loved to win, and win they did. In an incident-packed career that finished in 1955, Louie had chalked up 250 VFL games with Collingwood. Only three other men have represented his beloved club more often at Victoria Park.

It was fitting that this home grown product – educated at Collingwood Tech where his algebra might not have been up to standard, but he learnt a lot about bloodied knee caps, dirty faces and how to get a football when the going gets tough – should climb to the role of captain in 1952, and lead the side to a premiership over Geelong the following year.

There's no grey area with Lou, you either love him or hate him. He'd be the first to admit he upset plenty during the journey into the heart and soul of Melbourne's football media machine – as an outlandish journalist with the Melbourne *Sun* and focus for HSV 7's one and only "World of Sport". It's not surprising then that he didn't win Collingwood's Copeland Trophy for the fairest as well as the best player!

Louie's quick wit and acid tongue has got him into and out of plenty of hot water. Maybe that's why one of his many nicknames – Louie the Lip – came into being.

A man of his word and conviction, there's never a dull moment . . . he believes strongly in a football team's ability to win and is hardly ever right. He once told me he picked all six winners in a VFL round more than twenty years ago! That's a bit rough when the legend is supposed to be a football expert!

League coaches hate him to select their team to win because he's so often wrong – the "Kiss of Death" it's called. Sometimes he is committed enough to categorically state something stupid like "I'll jump off the end of Brighton pier at 6.00 a.m. on a freezing mid-July morning if I'm wrong."

As he dragged himself from the icy waters of Port Phillip Bay a couple of decades back, without a wet suit, he muttered: "I'll never do that again . . . can't be good for a bloke's sex life being this counter sunk!"

Several months later Louie the Lip had cracked it for another big one . . . this time sweeping Bourke Street, Melbourne, with a plastic toothbrush. It took a while!

He is one of the great characters of Melbourne and has been crowned King of Moomba, with the likes of Graham Kennedy, Mickey Mouse, tennis player Paul McNamee and that bulbous actor with the very proper voice, Frank Thring.

In the early Eighties I was invited to become Channel 7's cricket expert on "World of Sport". I was a little apprehensive at first, because the show had been running for twenty odd years with most of the same people, in the same format. Good luck Maxie, I thought. I was to need some too!

At Dorcas Street, South Melbourne – in a large barn like warehouse – I was to experience first hand the on-camera and behind the scenes pranks of Lou Richards and his co-stars.

The first week of appearing on tele was a pretty hair-raising experience. No instruction, no coaching, pick your own subject, and talk when the red light starts flashing on the camera.

Everyone else on the floor in the spartan old studios was joking, laughing and generally uninterested in what I was about to say. After all, District Cricket wasn't exactly the sort of television viewing that would make you put off going to make a cup of coffee or drop the washing-up to turn around to see who had won between Footscray and South Melbourne.

Actually during my inaugural "piece" to camera, I took a long, deep, nervous breath . . . and before I could make a second, hard-hitting point, the director, like God Almighty, somewhere upstairs in the control room, had slipped in a commercial break.

Now I should explain there is a lot of difference between being asked questions in an interview situation and being the up front person making the sensible comments as well as asking the pertinent questions, particularly if the first two or three thought-provoking prodders manage only a blunt "Yes", or "No" in response! So to perform articulately, and make some sense for say, three minutes, is a very difficult assignment.

GTV 9 newsreader Brian Naylor speaks at approximately five words per second. Yours truly is a fair degree slower at three per second – most Tasmanians do speak slowly! As you can imagine, sitting in front of camera as a terrified and nervous new presenter, 180 seconds can seem like an energy sapping 500 metre dash. It never ends!

Sometimes things don't quite go as planned . . . and that's when life really gets interesting. For example, the totally unexpected happened during my second weekend at Dorcas Street, much to everyone else's delight.

The culprit was one of Louie's best mates, a grotesque, bespectacled man, tipping the scales at more than 20 stone and affectionately referred to as "Uncle Doug" or "Unca"! He was one of the foundation members of this historic television program and over the twenty-eight years of the show's lifetime, the late Doug Elliott was the bloke most likely to plug the products. He would be Mr Patra orange juice, Mr Red Tulip chocolates, Mr . . . cheese, meat. You name it, Unc would be flogging as hard as his firm jaw and shaking head would allow.

A former Lord Mayor of Essendon, he had a sharp wit and a penchant for poetry which he often read on air. The big fella's appetite was legendary . . . it was stated often that if they X-rayed Unc's stomach they'd find three or four meat pies nestled comfortably inside without even a tooth mark on 'em! He wasn't a guts as some of his mates often suggested . . . merely a not so fussy connoisseur of all edible sponsor products.

Like most of "the team" Unc loved a practical joke. I know I do, as long as I'm not the subject. Unfortunately as the new boy on the show my "initiation" on the set was going to be much fun for everyone but Channel Seven's brand new cricket expert.

After less than thirty seconds regurgitating several well rehearsed comments on the leadership qualities of the blue-eyed boy from the West – Kimberley Hughes – a pear-shaped man with thick rimmed glasses appeared camera right. I couldn't believe my eyes!

Now I don't wish to sound rude and crude but this was how it was. Uncle Doug brazenly stood in my line of sight and in a rather animated manner, slowly undid the belt holding up his badly creased trousers. At this stage I was in a state of confusion . . . should I ignore him and continue trying to make sense to the totally unaware audience? I tried this for a few more uncomfortable seconds.

Then it all became too much when his trousers slipped past his nobbly kneecaps into a crumpled pile around his ankles, followed by his Hawthorn underpants – you know the type – yellow in the front and brown at the back.

I had a grin like Luna Park and the laughter was hard to suppress. Remember, there was no seven seconds delay, this was pure, LIVE television. Without even thinking, I'd blurted: "I don't believe it . . . he's just dropped his dacks!"

His reaction was to about face and touch his toes. Before my eyes were the worst set of hamstrings I had seen in many, many years – completely devoid of muscle tone and polar bear white in colour.

Meanwhile cameras were jockeying for position like dodgem cars with a view to capturing the mature gentleman dragging his trousers up to somewhere above the "plimsol line". I've never seen a pair of trousers and fly zip hoisted so quickly on the silver screen.

Yes, it was a memorable second day at HSV 7.

After my "initiation" Uncle Doug wrapped his arm around my shoulder: "That was great son, spontaneity is what this caper is all about . . . the show thrives on it!"

How true these words were. "World of Sport" was the only live television show I know that could be running thirty minutes behind schedule after only being "on air" for an hour – the madcap ad lib and semi-organised chaos was half the charm and attraction of this almost compulsory Sunday viewing in Victoria.

Day number three at the station turned out to be just as exciting – my motto should have been "prepare for the unexpected".

This time Lou got into the act . . . again yours truly was on the receiving end.

Many people had suggested Louie the Lip wouldn't be super helpful . . . after all, he barely knew which end of a cricket bat to pick up but he had done a lot of miles in front of camera. So when the chunky little ex-rover from Magpieland offered some advice, I thought, don't be quick to judge, maybe he's genuine. The straight look on his face was too serious to believe – but gullible old me did. This rough-hewn, loudly spoken master of the ad-lib suggested I use an "idiot sheet" like all the pros – Don Lane, Bert Newton and Mike Walsh.

My basic problem was not being able to say "Goodbye" quickly. In other words, they couldn't shut me up! Lou thought that if I was scripted, the problem wouldn't arise. How the shoe is on the other foot these days at GTV 9. My little mate still has trouble distinguishing the difference between a thirteen second chat and a forty-nine second conversation. On the Sunday Edition of "Wide World of Sport" we used to see that familiar rotating "wind-up" hand signal from the floor manager just about every story. It could be said we both like to have a chat!

At the completion of my District Cricket segment, Louie stood next to the camera, legs slightly astride, arms high with a huge sheet of butcher's paper. In the corner of his mouth his cigarette began to glow a bright red as he inhaled quickly. His mischievous eyes were dancing left and right looking for attention . . . he had all the support he needed.

My old architecture lecturer, Ron Centre, at the Royal Melbourne Institute of Technology, would have been proud of the lovely lettering on the beige coloured butcher's paper. This graduate from Collingwood Tech had obviously sat down with a chunky felt pen and neatly written my closing message.

What a lovely gesture, I thought, as I began to read, word perfect: "Well, that just about wraps up the District Cricket . . . "

I never did make it to the end of line two because, quick as a flash, Lou had dug deep into his Christian Dior trouser pocket and produced a cigarette lighter. No ordinary lighter either – a Dunhill, thank you very much! A sure sign the boy from the back streets of Collingwood had a few bob to spend on himself. Well, he doesn't spend it on anyone else!

What do you reckon he did with the tiny gold-plated flame-thrower! You guessed it! He licked the bottom two corners of the paper sign with the flame . . . everyone fell about laughing as I strained to concentrate on my line. Within seconds, the bottom half of the script was going up in smoke and Louie began to cough loudly.

" . . . someone call the Fire Brigade . . . and avagoodweegend!!" was about the best I could think of as a quick "out".

Well a lot of water flowed down the gutters of Melbourne in the next ten years – both Lou and myself crossed the tramlines to join the sports team at Channel 9 and still the fun continues.

After watching a troupe of female body builders complete their routines for the Miss Olympia title one morning on "Wide World of Sports – Sunday Edition", I asked Lou a simple straightforward question in back announcing the segment: "What did you think of Dianne – the one in the orange bikini?" She was the one he fancied!

After one more squinted look at our TV monitor, Lou let loose with a rip snorter of a reply: "She'd be pretty handy on a half-back flank for Collingwood wouldn't she?"

Needless to say we had about a hundred letters about his tactless quip . . . but at the time Collingwood weren't winning too many games and he probably meant it.

What about the full mug of coffee the little bugger poured over me during a commercial break . . . everywhere, shirt, tie, jacket, trousers. He was still apologising for making my underpants hot and sticky and I found it very hard to keep a straight face as the floor manager counted me in: 5, 4, 3, 2, 1 and his arm dropped! The light was on . . . and away I went introducing the next story.

Then he dared me to introduce the following part of the show trouserless! In other words, blazer and tie . . . and underpants! "Go on," he said. "You're gutless."

It never ends. The chatter is constant. "Did ya hear the one about the two hard-boiled eggs on their wedding night . . . ?"

I'd heard that one forty-five times, but with a new cameraman on duty he's worth a try. Well, that's Lou's theory!

Louie had once asked a question of a presenter, knowing full well that the segment had been taped earlier in the day. Then, when no answer was forthcoming, had the audacity to reckon the bloke had the "tom tits" with him . . . and wouldn't answer.

No doubt about it, there's never a dull or quiet moment with my little mate, Louie the Lip.

How to Tame Lions

"IT'S NOT THAT MY LITTLE MATE HAD A WEAK BLADDER, HE WAS GENUINELY TERRIFIED . . ."

Commonsense should have prevented us entering the lions' cage but it didn't – I guess that is a commodity that Lou Richards, alias "Louie the Lip", has very little of. Louie, my former co-host on Channel Nine's "Wide World of Sports – Sunday Edition" and yours truly were looking at the battered, rusty bars of the Sole Bros lion cage along with about 4,000 circus fans.

The majority were school kids with fresh faces and bulging eyes. They had paid good money to be there and it didn't matter that their bums were numb from sitting on the cold, collapsible metal seats. They were visibly excited in anticipation of the spectacle to come!

So too was Louie and myself, but for totally different reasons – Louie had already visited the toilet four times before he entered the ring! It's not that my little mate had a weak bladder, he was genuinely terrified at the thought of entering the lions' cage. To be honest, I wasn't exactly the Rock of Gibraltar either. I'd also managed to sneak in a nervous one before we had to get fair dinkum with the King of the Jungle.

When our turn to entertain the masses arrived, Lou was dead set shaking in his boots, all 74 kg of him. The little bloke kept sinking deeper and deeper into the smelly sawdust as his knees knocked against each other in perfect harmony with his chattering teeth. The noise was embarrassing! The possibility of the top drawer of his false "chats" sliding out – was very real!

We were both dressed in "Dr Livingstone, I presume" outfits complete with pith helmets, matching Khaki shirts and trousers. Sue from Wardrobe at Channel 9 had gone to a lot of trouble in outfitting us. The knee-high boots, for example, had been used in the Aussie film epic – *Gallipoli*. But I'm not too sure from where exactly she "discovered" our bullet-laden gun belts. Louie's oversized belt looked more like the supportive back-brace Dean Lukin wore during his heavyweight gold medal lift in the '84 L.A. Olympics. It sported, not one, but two very impressive brass buckles to thread through. At first I didn't realise this wasn't purely aesthetic. He had another belt wrapped around his belly underneath this one to hold up his saggy, baggy trousers. The best solution of course would be to pass Louie's salivating tongue through the buckles as well – after all Louie the Lip's flapper is in exactly the same proportion as his mouth – XXOS! To complete this otherwise bizarre outfit the former Collingwood captain had continued his fascination for large clothes . . . the wide shirt sleeves were at least 10 cm too long. I'm sure the little bloke would have preferred the freedom of a sleeveless Magpie guernsey.

On the other hand, the Anzac who proudly marched into battle wearing my boots must have been lean and hungry. I haven't developed the greatest set of calf muscles in the world . . . and after killing time in these cobbler's delights for an hour or so, not much circulation was making the downhill journey to the ends of my toes – they were cold and numb! The positive side of jamming both feet into an old pair of boots at least two sizes too small was that it took my mind off the unpleasant ordeal ahead.

Lou was still trembling all over when "beastmaster", Lindsay Perry, cracked his stockman's whip above his head like Indiana Jones in the movie *The Temple of Doom*. It was great showmanship and he was obviously a man chock full of confidence. For Louie and myself, that caged enclosure symbolised our "temple of doom"!

The mobile carriage used to transport the lions was backed up to the ring. Up went the barred door and we were treated to our first glimpse – unbelievable! Out they came one after the other. Real snarling, prowling, ferocious-looking lions! I counted four. That was enough! Lou suggested the quantities didn't matter, " 'cause there was no way known I'm going in there while they're still roaming around!"

Then I reminded him why we were dressed differently and peering through lots of sets of iron bars. We were shooting a "Wide World of Sports" promo. The initial concept dreamt up by our producer at the time, Stephen Phillips, was to film an enormous roaring lion jumping through a metal hoop framing a paper sign with the Channel 9 WWOS identification. As a visual concept, it was a beauty, but in reality it was frightening stuff . . . Thanks Stephen. I was beginning to believe there were more than nine dots next to the 9.

By this stage, Lou's face was as grey as his hair, for once in his life the legendary "Lip" had nothing cheeky or funny to say. And if I'm not mistaken, he was too busy praying to the big fella upstairs to tag anybody with the "Kiss of Death" . . . it's hard to believe but, yes . . . the little fella was on his knees in the damp sawdust. You couldn't blame him because Nero, a 300 kg, eight-year-old African lion, appeared to be "toe-sniffing" in the direction of Lou! He looked like a very hungry man eater!

We received a comforting reception from the capacity crowd under the big top when Lindsay, the lion tamer, announced our presence and objective. The worst thing that could happen to us, he told the anxious gathering was, "They could be eaten alive if they're not careful!"

The more I thought about it, the worse it got. I felt like a tail-end batsman waiting to get bounced by a manic fastbowler from the Caribbean.

Then a couple of the lionesses appeared upset when our cameraman, Mick Purdy, turned on the floodlights and pointed his lens in their direction. Remember, we weren't yet inside the cage!

Finally we could put it off no longer. On cue, me and my shadow entered the enclosure looking as confident as two guys could who had never even patted a real lion before and never wanted to!

I said to my little multi-media megastar mate: "Let's get this over and done with quickly; grab a hoop so the flaming lion can jump through it and we can get the hell out of here!"

"It's all right for you!" Louie snapped with some of his old fire. "You're only skin and bone (all 95 kg and 193 cm of me) since you went on that diet . . . they'll have a dash at me first! Where are they going to find another me?"

Mind you, that was a pretty good question. They definitely threw the mould away when they cast Lou!

"Anyway!" he stated arrogantly, "Channel 9 can always find another old has-been fast bowler or a batsman. They're two bob a dozen!"

As I gingerly took up my position between two stools, I could feel the hot sticky breaths of three restless animals tickling the back of my neck. None of them used MacLeans toothpaste either – their breath was dreadful!

At this stage the knot in my stomach was becoming unbearable and the lump in my throat had lodged somewhere between my ears. I don't know how Louie was doing beside me but I bet he was pleased to have his oversized trousers tucked in, so there were no tell-tale signs of his nervous condition!

We had positioned the hand-held hoop above our heads as directed. The exercise wasn't easy because of Lou's size. Somehow Melbourne's answer to George Burns hung on grimly to the bottom side of the hoop while standing on his tip toes. We were told to hang on tight because if the lion missed the paper target and hit the metal rim he'd be just as likely to knock both of us over and land on top of us. Don't even think about it!

One crack of the whip and around came Nero, a wonderfully fit-looking animal with his large black pupils focused only on the hoop. He knew exactly where he was going. Two bounding paces and his front paws reached the top of the stool, quickly followed by his powerful hindquarter. Lou's eyes were now shut tightly in much the same way as a child's – when they don't want to see the growling dog at the end of the street, roll up its upper lip to expose a set of sharp teeth.

But no problems with Nero – straight through the eye diddle diddle. A perfect leap. The cameras were rolling, lights glaring and even the odd flashbulb exploded as he landed on the other stool. Fantastic!

Louie looked at me with a, "What did I tell ya," look, out of total relief. The verbal diarrhoea was about to flow. Behind me the big cats were still showing us their stained teeth while clawing at Lindsay who had a chair in one hand and a whip in the other.

Louie was wrong again. The party wasn't quite over. He nearly fainted when our cameraman produced a second hoop. "An insurance shot!" he said. "Just in case!"

So back in position for take two. Nero did a lap of honour, flared his nostrils and away he went. Another direct hit. We just wanted to make a quick exit.

Before either of the human statues had made a move, Nero had completed a "U-turn" and was heading back towards us. Lindsay smirked at Lou ducking his head, as if appealing for a free kick. At the same time the other lions began running around and around and around us. I was getting edgy and very giddy watching their antics.

Fortunately Lindsay called them to attention and down they sat, side by side, like big puppies – butter wouldn't melt in their mouth.

Now with everything under control. Louie played up to the crowd. The chirpy little ex-Magpie performed a few pirouettes with the bare minimum of finesse. My exit was more of a modest acknowledgement that we were leaving in one piece – just a raising of the right hand.

As the stench of lion droppings filled the big top, we bolted for safety like Laurel and Hardy, "Shut the gate behind you please . . . the lions might get out!" was the parting tongue in cheek remark from the ringmaster. Colour was beginning to flush back into my cheeks. We had done the deed unscathed – one to tell the grandchildren about!

"Did you see them have a swipe at me?" Lou asked. "It was a bit dicey for a while!" he went on.

"Good thing you had me in there to look after you, Maxie!"

I thought to myself, "Yeah, Louie . . . there was no way you were even going near this cage if I didn't first agree to go in with you!"

But then again little blokes are all the same, aren't they? Those of you that are under five foot and finished growing will agree with Louie, but that's alright because he always get's it wrong, you only have to follow his footy tipping to know that!

As for aspirations of being liontamers, Louie will stick to the Fitzroy Football Club (The Lions) and I'll be content to see Australia whip the pants off the English cricket team. It's got to be easier than watching your life flash before your eyes inside a cage of prowling lions. Once is certainly enough for me, they can just keep replaying the same footage!

And no matter how often I look at that footage I keep returning to the same conclusion – Lou is not a pretty sight! Spare a thought for the lions.

I think "Captain Blood" Jack Dyer, the rough and tough Richmond ruckman was spot on when he told me: "That Lou was so ugly as a four-year-old kid, his mum used to have to hang the lamb chops around his neck to get their dog to play with him."

Many Unhappy Returns

"WITH A SICKENING THUD, THE BAG HIT THE TELEGRAPH POLE"

I don't know about you . . . but I definitely do not like having to return purchases to shops. Either because they are not exactly right or are faulty. In these days of greater consumer awareness there seems to be more and more people prepared to do it . . . and good on 'em.

As for yours truly – I'll get anyone I can to do my dirty work.

I know I shouldn't feel so bad – the shopkeeper is supposed to be providing the public with a service. Yet, more often than not, you front up at a counter wanting something you've paid hard-earned money for replaced, because it's cracked, broken or simply won't work, and they end up making you feel guilty because you've had the hide to bring it back.

Unfortunately, around Christmas of 1988, I was caught in exactly that predicament.

We had purchased a glazed pottery vase of 45 cm in height that was actually a bit like a terracotta agricultural drain pipe with an end. What attracted us was a large handpainted rose set against a pure white background on one side. On the other side was another stunning graphic flower arrangement. We decided to buy it because it matched a much larger vase we already had at home.

When anyone buys a nice piece like this, then you've got to use it as soon as you get it home, haven't you?

Out came the snippers and into the garden . . . only a matter of minutes and hey presto, a beautiful bunch of flowers.

Fill up the little vessel with water, pop in the flowers, plonk it on top of the television set in the lounge. Stand back and admire – looks magic.

So, there we were enthusiastically watching McEnroe serving against Lendl on the new rebound ace surface, underneath our new vase. It was just terrific! Except, after a few minutes, beads of water started to trickle down the screen, over the controls and down the back. What was going on! The umpire had not stopped play due to rain, yet it seemed we needed to put a waterproof cover on the television.

Obviously the new vase wasn't quite what it was cracked up to be! Out came the flowers – drop them into the sink. Up end the vase and chamois down the TV. At least that did us one favour and gave the screen a well needed spruce up.

Now to check out the new acquisition. Sure enough, there was hairline crazing or cracking almost completely around the vase. Now comes the hard part – who's going to take it back. Am I going to take it back, or is Kerry going to take it back? One look from Kerry said it all: I bought it and yes, I'm going to take it back! Good player out of luck. So away I disappeared the next day, down to Chapel Street, park the car, and rather sheepishly I enter the shop.

I pulled the wet vase out of a plastic bag. I said, "Have a look at this. It's not right. There's a crack here, a crack there." The sales girl blushes. "I'm a bit embarrassed," she said. "Look, we'll exchange it for another one."

Down the back she went, fetched another one, I go home grinning from ear hole to ear hole. How easy was that? No drama.

Out into the garden to snip a fresh bunch of flowers, fill up the vase with water, plonk the flowers in, pop it on top of the TV set. Gee, a bit more tennis, more big serves . . . and unfortunately more water dribbling down the screen!

This vase is only thirty-five minutes old! I just couldn't believe it. Help, I've got to go back to the shop again, Kerry won't. This would be the third time I had been to this shop. I'm a good customer but I don't need to be this regular.

The next day, after work, I hopped into the car and off I went. It's not easy coming up to Christmas to park the car close to Melbourne's busy Chapel Street shopping centre. I had quite a walk this time, before I would get to my favourite shop around the corner. Then I thought, "Hey, I'm running a bit late, the shop might be closed. Let's move it along a bit."

I started to stretch out into a gentle jog, which then became a run. You're not going to believe this . . . but about 10 metres from the corner there was a huge wind shift. A gust picked up my large, square plastic bag containing the vase. The bag filled like a sail on a windsurfer, and it, plus the vase, flew out to arms' length. With a sickening hollow thud, the bag hit a telegraph pole, and suddenly the shopping bag became very flat! I stopped in horror, and the bag and its sorry contents dropped limply below my knee caps.

I felt crook in the stomach. I get within 10 metres of this shop and now I haven't even got what I was going there to exchange. To regain my composure I slowly walked around the corner and tried to think positively about what I'm going to say to the poor assistant behind the counter. Is she going to accuse me of lying? Basically it was my problem and it was my mistake. But I thought, I'm this close to the shop so I may as well give it a whirl. A couple of deep breaths and the front door confronted me like a gaping Luna Park.

I walked in and the girl said, "Not you again!" She couldn't believe her bad luck!

I didn't know what to say, not being very good at this type of thing and never having been quite in this situation before. Well, here goes: "You know that vase I brought in yesterday? Well, I took the other one home, filled her up with water and it LEAKED!"

"Oh no! It couldn't have leaked too," she replied.

"Actually you're going to have to believe me – I can't show you, because it wasn't until about 10 metres away from the corner I had a bit of bad luck and smashed it. All I've got are the pieces."

I tried to pick out some of the big pieces to show her and prove that there was a hairline fracture where the water had leaked out.

She burst out laughing at this and the other people in the shop were looking over my shoulder. We were starting to gather a bit of an audience.

There was definitely a crack in the jagged 10 cm piece I had. But, she challenged, was the crack in it when I bought it, or from hitting the pole? I insisted it was before the accident. Then the boss came along and asked to hear the story. Well, it's your problem, he concluded. Typical of some bosses – authoritarian, show of strength in front of staff and all that garbage!

I tried to be logical: "You can't shovel all the guilt over to me. If I hadn't had a faulty one in the first place, I wouldn't have been run-

ning down the street at a million miles an hour, trying to get in here, to change it. You are partly responsible for me being in the wrong place at the wrong time."

"Well, for a start, you shouldn't have had water in it because it's not a vase!" he announced. This was a bit of new information!

"Now you're telling me! After three visits you finally tell me it's not a vase."

"It's a wine cooler," he huffed. "A terracotta wine cooler."

"You're kidding. You could have fooled me," I growled.

"It's not even glazed inside or on the edges, see . . . That's why water just flows straight through it. It's not my fault it's leaking. You used it the wrong way!"

After a deep breath I persisted . . . "But it still had a crack in it!" We were going around and around in circles, so I decided it was time to change tactics. "You know the one I brought back yesterday with the cracks in it? You can't tell me you're going to put that back on the shelf and sell it to someone else. I mean, as far as you and I are concerned, and all these other people here, you couldn't sell that one could you?"

He had to agree with me there, because my growing audience did! "And you can't sell the one in the bag because that's in a whole lot of little pieces!" That gem of Walker logic blitzed him!

"Well, let's come to a compromise," I continued confidently. "I'll take the cracked one back home and you hang onto the smashed one here! Your insurance policy is going to cater a lot better for breakages than mine. Then we'll call it quits! Is that alright?"

He reckoned that was a bit rough but by this time he had about forty pairs of eyes boring into him. He was under pressure and I don't think he had ever had so many potential customers near his cash register in his life. You could have heard a pin drop as the crowd watched him think this over.

"Well, OK!" he snapped and spun around to retrieve the original vase.

I headed to the door gingerly with both hands clasped firmly around the secondhand cracked "vase". My supporters applauded as I left the shop, and I could hear the cash register beeping behind me, tallying up all the sales that potentially could have been lost.

What is goodwill worth anyway – an empty vase?

. . . just goes to prove there are still a lot of good people around, and I would like to thank the staff of House in Melbourne's famous Chapel St for their understanding in what was basically a lost cause. Commonsense prevailed!

Recruit for the Fight against Evil

"HE WAS HAVING A LOT OF TROUBLE TRYING TO STAY ON THE PERCH"

Life's journey is so full of unexpected meetings. But in my wildest dreams I never expected to come face to face with that famous comic book hero – The Phantom! I had just sat down after about an hour on my feet entertaining a wonderfully receptive audience at the Western District Aussie Rules Football Club in Brisbane.

It was a hot, sticky night and the beads of perspiration were pouring forth from my forehead at an embarrassing rate and forming rivulets of good honest sweat down both sides of my face.

Showing a lot of class, I wiped my leaking brow and glowing cheeks with a bright red paper napkin I hadn't used after my main course.

Sitting on the top table at any function can be a bit like "spotlight on sport" with about 200 plus sets of beady eyes dwelling on your every movement . . . in fact it's very difficult to pick your teeth in private if the steak has been too tough, or if the gap between your front teeth is now clogged with a delightful piece of golden corn so elegantly gnashed off the cob earlier in the night.

Nevertheless the idea is to appear unruffled by all the attention and act naturally (a bit like Liz when she's on a royal tour, eh!) which is exactly what I was doing . . . just chatting away with the club president and signing a few autographs.

Then – I saw this strange character making his way to the official table.

I couldn't believe my eyes!

The humidity was stickier than a desert drover's armpits and here's a guy dressed in a full length overcoat, cravat, sunglasses and felt hat.

It was a capacity crowd. Yes, they were hanging from the rafters that night and as the masses made their way to the public conveniences in the foyer during a break, this joker forced his way against the traffic flow, to the front of the entertainment room, where we were seated.

At that time I said to the president, "'Ave a go at this bloke – I bet he wants to get in my ear!"

I couldn't help but add, "I bet he's a live one, this fella!"

Sure enough, he parked himself right in front of the decorated trestle and introduced himself: "Mr Walker . . . the ghost who walks."

I thought to myself, "Oh, oh, I wasn't wrong – he reckons he's the Phantom."

It was very difficult to prevent myself from laughing – and a sly grin did creep out from under my moustache!

He thrust his hand towards me in a positive manner of greeting and said, "From one Mr Walker to another, it's an honour to meet you!" Needless to say his hand was very clammy, but a vice-like grip accompanied the dampness.

My thoughts were: "He's fair dinkum, this bloke."

Then he started peeling off his clothes, bit by bit.

Off came the cravat, sun glasses and hat. Sure enough he had the distinctive hood and stark black eye mask to conceal his identity.

As he took off his overcoat, he revealed the skin-tight, grey body suit with the diagonal, black-striped jocks.

His chunky black belt flashed the famous Phantom skull symbol, and supported a dangerous looking firearm.

Yes it was him – the Ghost who walks.

But why pick on me tonight? How was I going to explain this fellow at question time, soon to follow? Surely the same name didn't warrant this sort of long, lost friendship!

And to make matters worse, he wasn't shy either. He quickly called for two glasses of milk so that Mr Walker could take the sacred oath – to serve the world, against evil!

Now milk's not one of my favourite drinks, in fact I can't recall the last time I consumed a whole glass full . . . but I thought any minute

now I'll be hearing the beat of jungle drums in the distance saying, "Drink the milk, Tangles, or you're dead!" Or maybe dozens of Pygmies would come rushing at me through the club rooms. The imagination was working overtime!

The other coincidence was . . . the Phantom's girlfriend is named Diana. Well, so too was the young woman waiting on our table that evening. This was all a bit too much!

But what could I do? The Phantom and the pure white liquid awaited . . . for unbeknown to me The Phantom Club of Australia had decided to present me with a life membership and this sports' night just happened to be the chosen occasion. Feeling very honoured (once I realised what the blazers was going on) I diligently raised my right hand above my head and read "the sacred oath".

"I promise to fight on the side of the weak against the oppressor with good against evil, and to do everything in my power to destroy greed, cruelty and injustice wherever it exists . . . and may my children follow after me."

The Ghost who walks then presented me with a special Phantom T-shirt emblazened with "Mr Walker's eleven" – and there I was . . . along with ten frizzy haired little Pygmies! With that, he turned and left as "unobtrusively" as he had come.

Actually my friend and Channel 9 cricket commentator Bill Lawry was nicknamed "The Phantom" because he always had a Phantom comic in his back pocket during his playing days, and as I later discovered, Bill was also a member of the Phantom Club.

In my case I was very proud to accept the life membership of the club and it really is quite amazing just where and when you run into Phantom "phriends".

For the uninitiated: some 400 years ago the lone survivor of a pirate raid was washed up on a remote Bengali beach. On the skull of his father's murderer he swore an oath to fight crime. He was the first Phantom, and the eldest male of each succeeding generation of his family carried on . . . as the unbroken line continued through the centuries the pygmy Bandar people believed it was always the same man. "The ghost who walks," they said. So the legend grew. A name whispered, loved, and feared . . . The Phantom.

And he is still a legend – The Phantom.

But I wonder how well he'd cope batting against the four-pronged pace attack of the West Indies. Maybe they'd respect him too much to fire too many bouncers at him!

It's amazing how a perfectly normal beginning to what would be a fun filled sports night could turn into a deadly serious commitment to fight evil at all times . . . all it took was a couple of milks, eh?

"Long live the ghost who walks" – and that applies to Bill Lawry, too!

CHAPTER FIVE

White Flannelled Fellas

My Dad pulled the well worn cricket ball high and hard.

The Great Cricket Teaser

"WE NEEDED TEN TO WIN, ONE BALL REMAINING IN THE MATCH"

Former Channel 9 cricket statistician, Irving Rosenwater is a man obsessed by the numerical aspects of cricket. His brain is like a computer, spitting out dates, partnerships, wickets and runs with efficiency plus.

His love of the game and his vast knowledge made him the prime target in our commentary box, for what I would call a cricket "teaser".

A typical morning prior to the beginning of a Test match could possibly begin with, "Irving, how is it possible to score "X" off two or three balls?"

Our man hated not knowing the answer and there have been very few times he's been stumped or caught out by his friends. He often came up with a few good ones himself! I once asked him to answer this question.

How can each opening batsmen playing for the same team be six not out and the total 0/12 after just two balls of the morning have been bowled by the opening bowler? Remember, there have been no wides or no-balls bowled! No tricks or no scoring mistakes either.

Easy? Not really! The answer is this: The batsman taking strike hits the "first" ball to deep mid-on for three. The return throw is taken by the bat pad fieldsman standing almost in the centre of the wicket. The umpire signals one-short as they scramble for three and the resulting wayward throw at the bowler's end goes for four over-throws! So after one ball, batsman number 1 is six not out and now at the non-striker's end after running three.

Off the "second" ball of the day, batsman number 2 hooks the bouncer for six, and the scoreboard states clearly both batsmen are six not out and the total 0/12. How about that!

I stumped Irving with another one too – "How could my dad score 10 runs off just one ball?"

First of all he asked if it was a first-class match. I said, "Not bloody likely, twenty years ago in Tasmania!"

Then the wheels in his head started to turn, his eyes focused on the ceiling . . . searching . . . "What if they ran three, got another three off overthrows, and then a further four overthrows?"

That's fair enough but when I canned the idea of no balls, wides and overthrows, he went an ashen-grey colour around the eyes.

Let me tell you what happened. My Dad pulled the well-worn two piece leather ball high and hard through mid-wicket. We needed 10 to win, one ball remaining in the match. True story!

Much to my old man's surprise, the small cork inner core of the cricket ball, with string intact, went flying over the crude boundary line and into the coarse prickle bushes "on the full". Six runs!

Now, wait for it – the loose leather jacket, looking like a fluffy, half-opened scallop shell, had just enough momentum and pace to trickle into the fence for four!

Add the two scores together, because they both occurred simultaneously off the same delivery and you've got 10 runs. As I often admit, this sort of situation could only happen in Tasmania!

Having then whet Irving's appetite for the unusual, I couldn't help but tell him of another occasion where Big Max, my father, steered us home to victory with a different 10 off the second last ball.

This was in a semi-final game of a Sunday afternoon competition – hardly Benson and Hedges World Series stuff, but it was certainly a good, clean, healthy and very competitive level of cricket.

The biggest problem in most of these games used to be clearing up the cow-pats from the area close to our home-made concrete wicket. There's nothing worse than diving to your right or left in the covers, and ending up with your nose in a fresh, warm, soggy pile of cow dung.

Nevertheless, the cows were very handy because most of our paddocks didn't justify the expense of a curator – the grass cutters had to be either cows or goats, and they did the trick! The only problem with goats is that they love the taste of willow cricket bats and leather cricket balls . . . it was goodnight if any gear happened to be left lying around!

My old man was captain of a social team selected from patrons of the Empire Hotel – he was the proprietor and of course supplied the liquid refreshments.

As you may well imagine the best cricket in these games is played late in the day when all the Dutch courage and confidence emerges. But not always with success.

The Sunday's proceedings went along very well, especially the morning session. Everyone had fun and a drink or two.

When someone finally tallied up the score card (on the back of a piece of cardboard) we became aware of an intriguing situation. The Empire Hotel needed 10 runs to win, and importantly there were two balls remaining. Possible but improbable!

I could sense the atmosphere around the ground. Everyone momentarily put down their amber-filled glasses waiting in anticipation, kids stopped playing and the dogs began howling. Electric!

The opposition bowler charged in to bowl off an unusually long run, his pocket full of car keys sounding like an eccentric belting away on a xylophone. I can still see the frenzied look on his purple-red face after running so far just to deliver one ball – a sort of distorted agony and ecstasy!

Big Max was "on strike" and I was at the bowler's end, backing up on nought, not out! The senior partner immediately moved onto the front foot . . . his size twelve sandshoes not quite to the pitch of the ball, but nevertheless his eyes were focused clearly on the well-worn cherry. It was so worn out that it looked more like a rag doll than a cricket ball.

The attempted cover drive wasn't exactly a reproduction from the *Art of Cricket*, by Sir Donald Bradman. My father's flashing blade could only manage a thick inside edge and the ball gently rolled away behind the square leg umpire, towards the fence.

We both took off and ran like hell, turned for 2, looked for 3, even 4. When it came to the sixth run, I said to my partner, "That's it, dad, we can only run 6!"

"Don't stop now, son," he replied, "just keep on running!" And so we did!

While we were scampering for runs . . . four or five fieldsman had gathered in the long grass down by the fine leg boundary. Dad and I just kept our heads down and continued running. By the time we'd run all 10 necessary to win the game, about eight guys were stooped in a circle about 60 metres off the bat, at long leg.

My dad was suffering from a distinct lack of fitness – it's not every day a batsman gets to run 10 in a row. We'd won the match with a ball to spare! "You little beauty!" I loved to win in those days, and I still do today!

Before we left the pitch, curiosity got the better of us . . . there were now ten players standing in a tight circle at deep fine leg up to their ankles in grass.

Yes! There it was. The lonely old cricket ball dead smack in the middle of a curled up tiger snake – must have been two metres long.

There was absolutely no way known that any of those blokes was going to put his hand down to pick up the ball! Not a hero amongst 'em!

Irving looked at me strangely. Maybe I am a touch warped, but my goodness, I did have a lot of fun playing cricket in the early days.

The greatest game of all.

Sunday Arvo Finalé

"THEY HADN'T CUT THE GRASS
FOR THREE MONTHS"

At the age of about eleven or twelve I was lucky enough to play cricket in the same team as my old man. Remarkably we played in a most memorable premiership. Irving Rosenwater, the former Channel 9 statistician, couldn't believe this one either!!

I should tell you that the curators in Tasmania are not too flash. They turn up about every three months to cut the grass. And even though this particular game was a Grand Final – Mathina versus Oatlands – I don't think anyone would have seen the match . . . it certainly wasn't televised.

And just because it was a Grand Final made no difference to the fact that there had been two and a half months between hair cuts!

Hence the grass stood about a metre high.

The situation didn't worry me because I had the ability to hit the ball in the air, but some of our other players were a little bit inhibited by this sea of green.

So, imagine the scene at the ground. Thirty-five of our relations and their dogs have turned up, and the atmosphere is absolutely electric. The buzz; the barking; the horns tooting all the way around the ground, you can feel the tension.

We require 17 runs to win. Normally we would romp in. But this time, it's just a little bit tight. There's only one ball remaining from which to score those 17 runs.

And to make matters worse, there's only one batsman left. His name is Big Max, or my old man. Just how good a player is Big Max, to be batting number 11 behind me in a Sunday afternoon competition?

The state of play doesn't improve . . . the previous batsman to be dismissed has chopped down so hard on a yorker, he's broken the handle of the only bat in the club.

We used to drop the bat and run up and down in between wickets in those days. There was no Kerry Packer back then and sponsorship was unheard of.

Now the opposition captain, he wasn't about to lend us their only bat, was he? No way! And the old man, very creative thinker that he is, walked out the gate, grabbed a picket from the fence – lucky we were playing at Oatlands – confidently strolled to the wicket and took block. Why he took block, I'm buggered if I know.

My old man is a dead set imposter. He possesses one shot and one shot only, and that is a slog straight down the ground.

Normally when you play on concrete or malthoid there's a stick of chalk behind the middle stump. You mark your own centre . . . don't you? Well, there's no chalk in Tasmania. And the old man's wearing the Dunlop rubbers, made in India, size eleven, and he's not having a lot of luck marking centre on the concrete pitch.

Then he had the audacity to look around the ground from third man to mid-off and way around to long leg . . . just like all the good players do.

Fair dinkum, my old man would not be good enough to snick a ball to Third Man. Still, the opposition were not going to let him off lightly – no matter what the odds!

And there beyond the umpire, 30 or 40 yards back, standing in the long grass, all you could see from the knee caps up . . . is a mad "quick".

No matter where you go in the world, every opposition side's got a mad quick. Haven't they? The West Indies have got five of 'em.

All they want to do is bounce the shitter out of the tailenders. Right? And this bloke's no different from the rest of 'em.

He's got the ball in his hand and is giving it heaps. He's polishing her up and down; really is giving it plenty!

Now I should mention there's a lot of science involved in polishing a cricket ball: Total maximum utilisation of one half of a cricket ball up and down your trousers, right?

I've been involved with my body for a fair while now and I can't come up with a better groove than that for polishing a cricket ball. Agree? The action's not just for women watching colour telly. It's for real!!!

Every fast bowler worth his salt has been known to rub a cricket ball up and down his trousers. Apart from one, Jeffrey Thomson. "Thommo" holds the ball in front, belt buckle high and gives it the gyrating pelvic girdle. It does pay to advertise, doesn't it? Well, it never hurt Thommo.

Imagine the mad quick in the long grass polishing the cork com-position ball . . . all the polishing in the world won't make this ball shiny, will it?

In the fastbowler charges, through the long grass. Up high on the toe-nails in the delivery stride – Tasmanians have got real long toe nails. With a huge grunt he has let the ball go and the old man gives him the big Colgate smile back down the track.

I'm 0 not out at the other end playing for the "red inks" (not out). Now anyone who knows anything at all about the game of cricket will realise . . . you must NOT bowl a ball pitched middle or leg stump to a tail-end batsman, okay?

Otherwise you'll end up being hit straight down the ground on the first bounce for 4, or depending on how much right hand is on the bat . . . a whack through mid-wicket for 6!!

So what does this bloke do? He bowls the big rank half volley – didn't swing a lot because there's not much red paint left on the ball. And like most number 11 batsmen, the old man plays straight down the track. Plonk. Almost trod on the ball which has got to be a bonus. Where do you think the ball's landed? Pitched middle and leg stump!!

So the old man's hit through the most magnificent on drive you've ever seen. We take off, run 1, 2, 3, 4, 5 . . . And there are five guys out at long-on, Can't find the ball anywhere in the long grass.

As we crossed for 6 I said to my partner: "Dad, that's it. You can only run 6." He said: "Bullshit son, keep running, keep running." 7, 8, 9, 10 and there are now eight fieldsmen way out at long-on and can't find the ball anywhere.

11, 12, 13. The old man has now got heartburn, dyspepsia, the whole catastrophe. You just don't come in first ball in a Grand Final and chip 13 off your toes, do you? I mean, that is really not on . . . no matter what grade of cricket.

14, 15, 16 . . . There are now ten of 'em out there at long-on . . . and still can't find the ball anywhere.

The wicketkeeper is the only bloke left – standing over the stumps for the run out. The rest of them are stamping down the long grass with their boots. A quarter of the ground is trodden absolutely flat. The rest of the grass is a metre high.

17 runs. What a fantastic performance! To get up and win the Grand Final, another flag for the dressing-sheds back home . . . against the odds. You beauty!

Great sportsman he was, the old man, looked across to the opposition captain, who was a bloody long way away at long-on, walked in his direction. "Do you really want to know where the ball is?" he asked with a grin.

Then he turned over the picket, and wedged deep into a nail at the end of the picket, was the lost cricket ball.

South Africa could certainly have done with a similar picket when they required 21 runs off one ball in that rain reduced shambles – the World Cup semi-final v England under lights at the Sydney Cricket Ground in March 1992. In a no contest finish England won but then were defeated in the final by Pakistan – an occasion at the MCG they too will never forget.

A Short Exercise in Being Nice

"I GUESS THE SAFETY OF THE DRESSING ROOM MUST HAVE BEEN A TEMPTATION"

In hindsight the English summer of 1975, and the inaugural World Cup competition was not exactly a great time for Sri Lankan cricketers, and in particular the batsmen!

I'd never heard of some of their names, let alone know how to pronounce them. We anticipated they'd be a bit of a walkover and it certainly looked that way after Australia scored 328 runs in the allotted 60 overs (6 balls).

Then, between innings the fun began to happen . . . inside the opposition dressingroom. The atmosphere was very tense . . . mainly due to the fearsome reputations of Australia's two demon fast bowlers – Dennis Lillee and Jeff Thomson! They hated batsmen from any country.

At that time we were having quite a few problems with our "image" as a team away from the ground. Consequently we were dubbed the "Ugly Australians" by the Fleet Street press gang.

Little did the Sri Lankans know that our boys had made up their minds to win some points back, as "good guys" and decided to go easy on the novices.

The opposition were not aware of that and when the two tiny opening batsmen emerged through the door into the bright sunlight . . . they appeared to wince all the way to the wicket . . . in an attitude of self doubt.

I believe they held a raffle for the two opening spots and no-one bought any tickets . . . and everyone pretended to tie-up a bootlace when the batting order was "announced" by the skipper.

Dennis Lillee and Jeff Thomson opened the bowling for Australia at a very friendly pace and kept pitching the ball up into the block-hole or on the half volley. Sri Lanka were going along quite smoothly – no problems at all.

I thought our behaviour was gentlemanly. We applauded their good strokes and we'd stop for a chat with the batsmen between overs to make them feel at home. No sign of the ugly Australian image now!

But when the score had reached 1/70, the public relations exercise had gone far enough. Chappelli, our captain, decided it was time for a few wickets – and quickly.

That instruction was like a red rag to a bull . . . Dennis the menace couldn't help himself and was soon in danger of bruising his big toe, so short was he bowling! Whilst at the other end Thommo got real nasty and bowled very quick.

One delivery from Thommo struck opening batsman S. Wettimuny right on the top of his front foot – it was a fearful blow. Much pain.

Wettimuny at this stage had been untroubled in making 53 excellent runs. But this crushing blow to the foot at about 95 mph made the slightly built righthander drop his bat and limp erratically beyond the square leg umpire before he fell to the ground in agony. Was it a broken toe?

The idea of "retired hurt" – 53 against his name on the scoreboard was not altogether unappealing. And I guess the safety of the dressing room must have been a huge temptation to the man. Nevertheless his captain down at the non-striker's end, wouldn't hear of it. "Bat on like a man!" he said.

What happened next was a strange sight . . . the front foot carefully cradled on top of the back sandshoe. He looked like a one-legged stork fishing in shallow water. I thought the draught from the next delivery would blow him off balance as it passed his right earhole!

Two balls later Thomson struck again. Same batsman. Same toe.

This time the vulnerable little Wettimuny S. definitely wanted out. He'd suffered enough. "No," ordered his skipper, "bat on!"

Standing at "mid-off" was the laconic gambler – Doug Walters. "Thommo, I bet you can't hit on the sandshoe a third time?" the dashing batsman challenged. Now the odds on Thommo hitting a sandshoe 3 out of 3 from 22 yards was not on, particularly a size 6 sandshoe. You see, one of Thommo's biggest assets was that he didn't have a clue where the ball was going . . . so at almost 100 mph what chance did the batsman have.

In a strange sort of a way the Queensland quick was excited by his achievement of "pinning" Mendis. At that stage of the tour Thommo wasn't experiencing too many plusses. The English ladies wouldn't talk to him, he hasn't received a letter from home, he couldn't get a wicket in a sports store and he was being no-balled on average fifteen times a match. But as Dougie chipped in . . . "it's nothing to brag about mate, this bloke is only four foot eleven! That's only a good length to a normal player like myself!!" But the banter was shortlived.

Bravely, Wettimuny faced the next Thomson delivery. Similar ball. Same result. Same toe. Same expression . . . the sandshoe-crusher had struck again!!!

Unfortunately for him it wasn't three direct hits and you're out! The batter tried desperately to occupy the crease for one more delivery with that throbbing toe supported on the arch of his back foot . . . which by the way had crept slowly back to the base of the middle stump, obviously to give himself more time and room to play Thommo.

This was all gutsy stuff, but the sight of the blond fast bowler, vigorously chewing gum and slowly polishing the red cherry by gyrating his pelvis, proved too much.

The diminutive opener overbalanced completely. Shouting, "I go off, I go off!" loudly to his captain who was still peering over his shoulder to see if Thommo again was on his way to the delivery stride.

So, nursing the most tormented toe in the history of first-class cricket our friend convinced his captain that fighting for his country was all very well. But being crippled was a bit bloody rough. Or words to that effect – he was speaking very quickly as Sri Lankans do when they're excited or frightened!

Wettimuny, 53 not out, hobbled unassisted for the first 50 metres back to the pavilion, then was propped up by two not so tall team-mates for the next 30. To a standing ovation he fell through the dressingroom door, just before the next man in, Duleep Mendis, was shoved out of the safety of that same pavilion. A point of no return. The door was locked behind him.

Years later Mendis became captain of his country but in this game all he had going for him was a pounding heart inside a small but robust frame.

The gutsy little Sri Lankan surprised us all. He played some sensational cover drives on his way to 32 and was just getting settled. Then, a few balls later a Thomson "kicker" reared nastily off a good length, deflected off Mendis' glove and struck him dead centre, right between the eyes! An awful blow.

Mendis collapsed. I thought Jeff had killed the guy . . . luckily as it turned out, not quite!

My mate Thommo always had this terrific knack of getting the cricket ball to roll back down the wicket towards him after he'd hit a batsman. It didn't matter whether it was the thigh, ribs or head – the ball used to still dribble slowly along the pitch towards the bowler. He reckoned it saved him having to follow through too far! Often he'd flick it up into the air with a boot. Takes practice that.

Well that's exactly what happened on this occasion . . . Thomson quickly flicked up the rolling ball and shaped to throw the batsman's stumps down for a run out.

The run out wasn't on though . . . because despite having fallen face forward, chin firmly embedded into the wicket the batsman still had both feet behind the batting crease.

Now what would any sport-loving fast bowler do in this same situation? Check out whether or not the victim would like any help . . . of course!

Thommo was just about to grab the poor fellow by the scruff of the neck and turn him over when he too said "I go off now, I go off!" We were all so glad to hear him speak. Naturally we called for a stretcher.

And I thought I'd seen everything but what happened next takes the cake! The KO'd batsman stood up, ran 30 metres towards the stretcher bearers and hopped straight on. He was then carried from the ground to an enormous roar from a majority Pakistan and Indian contingent in the crowd . . . he even waved goodbye!

Thomson copped a lot of outrage and criticism in the press over the incident and for his "wanting to see blood on the wicket" comment made prior to the tour.

Today, I take my hat off to the small country of Sri Lanka because in the big bad world of international cricket they've come a long way since that forgettable game in 1975 – now a talented Test nation.

Streaky Shot Claims The Master

"WE ALL GOT A LAUGH INCLUDING OUR CRESTFALLEN CAPTAIN"

Greg Chappell would agree that for him, playing matches against New Zealand hasn't been without its problems – for example the notorious underarm incident at the MCG.

Then, after the First Test debacle of 1985 – a loss by an innings and 41 runs in Brisbane – the Kiwis caused him a few more sleepless nights, this time as a national selector.

And I've still got very vivid memories of an incident during the second Test match against New Zealand at Auckland in 1977.

Greg invited NZ to bat first on a rain-affected wicket at Eden Park. Australia exploited the difficult conditions to limit the Kiwis to a first innings total of 229.

I'm sure our captain Greg Chappell was looking for a score of 350 plus and a lead of 150 on the first innings . . . and proceedings were going nicely for our boys until just before tea on the second day.

It was an overcast day and a maximum temperature of about 5 degrees Celsius was forecast – I wonder how Tony Greig would have described the cold against his "player comfort" conditions on the Channel 9 weatherwall? Well anyway it was bitterly cold . . . even watching from the player's enclosure, as Rick McCosker and Greg both posted half centuries and Australia's total moved beyond 150 for the loss of only one wicket.

Then it all started happening . . . a heavy dark cloud of smoke wafted across the ground from a house at the rear of the grandstand. The fire must have been serious because I remember the piercing shrill of a fire-engine ringing in my ears. As a batsman you really don't need that sort of interference to your concentration at the precise moment a bowler like Hadlee lets the ball go.

Using the smokescreen for distraction a streaker pranced out on to the Rugby Union ground-cum-Test match venue, from the seated area in the northern section.

After jumping the fence and conducting a brief "fashion" parade, he returned to his cheering audience. As he hurdled the white picket fence, arms raised in triumph, I thought he might do himself a nasty injury. No such luck. He regained his seat – still starkers.

With only minutes remaining before tea, NZ captain Glen Turner decided to give spinner Hedley Howarth a bowl. And while the bowler was busy stepping out his run up, another well-sozzled streaker

The streaker wanted to shake the great man by the hand.

bounded across the ground from the northern end of Eden Park.

This chap was "well-dressed" though. He wore an impressive suntan, goose-pimpled bum, a pair of heavy leather boots, socks and a pale blue towelling hat. As he raced past the square leg umpire he flung his hat into the air in victory then disappeared over the wire gate at the southern end and into the carpark . . . hotly pursued by a policeman.

I could see both Greg and Rick getting more and more agitated by these unexpected happenings. With the clock suggested it was well past the time for the tea adjournment, all they wanted was to be not out at tea.

After just a couple of deliveries . . . streaker number 1 was back over the fence again. Full of confidence and "ink".

So excited by the performance of master batsman Greg Chappell was he, the naked nutter wanted to shake the great man by the hand.

Incidentally, he was sporting a pair of radio headphones so he could hear a ball by ball description of his antics.

He had soared over the fence, evading Richard Hadlee at square leg, and continued lumbering towards our captain . . . who by this time was furious and staring glassy eyed at the naked man. The strokeplayers' famous double scoop Gray Nicholls bat was raised above his head . . .

You see, Greg Chappell has never quite felt the same about streakers after an incident in a Shield match the previous year. Three women promptly paraded naked towards Greg and his not out partner . . . on the centre wicket area at the WACA ground in Perth.

From what Greg told me, one of them had beautiful eyes. Though his mate tells me he wasn't looking at their eyes when he asked them to "hang around and have a chat".

Incredibly it all back-fired when the "young lady" that Greg fancied turned out to be a female impersonator. The man was shattered!

The whole exercise had been a publicity stunt for a local night club – similar to the brazen young blonde who bared it all in front of 100,000 people at a VFL grand final at the MCG a few years later.

Since being so "wrong" it would be fair to say that streakers have never been his favourite people.

But back to New Zealand . . . in Greg's mind this bloke was jeopardising Australia's aim of batting through the session without losing a wicket.

So Greg grabbed the man by his out-stretched hand and gave him a solid spanking across his polar bear white bottom . . . WHACK, WHACK, WHACK!!! Colour quickly returned to his bum.

I can still hear the smacks now . . . an incredible echoing sound.

Greg suggested he " . . . off!!!" And informed the intruder he was definitely not impressed. The streaker mentioned something about poking the cord from his earphones in Greg's ear-holes. This brought yet another couple of belts from the master's flashing blade!

By this time the policemen were in position and the offender was apprehended as he charged off in the direction of the seat he left vacant.

Next delivery, McCosker hit the ball firmly to mid-on but Chappell, thinking there wasn't a run it it, turned his back. Rick kept on running and was unfortunately run out at the striker's end by wicketkeeper Jock Edwards.

A disappointed Chappell left the field with his head hung low. The streaker was escorted out of the ground. Australia had now lost its second wicket.

At stumps that night, Inspector George Dwan, one of the policemen who arrested the streaker, searched out Greg for a chat.

When the inspector entered the dressing room, everyone shut up, silence reigned supreme. He said: "Son, you ought to be ashamed of what happened out there!"

Greg replied: "Hang on a minute, you mean the streaker don't you?"

The policeman answered: "No, absolutely disgusting," with a certain sense of finality about the comment.

Greg looked blankly at the inspector and said, "Why?"

The answer is the moral to this story: "Here you are, you play four cross bat shots," illustrating with a movement of his arms as if to play a pull-shot, "when one straight drive would have done the trick!" And he followed through as if to play a big straight drive at an imaginary streaker!

Behind that serious expression then beamed an enormous smile and we all got a laugh including our crestfallen captain.

We won the match by 10 wickets, with almost two days remaining, thanks to some great bowling by Dennis Lillee who finished the match with figures of 11/123.

But one of my fondest memories of that match was standing at ninth slip. Yes ninth slip! Greg Chappell decided to use a ten-man slips cordon, including the wicketkeeper Rodney Marsh.

Lillee was bowling to the worst number 10 batsman I have ever seen in my life – a guy called Peter Petherick, a silver-haired off-spinner. It was an amusing tussle with such a field. Nevertheless the terrified batsman with no talent held us up for the remaining forty minutes on the third day . . . long enough for us to have to come back after the rest day to take his wicket. We also had to score the necessary 26 runs for victory. Definitely a case of just not good enough to get out.

Effectively he was at the crease for three days and hardly made contact with a ball. Incredible. Well he can boast to his grandchildren that he batted against the legendary Lillee for three days. I can unassumingly suggest I once fielded at ninth slip for Australia!

Funny what sticks in your mind during a Test match. That was my last against New Zealand.

Cricket's Blackest Day

"IT WAS A PRETTY HUMILIATING EXPERIENCE WALKING OFF THE GROUND"

February 1, 1981, was one of the blackest days in the history of Australian sport. This was the day when Australia played New Zealand in the second final of the Benson and Hedges World Series Cup.

The match was well poised. Australia had scored 235 runs and New Zealand were 8 down for 229. One ball remained. There was no way the Kiwis could win the match but six hit from the final delivery and the match could have been "tied"?

Incredibly a totally unexpected conclusion happened. Captain Greg Chappell asked his little brother Trevor to bowl the last ball along the ground! Underarm!!!

I must say I was pretty disappointed . . . fielding way down at fine leg on the fence. Greg never asked me what I thought about the situation . . . in fact I've never been involved in the "big" discussions in Australian cricket. Yet I know in my own heart, and I'm sure all my mates seated behind in Bay 13 that day would agree, we could, and would have come up with a much different solution. And the directive wouldn't have been to roll the ball along the ground underarm.

With a new batsman at the crease, the possibility of him hitting the first ball he received out of the MCG, was just not on. I've never seen a batsman on the MCG, hit the first ball faced over the fence for six; the degree of difficulty rises when a fluffy old rag doll of a ball, 25 overs old, is bouncing only about two or three inches in height on its journey down the wicket! Afterwards Rodney Marsh reckoned it wasn't a bad delivery. He said, "It would've hit off stump!"

You had to spare a thought for the batsman, Ian McKeckney, the cauliflower-eared Rugby player from the South Island of NZ. He really didn't stand a chance. We could tell he was upset, because when he threw the bat on the ground it bounced back up in the air, about eighteen inches (half a metre)!

Seconds later, after the ball was bowled down at fine leg a deathly silence engulfed the huge stadium. I don't know what my dear friend Alan McGilvray was thinking, up in the ABC commentary box, at the time. No doubt he was dumbfounded by it all, and very, very disappointed.

The Channel 9 commentators were likewise shocked. What could they say? Not unexpectedly Ian Chappell bagged his younger brother Greg.

The stunned silence broke when the crowd realised that the under arm delivery, which has since been outlawed, was within the rules and allowed. Yes, it had actually happened and the game was over. Unbelievable! Soon the booing, hissing and shouting started to echo across the ground.

It was a pretty humiliating experience walking off my home ground behind captain Greg Chappell, head hung low and eyes focused on the grass. It seemed a longer than normal walk too – up the aisle of crowded people, most of them booing – through the green HOME dressing room door and down the stairs into the dungeon-like space below the huge, grey concrete grandstand.

As the old cliché goes, but very appropriate in this instance, the silence was so thick in the dressing room that it could have been cut with a knife. No-one was game to utter a word. Normally there occurs heaps of fun and frivolity after play. The first thing the players do is head for the fridge door and a nice cold drink. But there was none of this . . . not an appropriate moment to reflect on the glory of great deeds.

I sat on the edge of a timber bench, in amongst all the sweaty, smelly cricket gear and stared blankly at the floor, thinking to myself, "Gee, what a wonderful tight knit cotton-weave carpet we've got here today."

Finally, the dreadful silence was broken by who else, but team humourist, Dougie Walters. Dougie with a mischievous twinkle in his eye looked across to his dejected captain, "Mate, you've really stuffed it now, haven't ya?" No other player could have got away with the comment.

Gregory Stephen was speechless . . . what could he say!

That eased the tension and away we went. Still the dressing room doors were locked. No-one was allowed in or out, and the Press were predictably banned.

What had we done? NZ Prime Minister, Robert Muldoon, wanted his country to "go to war" with Australia . . . mind you, in hindsight. The dreadful event is perhaps one of the best things indirectly to happen to NZ cricket in a long time. It united a nation in anger behind her sportsmen. They haven't looked back!

The players travelled to Tullamarine that night by taxi to catch the flight to Sydney, for the next WSC final. The players were ushered in up the back stairs of the plane so as not to attract attention.

Vice-captain, Rodney Marsh and myself thought we ought to travel under more civilized conditions. So we played it pretty cool and travelled on the 10 a.m. flight, the next day. Like everyone else in the team we had a tight zipper on the mouth.

There were reporters waiting to talk to us from all of the TV stations when we walked off the plane. Rodney in the subtle style of John McEnroe cleared the way with, "No comment, thanks. No comment! NO COMMENT!!" He had his head shaking all the way to the taxi. But deep down the strong willed stumper would have loved to have voiced his opinion.

Waiting at the taxi rank, we had scored one of the last English-speaking taxi drivers operating in Sydney. Rod was rapt because he reckoned he might have one of his fans in this bloke. Bacchus (as in Bacchus Marsh) jumped into the front seat confident of a friendly chat. I was ecstatic . . . because I thought he's finally going to pay for a cab fare.

These days with Sydney cab drivers you never quite can tell where you are going to end up unless you give directions and take notice of where you are going. I hopped into a Sydney cab recently and asked to be driven to Sydney Cricket Ground.

The driver looked like he was on holiday from Saigon. He said, what suburb is that in? I almost felt like asking him to shift over and let me drive. It was only a couple of hook shots from the hotel where I was staying in the heart of Sydney. Diabolical.

Anyway, Bacchus soon suffered a dose of the "tom tits" – our Aussie driver hadn't recognised him! The man behind the wheel looked at Rodney and innocently asked if we were up here on holiday or business. Rod said, " . . . a bit of both!"

Rodney's eyebrows jumped as he looked at me in the rear vision mirror. "Where ya from?" asked the driver, very matter of factly.

The West Australian's expression said it all . . . gee, we've got a live one here. And he was absolutely right.

Marshie answered, "I'm from Perth and the big bloke in the back seat . . . he's from Melbourne!"

He obviously wasn't a cricket enthusiast. It was like seeing the lights on in a house yet knowing there was no one home!

He still hadn't recognised either of us and right in the middle of a major cricket controversy! Maybe this guy didn't look at bill boards, television or the front page of a newspaper. Maybe he couldn't read. Then again Marshie's head is unmistakable – one off.

"What do ya do for a living?" he rambled on automatically . . . and not really interested in the answer.

"We're both professional cricketers!" Rodney grizzled. The enlightened cabbie nodded casually. Still no one home!

Now I could tell from the next deep and meaningful question that he knew his cricket really well: "Who do you play for?"

How many professional cricket teams are there in Australia?

"I play for Australia and WA," Rod growled through his bristling moustache, "and the big gorilla in the back seat . . . he plays for Victoria and Australia."

"Aw! Right!" Finally after drip-feeding this fascinating sports fanatic the penny dropped, "You blokes . . . you were in that "underarm" game, weren't ya, yesterday at the MCG?" He was a different person with a couple of rightanswers.

He went through about four sets of red lights over the next few minutes, as he kept exercising the ball bearings in his neck looking at his passenger. And every time Rod's moustache bristled a bit more. I knew they didn't like one another a lot.

He looked at Marshie once more in the morning light. "So what do you do mate, bat or bowl?"

I still don't know whether the taxi driver was having a lend of us or we were having a lend of him. Australia's record breaking wicketkeeper was livid. (355 Test dismissals).

The Great Kiwi Debate

"NEW ZEALAND IS A PLACE WHERE MEN ARE DUBIOUS AND SHEEP ARE SLOW"

How does the idea of travelling to Wellington, NZ, for a live radio debate on the subject of "Kiwis Do It Better" sound? I was a bit apprehensive at first, until the organisers of the event mentioned I would be captain of a three-man team, including Tony Greig, the former England cricket captain, and Australian rugby union champion Roger Gould.

But the most attractive aspect of the trip was that our team would debate the negative side of the argument, which I must admit did sit rather comfortably with all three of us!

Our opponents were, as it turned out, three well-rehearsed and talented orators on the topic. A learned man named Jim Hopkins was leader of the opposition and unfortunately he was brilliant . . .

Batting number 2 for NZ was a batsman used to the position – John Reid, who's main claim to fame is being a cousin of ultra tall Test bowler Bruce Reid from Western Australia.

Third, was a grim, determined All Black named Andy Hayden who definitely looked over-dressed in a dinner suit – the attire mentioned on the invitation. Not a pretty sight . . . frighten a dog off a chain.

Obviously, Kiwis don't take any notice because Jim Hopkins was clad in anything but a "dickie-bird" suit. His white crumpled linen jacket and light brown shirt would have looked more at home on a university campus . . . and from the length of his greying hair and manner of speaking, he had obviously spent many a year doing just that – maybe even decades! A professional student.

Each speaker was given six minutes to verbally assault the subject through a microphone which carried our spirited joust to thirty-two radio stations around NZ – I thought they only had two and these went off air at 9 p.m.!

After five minutes of talk, a huge gong was belted . . . the loud message being simply – one minute to wrap up!

Tony Greig so correctly quipped, "Five minutes is ample time to present the positive side of 'Kiwis do it better' but six minutes is not nearly enough time to tear the statement apart!"

After the crowd of 500 (497 Kiwis) stopped booing, the tall blond haired all-rounder continued . . . "We'd need about forty-five minutes each!"

So as you can so clearly see, the visiting trifecta were on a hiding to nothing in front of a very parochial home crowd.

Our "three wise men" had been given absolutely no chance to recover from a torrid Air New Zealand landing (the pilot must have been a taxi-driver in his spare time) into a gale force wind on the extremely short runway at Wellington Airport.

Anyhow, we decided not to go down without giving 'em heaps! And we did.

On the stroke of 8 p.m. Kiwi-time, the exaggerated Kiwi voice of the Master of Ceremonies stated unashamedly, that he'd tossed the coin and Australia would speak first.

It was a lie, and I didn't want all of those New Zealanders who had turned into their crystal sets for the night's entertainment to think we were wimps, so I jumped to the lectern and set the story straight.

I took a "two bob" bit out of my trouser pocket, tossed it high in the air, where it sparkled like a jewel in the night against the bright television spotlights. I grabbed the floating coin as only a great fine leg fieldsman could . . . and shouted, "Heads or tails?"

Before I received even a semblance of an answer from the local boys, who by the way couldn't believe their eyes, I put the twenty cent piece back where it belonged in the pocket of my much hired dinner suit and quietly said, "Bad luck fellas, we win – you talk first!"

By the time my tail hit the seat, ten or fifteen seconds of pregnant silence had elapsed, and believe me that's a lot of black space (airtime) on radio.

So initially we caught 'em with their pants down, but I must admit, some six minutes later, we almost wished we hadn't pulled our brazen stunt.

The eccentric Jim Hopkins landed some very low body blows which even hurt Tony Greig, who has finally come to his senses after leaving South Africa and England, and settling in Australia.

It's common knowledge that the demographic centre of NZ is right plonk in the middle of Bondi Junction, a mere Aussie place-kick away from the Sydney Cricket Ground.

While thousands of Kiwis are on the dole in our country and I don't think they should be allowed to get away with it . . . only thirty-seven Australian born persons, from whom I wish to disassociate myself, are registered on the dole in NZ, I can't understand them because even with the drop in the Aussie dollar they're still getting paid less.

Needless to say, dingoes, beer, cricket and the Olympic Games were heavily commented on by the home side!

So I bit the bullet and went for broke. I doubt if New Zealand radio will ever be the same again . . . and not purely because of our strine and Afrikaans accents.

"Australia is a country where men are men and sheep are nervous . . . on the other hand, New Zealand is a place where men are dubious and sheep are slow . . . and the sale of gumboots very high – not necessarily to stop tinea," I stated.

More boos, but I continued.

"What about your Prime Minister? At least our PM can handle the Pritikin diet. The best your bloke can do is go on a "staple diet"! (The Kiwi PM has had his stomach stapled if you didn't happen to know.) And wait until the rust sets in – he'll travel real ordinary then!"

They didn't like it!

"How about 'Piggy' Muldoon (no offence) didn't he over-react a little after the under-arm incident? He practically wanted to declare war on Australia and now big American warships aren't allowed to park in Wellington Harbour. Whatever happened to the ANZUS pact?"

Deathly silence greeted that one!

When Tony Greig asked the women to take a long hard look at the fellas sitting next to them or opposite, more shouts of contempt.

"There must be some doubt about him, droopy moustache, longish hair and sideburns, pale face, pot belly, poor conversationalist . . . does he really do it better? If there isn't a doubt, then you haven't tried the REAL THING!" (Won the 1991 World Cup.)

That one went down like a lead balloon, but I liked it!

Roger Gould gave 'em plenty on the rugby union scene where coach Alan Jones and Australia was dominating the world – STILL ARE!!!

New Zealand is a place where men are dubious and sheep are slow . . .

"I haven't forgotten about the K-27 or 'plastic fantastic'," I said.

Unfortunately, it took a Belgian-born Australian businessman to have the foresight to enter a challenge for the America's Cup on behalf of the Kiwis.

Do they do it better?

Nice of the Kiwis to take their plastic toy boat out of the bath and finally give it a go in some real water off Fremantle.

There's nothing to write home about in NZ either . . . they spat the dummy when a core sample from their yacht was mentioned. That story hardly made a ripple in Australian waters but was front page for three days in NZ and even then the papers were a day late.

The pilot of the plane said, "Turn our watches on two hours when we arrive." I reckon the clock should be turned back ten years.

Sorry if I've offended any Kiwis, but it was a great debate . . . I'll admit we lost, but not by much.

Also I should mention the new DB Kiwi Lager – the reason for our gathering was to launch this new export lager. It's not a bad drop. I especially like the label colours, Australian green and gold.

C'mon Aussie C'mon!

Perils of a Nightwatchman

"HE'S NEVER SMILED AT AN AUSTRALIAN BATSMAN IN HIS LIFE"

It was well after dark at one of Melbourne's largest football stadiums, VFL Park. The digital clock at one end of the ground suggested it was 8.35 p.m. No-one occupied the electronic scoreboard on which the clock was mounted and the huge concrete grandstands were empty, cold and uninviting.

But there was some activity. The cluster of lights hanging in the sky focused like laser beams on twelve of Australia's finest crick-eters. They were huddled around a plain old cardboard carton, intent on taking the gentleman's game into a whole new era.

Inside the much used carton were between twenty to thirty cricket balls. Every colour in the rainbow seemed to be present – there were yellow ones, white ones, pink ones, pale blue, orange, even a bright red one!

Yes, this was how night cricket began, as an experiment with coloured balls under lights at VFL Park. I must admit I arrived at the ground that night thinking it was just a crazy idea. How could any batsman be expected to see 5¹/₂ oz. of leather hurtling down the wicket towards him in the middle of the night and consistently hit it. Well, by the end of the night it was obvious that cricket could be played at night and Kerry Packer immediately spent millions of dollars on it. The cardboard box and coloured balls was the "cheap" feasibility study, what followed was groups of monolithic light pylons at the Sydney Cricket Ground, similar at the MCG and the WACA ground in Perth.

White balls were selected and coloured clothing and protective gear quickly followed, mainly because of the umpiring difficulties in "seeing" the white ball against white pads.

Australia was given lemon, which really set off the road maps in the eyeballs after a night out on the town. Wicketkeeper, Rodney Marsh, the man with billiard table legs, was the Aussie model. The West Indies were given a colour which very much resembled "nipple pink". Can you imagine the world's Number 1 batsman, Viv Richards, in nipple pink? It was an amazing sight, particularly if he batted all night, which he often did. The other problem with the "Windies" colour was that pink in the Caribbean was the gay colour. I couldn't blame 'em for grizzling. And giant South African-born Tony Greig looked like an oversize plastic clothes peg, the first time he strutted his stuff in the pale blue of the World XI colours.

The introduction of night cricket changed many aspects of the game. It had a dramatic effect on me, especially as a batsman. You can't overlook talent forever and the good judges of a batsman in my time – like captains Ian and Greg Chappell – didn't. They looked very seriously at the talented batting ability of Maxwell Henry Norman Walker for the role of night watchman and I didn't let them down! Well I didn't in the daytime.

Now the "nightwatchman" is usually a batsman not good enough to bat high in the batting order regularly. Against his will or better judgement he has to be prepared to go to the wicket for a few desperate minutes before stumps to protect the so called "good batsmen" for another day! Usually these better players are settled back in the dressing room; boots and socks off, feet up on the window sill, reading the paper . . . completely devoid of anxiety.

Whereas the poor old "nightwatchy" is usually poised on the edge of his chair, buttock muscles tensed and trying not to stain his jock strap. At the same time attempting the impossible – biting his nails through the heavy padding of sausage batting gloves. He has one eye on the cricket – playing each ball from the sideline, heart pounding against his ribcage – while the other eye watches how slowly the second hand moves around the clock face.

When I look back on my evenings as a nightwatchman I guess I was pretty lucky. In Test matches I never did get to make that agonisingly long, lonely and slow walk, to the centre wicket area as 11 sets of beady eyes watch your every move to add to the mounting pressure. But during the two pioneering years of World Series Cricket, a lot of things changed under the tee-shirt slogans of "Big Boys Play at Night" and "Come see the White Ball Fly", including the role of the nightwatchman. For no longer did he have to go in at ten minutes to six. Try something like 10.20 p.m. at night!

The great players do it and if an average player goes through the same routine it makes him look more confident. Have a bit of a look around the ground, from third man, through mid off, way down to long leg. You just may bluff the opposition "quick" into thinking that you have the ability to play shots all around the wicket – and we all know that the worst thing a fast bowler can do is think, don't we? Not too many of 'em are Rhodes Scholars and I mean that in the nicest possible way because some of my best mates are former fast bowlers! The moment of truth is getting fearfully close. This is how it works. Sooner or later you will have to more than just look good. A batsman is only allowed to fiddle with his boot laces and tighten the top buckle of both pads for a few moments, otherwise it will appear suspiciously like you're stalling for time and an umpire doesn't have to be Albert Einstein to come to that conclusion.

Ready. Place one foot either side of the batting crease and start tapping the bat on the ground in anticipation while holding the handle with the tight grip of a wood chopper. Now, you look like one of those black and white photographs in Sir Donald Bradman's coaching manual *The Art of Cricket* – chin tucked into the shoulder and eyes focused towards the umpire. Even though the visor of the crash helmet is fogged up through being hot under the collar and the adrenalin is starting to flow freely through the body, try to manage a smile at the umpire. He may just keep his hands in his pockets a little longer . . . especially if it's a cold night. It's possible he is recalling what Confucious say, "Little boy with one hole in pocket feel cocky all day!" and "Little boy with two holes in pockets leaves no stone unturned!" Anyway, all the men in white used to be little boys at some stage of their life and dare I say it, many still are!

Okay look back beyond the umpire. There he is – Joel Garner – the giant calypso quickie, standing in front of a black sight screen. The "Big Bird" is not half past eleven, he's midnight. A very dark man. He's never smiled at an Australian batsman in his life and isn't about to now. Even if he did all you would see would be a massive piano keyboard!

Garner and three or four of his long-legged team-mates all have the ability to bowl at about 150-160 kmh. This means you've got about 0.25 seconds to play forward, back or simply duck to get out of the way! How are you feeling now? Decidedly sick and scared I bet!

Brace yourself as the "Bird" pushes off the sight screen. Honestly, all you can see at first is a white cricket ball suspended in space about a metre above a white shirt. As he charges in towards the umpire, set against the black background, his bulging eyes look like ping pong balls. The pounding of his massive feet sounds like a herd of elephants. Still a few paces to go. Then he gets up high on his toenails in the final delivery stride . . . an awful, awesome sight!

Now, just as his huge bunch of fives is about to launch that leather missile, imagine that one of those fat moths that buzz around the lights at the SCG flutters into the gap between the helmet visor and your perspiring face. What do you do? You can't extend your hand down the wicket like a traffic cop to stop all oncoming traffic! You can't shout at the top of your voice, "Hang on Joel . . . till I get rid of this dirty big moth!" There is no way he will hear over the roar of 40,000 fans. You can't stick a hand up the visor because your fingers and thumb are double the thickness in gloves. They won't fit!

There is only one answer – open your mouth as wide as you possibly can! The moth's legs wedge in your throat and the clapping wings soon stick like glue to the saliva on the roof of your mouth.

While this activity is taking place inside your mouth, Joel Garner has let one go, straight at the target. You know very well that the ball is going to crash into your rib-cage with a sickening thud. It's pitched about half way down the wicket, climbing rapidly and those six lines of stitching are steering the sphere at you. Bullseye!

You can't help but swallow and the jerkin juice gives you heartburn on the way down!!

It's often been said that pain is only bone deep and I couldn't agree more! Ask the bloke down at the non-strikers end, smugly leaning on his brand new bat, if he knows what it feels like to have a couple of ribs broken by a cricket ball. Most probably he explains in an understanding manner that he knows exactly how much it hurts. But you know bloody well he's lying – the alarm bells are ringing inside your ribs not his.

With that kind of experience behind you, I'm sure that you'll agree that watching a "nightwatchman" trying to get his act together against a great fast bowler, back into the attack after a spell at fine leg, to take the new ball, is a very entertaining exercise for everyone except the poor old nightwatchman.

It's been many years since I was last called in as a nightwatchman. But those other good judges of talent – the Tattslotto management in Melbourne – looked closely at me and put me in to "bat" at 5.58 p.m., six nights a week, on TV.

This was to launch the new gambling game of Keno. With my vast experience . . . and eye for the clock around that time of night, I guess I was going to be a natural. Playing Keno and being a "nightwatchie" is very similar. Both are played with coloured balls. In cricket, it's a matter of spotting the shiny red or white ball (depending on when you play) and matching your batting skills. If you're lucky and play the correct shot, you're still in the game and you get another chance. Not so different really to spotting a series of numbers at Keno and matching them. If you're skilful, or should I say lucky, you're a winner in this game. The simple sporting elements of spot, match and win.

Grass Growing, Seagulls Landing

"WHEN I FINALLY SANK INTO MY POSITION MY NERVES WERE SHOT"

How does a first class cricketer, especially one qualified in the profession of architecture, become a member of the Poison Typewriter Club? That's how most Test cricketers generally refer to the printed media – and some commentators. Use the wrong tone of voice, and commentary can be quite cutting and caustic!

Yet today, many summers away from the first class arena, I find myself a fully-fledged member of the Poison Typewriter Club, as a cricket commentator.

The direction of my life has been drawn like a magnet towards the media.

Unfortunately this has resulted in a departure from my profession – architecture. Nevertheless I'm sure the demand for architect-designed chook houses with 30-degree, sloping metal deck roofs is not so great today anyway!

After my retirement as a player I made my debut as a cricket commentator at Kardinia Park, Geelong, in January 1982. Drew Morphett and I covered the match between Victoria and South Australia for ABC-TV from 10.59 a.m. on day one till 6 p.m. at the end of day four!

It really was a gruelling initiation. The wicket at Geelong was perfect. Hundreds of runs were scored between many slow moments. I can tell you it was difficult at times describing grass growing, seagulls landing, and the odd stray dog trespassing onto the field at fine leg.

At the end of the game Drew, my senior commentator, was asked how the "big fella" had performed? "This bloke's unreal," Drew replied. "He can talk underwater with a mouth full of marbles!"

Several weeks later I found myself progressing to calling a one-day international between Australia and the West Indies in front of a huge crowd at the MCG.

On that occasion I shared the microphone with the doyen of Australian radio commentators, Alan McGilvray. I'm sure I was more nervous of fronting up in the commentary box than before playing in my first Test match almost a decade before on this very same ground.

Before going on air, "Mac" gave me some invaluable advice. "Son," he said, "if you imagine you are talking to a blind man when describing the game you will do alright – call it colour radio."

I have since used Mac's words of encouragement in combination with my own philosophy – it is invariably easier to be an armchair critic than actually be out in the middle doing all the hard work, taking all the risks.

Now, before each day's play commences, I write at the top of my pad of notepaper next to the microphone: *"Cricket played at this level is a very difficult game!!!"*

Those words I hope help me to get the contest into the right perspective . . . and not become an instant coach, critical of every shot.

I have been lucky enough to enjoy the company of three of the games finest voices – each a magnificent communicator.

On two tours of England it was a wonderfully enriching experience to make friends with the gravel voiced historian and wine expert John Arlott. While visiting South Africa in the Seventies it was a pleasure to meet Charles Fortune, a man whom I listened to as a boy for many a long hour . . . and of course our own Alan McGilvray.

Each of these gentlemen had a burning passion for the game based on a lifetime involvement. They also had the ability to put into words a rare insight into proceedings no matter what the predicament – common sense and unflappable composure.

Unfortunately John Arlott died, in his eighties, in 1991 but he left cricket lovers with a rich tapestry of his time at the crease.

Because of their talents it would appear to listeners that there are rarely problems . . . but let me share a few occasions where things didn't quite work out as planned!

In fact the Australia v West Indies limited over match mentioned earlier was just the beginning of several testing moments.

The ABC radio commentator's box in those days was not the most aesthetically pleasing piece of architecture at the Melbourne Cricket Ground. Located at the back of the cigar smokers stand (M.C.C. members) on the top level it resembled a crude chook house – split level over two seats approximately two metres by three metres – with a corrugated iron roof but without the wire mesh (sliding glass windows) front.

On that unforgettable day the temperature hovered around forty-five degrees Celsius – very, very hot!

In order to occupy my position at the microphone as expert comments man, I had to climb bodily over the shoulders of both Mac and our ever reliable master of statistics, Jack Cameron. With a nickname like Tanglefoot, standing 6'4" tall and sending the rev counter on the scales racing towards seventeen stone I was never going to achieve my objective without incident. Even the doorway into the confined space presented a struggle – it sloped across the top from right to left about 5' to 3'6".

I felt like a dog entering his kennel. Batting hero of the Sixties Norman O'Neill had just completed his hour long stint . . . as he stood up it was clear to see not a stitch of his clothing was dry – he could not have perspired that much had he scored a century. My leading knee cap clipped dear old Mac smack bang on the back of his head . . . the pair of binoculars he was holding went close to shattering his reading glasses and the veteran student of the game almost swallowed the cigarette he was enjoying. I knew I was in trouble when he started coughing with an unhealthy barking sound. Step number two got me into more strife. Remember there were no Unisys computers spitting out green figures on a backlit screen in those days – Jack either stored them in his head or in several shoe boxes that he never let out of his sight (fifty years of accumulated averages, aggregates and match results painstakingly handwritten onto small cards). As my size eleven shoe landed on the lid of his priceless shoe box, our scorer let out an almighty shout in disbelief. While his words echoed around the Members Stand . . . cards spewed out onto the rows of spectators like a pack of cards. Two out of two . . . and the new boy still had a pace to go.

No commercial breaks on the ABC . . . the broadcast box was in a state of upheaval. Mac and Jack eye balled the intruder with looks that could send a keen mind blank. The two technicians were trying desperately to suppress uncontrollable bouts of laughter.

By the time I finally sank into my seat my nerves were shot . . . but both forgave me in a big hurry and "nursed" me through the next hour together. Somehow it was difficult not to think about who called the first hour – Norm O'Neill. Now Norm is the sort of bloke who enjoys a drink *even* on a cold day . . . The pair of headphones had filled like cups with stale sweat 'n' beer . . . as I exercised my jaw Norm's stay in the box trickled down my neck and lingered longer than any after shave.

My new Pierre Cardin suit, especially obtained for the occasion, looked as if I had been swimming in it! Bad luck about the under armpit odour – even Aerogard wouldn't have worked in these conditions!

Yes, my work in the media has not been without its moments – some funny and some moving.

During the Adelaide Centenary Test, ABC colleague Jim Maxwell arrived into the commentary box with a batch of Mars bars. He offered one to me and then took his place at the mike, ripping the paper from his chocolate bar, apparently all ready to take a bite . . . much like tackling a banana.

I acknowledged him by taking a big bite. Jim who was just starting his stint, immediately asked a very short, sharp question. "Max, this bowler has got a beautiful approach to the wicket . . . talk us through this delivery!"

I had trouble for the next thirty-five seconds or so trying to separate my tongue from the roof of my mouth, my upper teeth from my lower teeth and trying to answer the question at the same time.

By this time Jim had put his Mars bar down and swayed away from the mike with his hanky over his mouth enjoying the prank and chocfull of laughter. This medium pace bowler momentarily lost his line and length.

Often, in Sydney for the night cricket, one or two of the kinder souls make cakes and send them up to the commentary box. As with the Mars bars, the difficult decision will always remain when and how to take a bite.

And to those with a devious sense of humor like myself, the object of the evening often is to see which one of the ball-by-ball commentary team can be caught out with a mouthful of cake.

There also have been some very serious and emotional moments.

During the 5th Test between Australia and the West Indies in Sydney in 1985, Alan McGilvray was calling his 219th Test – his last in Australia.

During the fourth day's play we had witnessed the emotional departure of one of the games greatest ambassadors – Clive Lloyd. The big cat snaked his way from the ground, dragging the 3 lb 5 oz piece of willow in his shadow, lingering as if to slowly soak up the standing ovation afforded him for his marvellous contribution to the game of cricket.

At tea-time . . . only two West Indies wickets remained intact . . . this would be a memorable victory for Alan Border and certainly this session would be Mac's last. Coincidence had Max Walker rostered to share the time slot.

Alan Marks, the executive producer for ABC cricket, had asked Mac if he would be in the box five minutes early to give some special comments.

The real reason was to hear a special taped tribute to Alan from the then, Prime Minister, Bob Hawke. This had to be taped because no-one could pre-determine the conclusion of the Test match or Alan's last shift on air.

Mac settled into his chair then he heard his name come over the public address system.

There was a mix-up. The high-tech electronic scoreboard had begun to broadcast the PM's tribute for all to hear – 45 seconds earlier than ABC radio.

Once Mac had recognised the voice he took off his headphones and pulled the sliding glass windows open in order to hear more. Then we had drama as Alan Marks asked Mac to close the windows and trust him. Firstly he refused – and only agreed when he heard that same voice come through his head-set.

What Bob Hawke had to say obviously moved the veteran commentator . . . Alan looked at me and said quietly "My goodness gracious me what have I done to deserve this . . . I'm just a cricket commentator . . . I do my job like everybody else!"

Then, as the game was due to get under way for the final session of play, the diamond-vision screen of the huge electronic scoreboard came to life in a kaleidoscope of colour with the words "Thanks Mac, you are the greatest" etched into the 40,000 light globes that constitute the screen.

Simultaneously 25,000 stood to a man and turned away from the game with eyes cast high to Alan McGilvray in the commentary box at the rear of the Sir Donald Bradman stand. Hands above their heads they gave the man who belonged to the voice, who so many people had loved and respected for almost fifty years, a thunderous, standing ovation.

Two balls had been bowled in the middle as we both stood before the crowd. Mac lifted his hands just as royalty would. Here was a moment very special in Australian sport.

I thought to myself . . . "Might as well go out in sympathy with him," so I stood up. The old bloke was choked with emotion.

At this stage there was a steady stream of tears rolling down . . . past the purple nose of the silver-haired legend . . . several splashed on the exercise book below. Back went the sliding glass window again . . . in came a huge lens mounted on a television camera. This time I asked myself a question, "Gee Maxie, you want to look good on the ABC News tonight . . . get that rib cage up where it ought to be!" So I sucked in one almighty great breath . . . and hung on! Mac might have been crying but I was in real pain and my face too was going purple – how long can a mere mortal hold his breath for?

Then like the true professional, Mac sat down, regained his composure, thanked several people for their contribution to his career as a communicator . . . and called the remaining deliveries of the over.

Alan McGilvray isn't just another commentator – for almost half a century, from the 1938 synthetic Test match broadcasts – he was the undisputed voice of cricket in Australia.

He ended his innings with grace a few minutes later at the end of the second over when he asked Alan Marks, "Is it possible to have another commentator in the commentary booth please, I would now like to leave."

The old bloke just stood up, turned and immediately walked away from Test cricket in Australia.

Then, with the Master's chair momentarily vacant, I was left with three options, realising that the lump, formerly in my throat, was now somewhere up near my ears and the atmosphere in the enclosed booth was very emotional – as thick as a London fog.

Firstly, I could commence a ball-by-ball commentary, something I hadn't attempted in the past; secondly I could give my expert opinion on the last 10 or so deliveries bowled, none of which I'd taken much notice of; or finally, I could put in a few well-earned words of praise.

I opted for the latter.

Conditions might have been difficult in the middle for the West Indies batsmen trying to cope with the spin of Bob Holland and Murray Bennett but I can honestly say it was also very difficult batting from behind the mike . . .

I was pretty pleased to finally see Dennis Cometti sit down next to me. He, too, was stunned and speechless for about fifteen seconds – it seemed like eternity, but as we say in the box. He was the batsman on strike.

Ready to show the world

"DOUGIE BATTED FOR HALF AN HOUR AS BUDDING FAST BOWLERS LINED UP FOR A CRACK AT HIM"

It was 3 o'clock in the morning. Two young boys sat on the edge of their dormitory beds, feet barely touching the floor. Inside their tummies huge butterflies danced up and down . . .

The occasion was the final day of the live-in Max Walker Cricket Camp held at the famous Assumption College, Kilmore, Victoria in February 1986.

Today they would be playing a cricket match . . . for many young-sters it would be the first time they had ever played in an official cricket match. A mighty step forward!

It was a real pleasure to witness the pride each of these budding cricketers had in their own ability . . . they wanted to show the world they could play the game! And that alone was a wonderfully healthy attitude to have.

Each of these junior "champions" had his bat gently resting on the floor. They weren't going to waste any time either, for both were fully dressed in their all-white cricket gear, glowing in the dark.

When questioned by the housemaster on duty that night as to what they were doing, their wide-eyed reply was brief and to the point. "How long till the game starts?" It was almost enough to make a grown man cry with joy.

Yet today we see our Test players using former greats like Dennis Lillee and Rod Marsh to get them motivated. Surely a Test cricketer doesn't need another person to tell him he should be giving his abso-lute best when representing Australia!

The beautiful truth is that all these juniors want to play Test cricket . . . and I reckon they all dream about striding to the wicket at the MCG just about every night they put their weary little bodies down to rest after a solid day's work out.

Every camp has its characters and this year was no different. In all we conducted three camps – two at Kilmore and the third at Launceston. The boys travelled far and wide to improve their game.

In fact one young fella named Rhys became the darling of all the coaches. He had been holidaying in England with his parents and came straight from Tullamarine airport to Kilmore . . . no jet-lag with Rhys.

The nine-year-old "Bradman" was so small he commanded a great deal of respect from his peers. Add his cheery nature and bright beaming smile and the diminutive little Aussie had his mates eating out of the palm of his hand.

One boy came all the way from India to join the camp. It didn't take long for the lads to nickname him "Kapil Dev" . . . and what's more he loved being identified with his native hero.

Then there was "an individual" named Mark Jackson – he even had the prickly, crew-cut hair-do. You'd never guess, he was called "Jacko".

Another kid they called "Rambo" because he wore the same jungle greens and black track-suit trousers for four days.

They were quite an incredible bunch. At shower time they all became very scarce – some of the nine to ten year olds needed an operation to get their clothes off. In fact some of them used to hide in the cupboards and under the beds.

And then there was "The Professor" who came back to us for the second year . . . he knew everything. He just wouldn't shut up – like a tape recorder with a new set of batteries.

On the first morning he said, "Remember me? I'm the fellow who bowled two balls into the nets last year and got a wicket with each delivery!" How could I forget . . . he mentioned it often enough.

One kid used his protector (box) when he was bowling because his follow through arm usually ended up between his legs. He had a very awkward action. So much so that we nicknamed him "Richard Hadlee" – rather unfairly in hindsight.

The coaches were the key to the camp's success. Each and every one of them was of the highest possible order and a successful communicator. But they also copped some flak from the boys.

Kerry O'Keefe, former Australian and NSW leg spinner received a beauty from young Jeremy Stebbings. He said, "I bet you don't know what that 'brain sucker' is doing on your head?" Kerry didn't have a clue. The kid gave him a rather cutting answer, "Going hungry!" I liked it.

Then we had everybody's favourite and one of the greatest players ever to put on a green baggy cap for Australia, Doug Walters.

One night Dougie batted for half an hour as budding fast bowlers lined up for a crack at him. Much in the mould of Sir Donald Bradman, Dougie didn't let 'em down. He kept middling the ball beautifully. One straight drive cleared the sight screen sixty metres away . . .

Then came the acid tongue of Kerry O'Keefe trying to discipline one wayward leg-spinner. Subtle as a sledge-hammer.

"That's the worst ball I've every seen bowled in my life!" he screamed as the ball landed twenty metres to the left of where it ought to have. "I think you should go and lock yourself in the toilet for half an hour and think about it!" And the kid was so upset he did.

There was never a dull moment, even at night. One of our night staff discovered a sleep-walker . . . he had no alternative but to wake him up because he didn't have his name tag on and he didn't know where the poor kid came from.

Limited over star Simon O'Donnell used the three camps to overcome an injured hip. It was the same injury which side-lined him during the Australia v New Zealand Test match at the SCG in December 1985. He was a huge hit with the group – so were our two West Indian coaches.

Ken Benjamin, a fast bowler from the island of Antigua, soon became very popular with his outgoing nature and madcap sense of humour. He was in Australia on an education scholarship along with Guyanese batsman and off-spinner Carl Hooper. Hooper won rave revues for his performances in the 1985 West Indies domestic season and these days is a Test regular.

At night there was plenty of entertainment. During the screening of the Centenary Test film in Launceston the roof almost came off the theatre when 220 schoolboys chanted, "Lill-ee, Lill-ee, Lill-ee," as the champion fast bowler took apart the Englishmen in March 1977 at the MCG. Dennis Lillee took eleven wickets for the match – they had plenty to shout about. What a legend and a role model.

There was not much need for punishment throughout the twelve days of coaching . . . but Brother Pius at Assumption College had a good method of discipline! One night at 11.30 p.m. two boys had to do four laps of the oval in the rain and in the dark, on separate ovals – a bit scary!

The young man who received my courage award was Jason. Jason had a physical disability that would have stopped a lot of boys participating – he only had the use of his left side.

He bowled off a lengthy run, by dragging himself along, if only to be like the other boys. We cut his run down and within a couple of days I was amazed at his improvement . . . the way the ball left his hand, seam vertical. I was really proud of him.

When he batted in the nets he quietly asked one of the coaches if the boys would mind not bowling so fast at him – they didn't.

When Jason played his match on the fourth day his new mates clapped him all the way out to bat . . . he scored a one-handed boundary which was a gutsy effort . . . and his mates clapped him all the way off.

The shy youngster acknowledged the applause by quietly stating, "It was an easy hundred boys!"

There were so many stories of humour, courage and sadness amongst the 750 odd boys we shared our time with.

Sure there were some tearful beginnings as is always the case when a youngster leaves his parents behind for the first time – a painful necessary learning experience. Part of growing up.

Michael took his stuffed dog to bed with him, another had the Sesame Street phone book on the window-sill.

With all those mixed emotions thrown in it was great to personally hand them all a certificate of proficiency at our wonderful game – to watch them smile was a priceless gift.

It was also wonderful on the first day in Kilmore to overhear two young mates saying to each other, "I'll write you a letter!"

For many it was a chance to make their first real friend outside of family and school – they shared so much under the common bond of cricket.

We never stop learning about the game – when you do, it's time to give it away!

CHAPTER SIX

The Trauma of Travel

The sky's the limit

"HAD VISIONS OF SOMEONE – HOPEFULLY NOT ME – BEING SUCKED OUT OF THE OPEN DOOR"

"**W**e all ought to be certified for getting back into this bastard of a plane!" shouted Sam Newman from the rear of our temporary prison. For surely, we were doing time the hard way – trapped in a tiny flying machine.

Sam, the former Geelong VFL footballer and now a Melbourne radio and television sports personality, was sharing the second, or back row, of a four-seater, twin-engine Cessna next to notorious Melbourne television character, Peter "Crackers" Keenan, a veteran of more than 250 games with VFL clubs Melbourne, North Melbourne and Essendon. Today he is a member of the coaching staff at Collingwood.

Yours truly was in the cramped cockpit – in the seat reserved for the co-pilot. From the beginning, I had been almost hypnotised by the glaring mass of illuminated green and yellow gauges before my eyes.

Graeme, our young pilot, was responsible for safely transporting Sam, Crackers and myself to and from a speaking engagement in the small town of Cohuna, in the north of Victoria.

The aircraft was being buffeted continually, like a lost balloon, in strong wind gusts. The plane had just fallen abruptly – about 1,000 feet – when Sam made his timely comment.

Crackers and I agreed, and he replied quickly: "Gee, I feel close to God, but I don't want to meet him just yet!"

The flight wasn't exactly a religious happening, but the time we shared in that cramped, dark interior of the plane certainly was soul searching stuff! I kept thinking about what a terrible bloke I'd been all my life . . . and how I might live if ever I received another chance!

I've got it on pretty good authority that there was some good money within the four of us to say that we would not make it back to ground in one piece! And I'm not telling any lies when I say we were all very bloody frightened. Maybe it was the bad beginning to our epic journey?

What a way to start! As we calmly taxied down the black bitumen tarmac, there was very little discussion, other than the preceding week's events. At near top speed, our wheels left the tarmac of Essendon airport.

A perfect take-off I thought. Sammy and Crackers didn't really care as they dissected VFL footballers' recent performances. Whatever the field, old players never die, they just become experts in their sport, or maybe commentators like myself, eh?

"Bloody hell!" Sam screamed, as we were barely 300 feet above the ground, and still climbing, because the pilot's door flew open. Wind at about 160 kmh gushed into the cockpit. My heart began pounding very loudly – I was terrified! And I know that I wasn't an orphan in feeling like that!

I flung my left arm across the pilot's back, like any "great" slips fieldsman might, to grab the flapping door. Simultaneously, both hands from the 6'4" ruckman from Geelong appeared from the other direction, desperately trying to pull the door shut.

Crackers was issuing the obvious instruction at the top of his voice: "Shut the bloody door, quick shut it, c'mon Sam shut it!"

The door would not close, despite superhuman efforts by Sam and me.

Through all this, the pilot was huddled grim-faced over the aeroplane's controls to give us a better chance to slam the door.

The lights of Essendon were all too bright below us – barely 500 feet off the ground. For some reason, the door still would not slam shut after several more vigorous attempts. Graeme struggled with the joy stick as we banked steeply round the control tower.

At one stage, I reckon we must have been flying side-ways at ninety degrees to Earth and hanging on for grim death. I felt the long legs of Peter Pius Paul Keenan almost pushed through the back of my seat as he fought the forces of gravity.

A unanimous decision was made to land the plane and see what was wrong – who said footballers had no brains? On this occasion, commonsense prevailed!

I had visions of someone – hopefully not me – being sucked out the open door into the cold dark night air, never to be seen again! Did you ever see the film *Airport '75*??

The very large lump in my throat had moved and lodged somewhere near the back of my ears as we levelled out over the Tullamarine freeway . . . if only we can land this plane safely?

I should not have doubted Graeme's ability, for the Cessna came in for a smooth landing. The "team" was right back where we started five minutes earlier.

Without even stopping the plane, the door was much easier to close when we were rolling slowly along the tarmac. I wonder why?

Nerves frayed, but confidence restored, we powered down the runway for the second time. Crackers suggested that the air traffic controller in the tower probably thought he was drunk seeing the same plane take off twice in seven minutes. It was good to hear some humour again!

But it didn't last long as we struggled into very strong headwinds. We should have been travelling at 160 knots, instead we were averaging only 105.

Long before we reached Bendigo, we agreed that it was the worst flight we had ever been on, except for Graeme, who was showing a brave face.

Then the small charter plane pressed forward relentlessly into the face of a very nasty storm. Thunder punctuated the unhealthy silence inside, while outside heavy rain pelted the windscreen, and lightning forks etched golden lines into the night. Visibility could have been barely ten metres – we truly were flying blind.

Graeme would not dare let his hands leave the controls as we continually dropped out of the sky with devastating effects on my stomach, which had become horribly knotted.

Our plane was taking a battering in appalling conditions – it was a real effort to fly horizontally.

We were told that sick bags were in the seat pockets. I was too scared to be sick . . . Crackers said that if he was going to be sick, then it was only right the pilot should wear it. From where I sat it was odds on that I would wear it.

I should mention too that Crackers had been out to lunch: and garlic prawns had been on the menu. Every time he opened his mouth it was like an Indian flame thrower at work and the plane's interior was beginning to smell like an oven full of garlic bread. Very selfish that . . . I'll get him . . . but it did take our minds from our dangerous predicament.

My palms were very sweaty, and I'm certain that the giant ruckmen behind were holding hands as we plummeted through the clouds.

The rain on the wings now looked like huge sparks illuminated by the flashing wing lights – heavy drops were pounding on the windscreen.

I never have felt so insecure for such a long period of time! The two lads in the back were joking nervously about the possible news stories if we went down. A lot of those little planes do!

Something along the line of: "Football will miss Peter Keenan and Sam Newman, the two VFL champion footballers tragically killed with their friend, former Test cricketer Max Walker, when their light aircraft crashed north of Bendigo last night on its way to a speaking engagement at Cohuna."

As funny as it may sound, it could have been all too true! Nevertheless, we exchanged versions like jokes – I don't think our pilot was impressed. But I'm sure he realised our grave situation. As

Crackers said: "Don't worry Maxie, he's a mature twenty-one-year-old."

I thought here we are, our lives in the hands of a fragile, metal machine with two props and a twenty-one-year-old pilot. Unreal, and for what? A few hundred dollars for the night.

But it soon was established that we were being paid three times the amount the pilot was getting – absolutely insane!

Graeme could have been at home watching telly for that money – mind you, so could we! Sam said: "How far is it to Cohuna, one and a half hours? We've been going for one and a half hours and haven't looked like making bloody Cohuna!"

"Yeah," Crackers said impatiently, "we should've driven up – could have saved a few bob and a lot of heartache!"

Finally, almost two hours after our original take-off, we were in the vicinity of our flight destination, Kerang. We were flying at about 4,500 feet, give or take a thousand feet depending on the clouds and rain. All we had to do was find the airstrip – not easy!

I watched the altimeter spin from 4,600 feet to well below 1,000 feet – still no sign of the strip. My ears popped and I hung on tight, hoping there was no radio tower or mountain tucked away secretly in the darkness below us.

Then, from nowhere, the two parallel blue lines appeared to our right – I didn't think that two blue lines could ever look so good. We did one arbitrary lap of honour before we made our final approach to land.

The nervous tension had got to us – we all started laughing as Graeme again put us on deck with a beautiful landing in pouring rain.

While the propellers unwound, and our aeroplane came to a standstill, I thought: no way am I getting back into this kite, unless we've got clear skies. Judging by the amount of water bouncing off the wings it looked like overnight at Cohuna.

You are not going to believe me when I tell you this, but about 12.30 a.m. we left Kerang in clear skies. But around Bendigo we hit the storms again and sat through the same fear for another hour.

We could not get Graeme to admit that it was the worst flying conditions he had flown in. But he did describe them "as a long way from the best!"

I can understand why people hate small aircraft or flying full stop – you feel so helpless! Never again!

A Gamble in the Clouds

"OUT OF THE POCKET CAME A WAD OF BANK NOTES THE SIZE OF A CAN OF PEACHES"

Seat allocation on an aeroplane can be very much a gamble, especially when travelling alone. The random manner in which the airline computer spits out the all important seat number is like a lottery. You can never tell until you've actually planted your bum on the seat, whether you're a winner or loser, whether you've got the window or the aisle, who's next door or in front.

If you're a non-smoker, there is nothing worse than spending an hour or so sniffing the breath of a chain smoker . . . even a blast from the airconditioning vent won't stop your eyes from watering.

And how about if you draw a "Black & Decker drill" as a partner – someone who doesn't draw breath from the moment the pointy end tilts to the sky for fear of losing "airspace", or should I say, conversation space.

The only way to deal with this sort of bad luck is to bite your tongue, close the eyes, incline the head to one side, and force yourself to go to sleep. Then, when you feel the undercarriage make contact with the runway below, awaken to the screech of burning rubber, as the tyres tear up the tarmac . . . you sheepishly look across the armrest to your frustrated companion in travel, and apologise for having gone to sleep half way through a sentence!

Believe me it's really very easy to do, especially if the person has had a big night out on the garlic! Even looking straight ahead at the seat back – which by the way, is very rude when the person on your left is trying to speak to you – the stench of a dead prawn drowned in a garlic bath hits your sensitive nasal passage. There is no escape!

And how could we forget the poor little overworked business executive sitting in front. Resplendent in a pin-stripe suit, conservative navy tie, receding hairline, commuting daily between capital cities and treating the plane like his personal transport. How can I tell he's going bald? Easy! Thirty seconds after take off he and the other little buggers push their seats back just as they must have done in their thrill-seeking teenage days at the drive-in. Nothing quite like the old lay-back seat, was there? Except when you're 6'4" and sitting behind one, on a commercial aeroplane, headed for Melbourne.

It's very difficult for a little "exec" to understand how uncomfortable air travel can be for a long limbed gentleman like myself. There is only one course of action . . . dig the nobbly knee caps deep into the seat in front of you (this happens automatically, the moment the seat is reclined) so that the little bugger's collarbones span awkwardly between the two offending lumps.

Apart from cutting off the circulation of blood below the knee, the other problem with unco-operative passengers in front, is getting the tray table down to a horizontal position. Mission impossible! When this occurs, the only thing to do is to be a pest, don't be shy, interrupt his sleep and make him sit up straight like a good boy so you can enjoy your coffee without fear of wearing it all over your lap. He won't be happy, but who cares? He didn't worry too much about who was behind, did he? An attempted plastic smile may help.

Then of course there is a drunk, or should I say, the overindulged traveller. There's not a lot either you or the hostie can do with this sort of customer. Generally his attitude will be one of having paid for his trip like everyone else, and he's going to enjoy it by participating in a few extra sips to ease the nerves.

Now, this was exactly the case recently. My wife Kerry and I were returning to Melbourne, on the 6.45 a.m. early bird "special", following a speaking engagement in Launceston. This is always a bad time of the morning to travel, as it's possible to crack it for customers on their way home from the casino. We hit the jackpot, not one but two

– both men had bulging pockets and obviously had enjoyed a truck load of bourbon and coke before the sun rose above the horizon.

Initially we thought how lucky we were to have been "upgraded" by the friendly officer at the check-in counter of Australian Airlines to seats up front. A comfortable, roomy flight and a hearty breakfast to look forward to. Well, that was until our two would-be wobbly friends climbed the access staircase at the rear end of the aircraft. Against the general flow and wishes of the passengers, they pushed, shoved and jostled their way loudly to their seats at the front. Our not so well slept hostess was unimpressed by the impatient waving of their boarding passes beneath her powdered nose. You see, no amount of makeup was going to conceal the red lines at the edge of her bloodshot eyeballs. They looked like chook's feet! There was no mistaking it, the lady had obviously been on a bender and was in no mood to tolerate fools. Particularly drunken fools.

She couldn't believe her misfortune in copping this terrible two-some. It was quite funny – until she extended her right arm stiffly, gesturing the pair into seats directly in front of us! The crotchety attendant in the dark blue uniform could walk away. We were going to be stuck with 'em.

The younger man of the ill-mannered double, was rapt to get the window seat. His partner was a lean 'n' hungry bearded man with darting eyes, mostly focused on the coca cola bottle shape of the blonde hostess. His smile was an ugly giveaway – forty years of drinking and smoking had left him with some teeth but they were badly in decay; the colour of a urine-stained toilet bowl. His black hair and grey beard hadn't experienced the excitement of a comb since leaving his hotel room many, many hours before. Yet above all, he was obviously happy to be alive and convinced the world was a great place to live in.

Whilst he searched for the seat belt, his unshaven apprentice did a double-take – he spotted my ugly dial above the head rest. He couldn't believe his eyes . . .

"MAXIE BLOODY WALKER! JESUS CHRIST! What are you doing here?"

"Just grabbing a ride back to Melbourne like you!" I explained.

"Wow, what a buzz! I used to watch you when you played footy with the mighty Demons!"

Obviously a Melbourne Football Club supporter since he was weaned off his mother's milk. Words just kept flowing from the heart.

"I never thought I'd see the day. Bloody hell! Colin, do you realise who's sitting behind us?"

"No . . . who?" questioned the senior partner.

"Don't you recognize 'im? Maxie Walker!"

With a blank look of nobody home, "Naah!" he whined mischievously. "What's he do? I bet he's never played for Collingwood!"

"You can say that again!" I bellowed back, and I meant it.

As I said that, it reminded me of a question I was once asked by a Collingwood detractor: what's the difference between a Collingwood supporter lying dead on the road and a dead pig? And you're not going to believe the reply: obviously the skid marks are in front of the pig!

We hadn't even taxied along the runway and the trip looked doomed. There we were, Kerry, no great Aussie Rules lover, and myself, on a hiding to nothing, sharing a back seat with two inebriated winners – one of whom couldn't see past his nose or Collingwood.

At least one was a Demon through and through, and for only that reason could the trip have been bearable.

In a complex volley of slurred words, he attempted to explain to his slippery mate who I was. "You know, the bloke on television. He used to spray that little kid in the face with a can of Aerogard every time he went out to play cricket. You remember, Lillee and Thomson, when they blitzed the Poms?"

"Yeah, but I can't remember him," he barked with a sarcastic sting to it. It was now obvious we didn't like one another and the chances were that the temperature wouldn't get any warmer.

"What did he do? Bat or bowl? Or just hang around in the field while Lillee stuffed 'em?" he teased.

At this stage the ball bearings in each man's neck were doing as much overtime as Ossie Ostrich when he cranks up Daryl Somers on "Hey Hey. It's Saturday". Mind you, if they continued to unleash much more verbal diarrhoea, then my intentions were to stretch the ugly Magpie supporter's "Adam's apple" about a foot above his shoulder blades!

The signs were now illuminated NO SMOKING, FASTEN SEAT BELTS. The focus of attention moved back towards the blonde, complete with the yellow inflatable lifejacket and red toggles.

She was standing in front of the toilet sign which must have caught the eye of Colin in front. As he lent across into the aisle for a better squiz at the young woman's legs, the call of nature urgently registered somewhere above his bushy eyebrows.

Like a school boy, up went the hand in question to the hostie. "Lady, I need to go to the dunny." This broke up the occupants in the front of the aircraft which only served to encourage him.

"You'll have to wait sir, until we level out. And do up your seat belt for take-off!"

She continued her well rehearsed routine, "Pull this, blow that . . . don't inflate your lifejacket until you're outside the aircraft!"

It was all too much for our gambler, "I'll never make it till 30,000 feet! I'll explode!" he painfully pleaded. "Well, you'll just have to keep your legs crossed and mouth closed!" she snapped.

"That's your caper, lady! I'm telling ya, I've gotta go to the bloody toilet!"

The exchange was very funny for everyone except our intrepid gent. For him the pain was very real as he waited impatiently.

Not much happening out the window, only grey concrete and grass rushing by, so my Demon mate suggested: "Let me buy you and your lady a drink Maxie!"

Just as well the no smoking sign was on because I'm sure if anyone struck a match, the plane would be up in flames – his breath was ninety per cent alcohol.

I was conscious of trying not to offend the odd couple because drinking, and drinking heaps, was a subject very dear to both of them. As we angled towards the clouds I declined the offer, "It's a bit early yet!"

"C'mon, Tangles, I thought you'd be a real drinking man like us. You know, Dougie and you . . . you're always drinking on them ads!"

I didn't have the heart to tell him they basically are the same commercials played over and over again. Then again it would be very fair to say that my former cricketing mate and co-star of the Toohey's 2.2 commercials did take the opportunity to "sink" quite a number more cans than was necessary to complete the thirty second commercials. Dougie was never one to pass up the opportunity to have a beer, especially a free one!

As we levelled out, the OCCUPIED sign was illuminated by our impatient drinker. Now with one seat vacant, it was easier for the Demon fan to turn right around to face us. He ran his eyes quickly over Kerry from the top of her head of dark brown hair all the way down to the carpet supporting her shoes, and I'm sure he approved.

"You must do a lot of walking to have calves like that!" he questioned. Kerry continued reading.

His mate, who looked like a prawn fisherman back from a haul, returned with a real wild card comment, "You know listening to golf on radio is as boring as listening to you!"

What could I say? One of 'em loved Kerry's legs and the other hated my commentating!

He went on, "McEnroe's my idol. He's got so much aggro in him!"

"Yeah, and he's got a lotta beaver in him too!" his mate replied.

"I like champions . . . they're great . . . 'cause they always win!"

I thought to myself, "He doesn't kick with the breeze much this bloke, does he?" They wouldn't be bloody champions if they kept on losing! I bit my tongue and kept quiet. No need to keep the fire burning and what's more, I understood that no amount of discussion was going to alter the way they thought about anything. Tomorrow they would be nursing a nasty hangover and amnesia.

Kerry thought about a sleep but gave up – too many loud-mouthed interruptions. Next thing, up went the arm in front, like a Heil Hitler salute . . . bang, flush on the service button. This time a more matronly hostie arrived and I decided to take a few notes on proceedings while they ordered.

The elder statesman, with the track-suit top and tee-shirt couldn't help himself. You see the hostess had an open-necked shirt on and from where he was sitting, she looked great. So out of the pocket came a wad of bank notes the size of a large tin of peaches. The body language was very much c'mon . . . wink, wink . . . nudge, nudge . . . what do ya reckon! Our senior hostie wasn't impressed.

"Ya want a drink love? You name it, you've got it!" followed by a big, beaming grin. Tiredness must have set in because he couldn't hold the smile, or maybe he recognised his offer was just not on!

"We don't drink on the job," was the cool reply.

"Aw, c'mon, just one won't hurt ya!"

Not to be outdone, our Demon supporter stood up – he too had a bundle of notes larger than his fist could hold.

"Do you reckon we haven't had a good night!" he bragged.

"We blitzed 'em on the tables, didn't we."

"Sure did!!"

Then the bearded one turned around and in a more pleasant manner said, "He loves you Maxie!"

"Anyone who plays for Melbourne is alright by me!" his mate declared.

"Na . . . Collingwood forever!"

"Up the Demons!"

"Go on, prove you love him, you miserable bastard. Give him half your winnings! See, now he doesn't love you. He's only saying he does!"

At this stage I thought we were set for a right old barney, but the hostie did her bit.

"What did you ring the button for?"

"What do ya reckon . . . a drink of course!"

"You'll have to wait until we serve breakfast!"

"Breakfast?" Colin exclaimed. "It's a bit early for breakfast . . . we haven't been to sleep yet!"

"We ordered a cab for 3.00 a.m., it didn't lob and we had to ring another one . . . !"

I noticed a few spots of blood on the tee shirt. Yes, it really had been a huge night. Then again, he could have had a bleeding nose. I suppose I shouldn't pre-judge. Maybe he fancied himself as a potential Mike Tyson and I wasn't about to find out!

Commonsense prevailed and they soon got their bourbon and cokes . . . before breakfast!

But far from keeping them quiet, this was merely another reason to argue about whose shout it was and the splitting of the taxi fare.

"What about the four miles you owe me?"

Kerry and I couldn't help but laugh – it was spontaneous slapstick entertainment.

As a good gambler always out of luck, the obvious thing to do was to ask if they worked to a system, or if in fact they did play the roulette table. So I tapped my tired Melbourne supporter on the shoulder and popped the thought-provoking question.

His reply was wonderfully simple. "Nope! We just sit and think . . . and watch a bit!"

Soon, with all the twisting and turning in their seats, it was bound to happen. Off the tray table and into the lap slid the plastic cup. Nothing like the cold shower treatment with the bonus of a few ice cubes . . . and a nice wet telltale patch on the front of the trousers to go with it. Not that either men cared – the remains of the bourbon and coke were brushed off the tray and onto the floor. The problem was easily solved with the hasty order of drink number two . . . neither of 'em was feeling any pain or discomfort at this stage.

Nevertheless, one must give them full credit for having enough sense to stop when they were well in front – breakfast was coming!

The food silenced the entertainers for a short while. Still, I kept jotting down some classic one-liners like these:

"How do me eyes look!" Colin quizzed.

"Dreadful! Road maps everywhere!"

"Gee!" he said, "you ought to climb inside my head and take a look at 'em from this side!"

I was beginning to warm to the Collingwood guy. At least he was loyal – even the hoops on his tee-shirt were black and white.

The pair confided in us that about once a month they make the pilgrimage to Tassie to watch the little ball roll and clatter its way around the coloured edge of the roulette wheel. But as is the case with anyone who is unfortunate enough to be a victim of the gambling disease, they never lose, or you never hear about the losses.

Next, the overnight winners were keen to enlighten their captive audience on last year's journey overseas to the bright lights and glamour of Las Vegas.

"Didn't we take 'em apart over there . . . ?" The memories came flooding back in black and red, odds and evens, 36:1 chances.

"We collected two big ones (I think they meant thousands) after the first hour. Then we had a tub (shower) . . . might as well, seeing they laid a free room on us!"

You could see the sparkle in their eyes.

" . . . $9000 each we peeled off 'em. Like taking candy from a kid!"

"Yeah, we really loved it in Vegas," with almost a hint of American twang in the voice.

I became the subject of conversation again as they noticed the pad beneath my hand – they didn't miss a trick.

"Don't make out you're intelligent."

Then in popped the other. "Trying to make your $5.00 shopping list?"

The interrogation in stereo continued.

"What's it like living with a spendthrift?"

"Gee, I thought celebs looked after their women – he won't even let you have a drink! What a tight bastard he is!!"

They had their fun. Now it was time to lighten up! Neither Kerry nor I smoke. I gave it up at eight years of age when my mum detected the smell of cigarettes on my breath during an evening bath (big trouble that) – so we suggested they were sitting in a non-smoking seat. That didn't worry them. Both of 'em were puffing away . . . one off the end of the other.

Then our eagle-eyed hostie – the matronly one – spotted the grey, polluting haze hovering around.

"You guys know this is a non-smoking area? It's illegal!"

"What . . . wee wouldn't do anything illegal . . . would we?" They mooned at one another in a mimicking way.

"Give these to the captain . . . we don't want the cops on us!"

They handed over two well spent cigarettes – still alight with sticky saliver clinging to the filter tips. I guess the floor of the cockie's cage, which was what their mouths must have been like, was pretty awful after the night's events.

Thank goodness the airlines have finally come to their senses and banned smoking on all our domestic flights – much more fun to fly.

Now it was time for philosophy corner with about twenty-five minutes to touch down.

"What a lovely lady that bird is," referring to the hostie. "You know, if you give your respect to people . . . then they'll be all right."

Poetic words considering the waitress in the sky had two cigarette butts in her hand – a fine way of showing their respect! I imagined that next up they'd be bearing their soul in this moment of seriousness. No, they broke into a teasing banter again and began discussing their other halves.

"Will the missus be there to meet ya?"

"Yeah, she'll be there."

"No she won't!! She doesn't finish at the parlour till 8 o'clock!"

A loud gravelly guffaw accompanied that little gem. The girl across the aisle jumped in fright. She thought she was having a bad dream, only to discover it was real! It was two gorillas having an early morning romp above the clouds.

"That's where we should go!" the bearded one suggested on realising they were about to arrive back in Melbourne on a Saturday morning. " . . . the races!"

"No, let's go to the pub and have a drink!" Obviously the grog was doing a fair bit of talking.

"Where are the races . . . ?"

"What about the greyhounds? They're easier!"

Their discussion was interrupted by a thud as Tullamarine airport rushed past the windows. We were back on deck. The journey seemed to take no time at all. You know, time flies when you're having fun. We had no alternative!

Now for the deep and meaningful grab of the hand, overlapped by a few sincere words like, "Lovely flight. Hope to share your company again soon," that signal the end of most airline travel. Like hell we would.

One hand had come bolting over the headrest with the speed of a Lionel Rose right jab to the midriff. I was lucky to cut it off before it scored a point. The other hand found its way between the seat backs. There was a crunching sound and the sensation of having just extracted my right hand from the mincing machine – I hadn't pushed my right thumb into position quickly enough between the index finger and the opposition thumb. This is very effective in nullifying some smartie who wants to show off his strength. You can't tell them to go squeeze a few extra tennis balls so you must hit 'em hard with the thumb where it counts – or suffer the consequences.

Exiting was a slow process off the plane and into the terminal in the shadow of our new bosom buddies. For them it was five steps forward and three back. Going nowhere fast! Or were they?

"Let's head straight for the international bar – we'll get a drink there!"

That was the first time they had agreed with each other since Launceston. The time was still not 8.00 a.m. . . . . there was every possibility the lights would go out early for Col and his mate!

Hope you had a good weekend fellas, it sure got off to a flying start!

The War of the Suit Carrier

"HAD LOST THE ARGUMENT AND WAS RATHER SHEEPISHLY HEADING BACK THROUGH THE GLARING CROWD . . ."

The cruel thing about travelling these days is that you can't get away with anything – your baggage has to fit in a special frame. The situation is the same with anything else you want to bring on the plane, like a suit carrier – that also must pass the pinch test . . . through a skinny metal slot.

Then of course there's the X-ray machine. I've got no problems at all with them . . . if they can detect a terrorist bomb, or weapon I applaud their work.

Let me tell you a true travel tale about my favourite piece of baggage. After years of searching I finally managed to find what I'd always wanted while visiting Egypt – a beautiful soft black leather suit carrier with stacks of zip pockets and saddle bags. The best thing was that it was long enough to fit a size 46 inch jacket in without the bottom being crumpled. Also for the quality, the price was dirt cheap . . . unlike the airline ticket – Melbourne/Cairo/Melbourne.

It was like a faithful puppy . . . following me wherever I wanted to go and I never let it out of my sight. The last thing you would want to happen to your pet dog is for it to be roughly manhandled, placed on an electric caterpillar, dumped into the hold and then have tonnes of other baggage stacked on top . . . what I'm trying to say is that under any circumstances I didn't want to see my leather suit carrier bundled off to be stored with all the other heavy items in cargo.

Commentators generally travel light, particularly for day/night games . . . so all my suit carrier contained on the return was a blazer, a couple of pairs of trousers on the one hook, one clean shirt and another used one crumpled down the bottom, a couple of sticks of underarm and a dirty pair of underpants. Not much really.

Now because the suit carrier is leather, it is fractionally wider than the normal carrier but nevertheless it hangs up inside the first class coat storage area, no worries!

So with the best intentions I head into the terminal at Brisbane Airport. With me is Bill Lawry who is also travelling back to Melbourne. All I am burdened with is my suit carrier and briefcase – I don't want to be hanging around for forty minutes at the other end waiting for luggage that may not even arrive.

Bill and I walked up to the waiting lounge and greeted the two duty hostesses, "G'day girls. How are you going?" No problem checking in! Walk through the gate, down the elbow-shaped tunnel into the plane . . . and then it started!

We visually confronted the purser who was dead set straight out of a concentration camp. She was probably forty going on ninety and not a pretty woman. The lady had the bun on the back of the head, hair pulled back, eyes close together, ears back and lips pursed like a purser's should be. She had that lean, mean look of a racing greyhound – no matter what happens I'm in the lead, number one. She was the head honcho alright, the one who makes all the decisions in the cabin.

I walked straight on down to her, ahead of a fairly long queue. Luckily I was ticketed to be sitting in 1A – and was about to turn right into the cabin when I was stalled in my tracks . . .

"You can't bring THAT on here," the painful-looking purser barked pointing at my beloved suit carrier.

I was not happy. "What do you mean I can't bring that on here. I have been travelling around Australia on this airline for the last six months and I have brought it on every flight!"

"Well, you are not going to bring THAT on THIS one!" she demanded.

I protested. "The last thing I want to see is my valuable suit pack down in the hold. Being soft leather it will probably get torn, if I in fact ever see it again!"

"If you don't get it out of here IMMEDIATELY, it won't even be on this flight AT ALL!" she shouted with a rigid bottom jaw.

That sort of freaked me a bit, but I persisted. "Well, what happens if there is a tear in it?" I persisted.

"That's YOUR problem. You can't bring it on!"

Obviously she had a fixation that I was not going to bring my favourite suit carrier on the plane. There was no point arguing with the female brick wall.

By this stage there were about thirty or forty people queued up like sardines impatiently waiting to get on. The queue had developed way beyond the gate to the loading arm and there were airline staff running around, wondering what was going on. My clobber and I had to part or else there would be no travelling tonight.

Incredibly I had lost the argument and was rather sheepishly heading back through the glaring crowd until another of the hosties caught up to me, grabbed the offending article of hand luggage from me and ran it back to the two girls at the gate where they had only minutes earlier screened the same piece for "unsuitable" hand luggage and cleared it.

I elbowed my way apologetically back through the crowd to discover our "watchdog" had bailed up five guys out of the next seven behind me.

Meanwhile Bill, who had a ringside view of all this, seated in 1B, was doubling over in laughter. He reckoned it was marvellous entertainment witnessing me walk my carrier back out.

"See I told you. I told you you wouldn't get it on. Don't you try and break the system, Maxie! If it is good enough for everybody else, then it's good enough for you!" he sarcastically stated, looking down the slope of that large angular nose of his.

I slumped down beside Bill. "Don't you say a thing, Bill," I scowled in reaction. "You have been wearing the same bloody shirt for two and a half days!" Well . . . it didn't hurt to exaggerate a little to make my point!

All the other blokes she had cornered and delayed because of luggage were First Class passengers, so the plane was still basically empty. One businessman was livid – the majority of the heat from your body disappears through the top of your head – this gentleman had steam coming out of his ears, nostrils and mouth. The veins were popping out from his forehead and his face was going purple! He had a matching brown Gucci briefcase and suit carrier which cost twice as much as mine!

Like a naughty schoolboy, he too was forced to make his way back through the crowd, followed in succession by four more humiliated gents with freshly rejected hand luggage.

The annoying thing was that the door to the VIP wardrobe at the front of the first class bulkhead was open and there was nothing in there except the purser's coat hanging up, her overnight bag and Bill's limp plastic suit carrier – a 1979 Benson and Hedges World Series Cup hand out!

I was fuming and Bill was still sniggering. Sensing he could have more fun, Bill prodded me, "Go on," Bill pressed, "Go on Tang, call her a bitch!" Well she was a bitch but I didn't want to be totally rude and tell her to her face.

Once we were up in the sky she came visiting the first class passengers . . . all the offending men refused to accept drinks from her. In fact they ignored her, preferring to go without everything on offer from her . . . but she didn't seem to care!

Meanwhile the other hosties were quietly apologising for her unusual behaviour. There was nothing they could do – she was the boss. Everyone was dirty on her for holding up the plane for so long . . . so her coat could hang in the locker, unencumbered by the baggage of paying customers. Great priority.

Normally the purser displays a name tag but she wasn't wearing hers – I could understand why! Her badge said only Purser. After a little while I asked one of the hosties for her name. She couldn't remember exactly but bravely said, "Wait a minute and I will go and ask her."

A few seconds later, a familiar head peaked around the corner, "Yes, it's me," I mimed and pointed at my chest as I fixed her cool gaze, "I'm the one who wants to know your name!"

She rather self-consciously showed her face the bare minimum amount of times after that!

Most airlines have cards on the planes on which you are encouraged to write a report about the service. You write, "Well, this girl was terrific", and they put the comment on her file. We all asked for cards! A couple each.

She was glaring at us while we were madly writing down our abuse in large capital letters . . . we were within our rights because she had flung our bags off the plane which I felt was unjust. My only right of reply was through this report.

In all my years of travelling, I have never come across a person in a service industry – particularly in tourism – who had a worse attitude towards people.

The purser had probably alienated at least five First Class passengers – the most profitable customers. The possible ramifications were that maybe those five guys don't fly First Class any more – in fact they are likely to travel down the other end or change to the opposition airline. The direct cost of those few minutes of unnecessary superior tongue-wagging could equal tens of thousands of dollars for each passenger. They probably spend that much a year flying around the country. The woman was obviously in the wrong job.

I wouldn't have minded if my carrier wouldn't fit because then I would have been trying to bust the system – nobody can argue at being stopped for that!

I use an aeroplane so much and travel so often that's why I bought my special leather suit carrier – precisely so I could walk on and off without worries and delays with luggage.

The story didn't have a happy ending either. After waiting half an hour for the suit carrier to be spat out onto the revolving platform, something looking like it slumped down the slide.

Yes, sadly, that was my pride and joy! The solid brass handle had been yanked off, the buckle was broken and it was basically looking like a cricket ball after sixty odd overs . . . but that's the way it is with air travel sometimes.

Maybe there's a lesson in all that . . . only use cheap baggage.

Running into a Fan

"THERE WERE ONLY TWO WHEELS ANYWHERE NEAR THE GROUND"

Like most young adolescents I couldn't wait until the day I turned eighteen – old enough to legally drive a car. Looking back on a career spanning twenty-five years behind the steering wheel of a great variety of vehicles I can honestly say that motor cars are both expensive and dangerous.

I'm still alive to describe some of my close encounters of the four wheel kind, but not without a fair amount of luck.

The first new car I owned in Melbourne was a beautiful box-like, but shining white VE Valiant, or as the boys would call it – the Greek Mercedes. It really should have been a VD Valiant, because the previous year's model was given the initials VC. Maybe the sexual overtones were too hot to handle for the manufacturer, Chrysler.

Anyway what's in a name – I loved this pure white machine with all my heart. I had qualified for my driver's licence in amongst the hardly bustling 4.30 p.m. peak hour traffic of Hobart, eighteen months earlier. So, by comparison, the congestion and driver aggression of downtown Melbourne was a frightening experience for a young fella from Tasmania.

Add to that the peculiar right hand turns that could only be made from a left hand lane and the overall result was one of fearful confusion. . . so much so that I only had the confidence to drive my brand new showpiece once or twice around the block in Camberwell, where I lived.

Then when I did eventually, take it into town, for the first big trip, it happened – smash! A bingle. Yes, in the back streets of Collingwood, a stupid driver in a blue Falcon, failed to give way to his right. Even though I stood firmly on my brake pedal, the sparkling body work and chrome grille came to rest crumpled and hard up against the other driver's front door and fender.

Words failed me at the time, especially when he hopped confidently out of his undamaged passenger side door, and confronted me with the unexpected words, "You're Maxie Walker aren't you? I barrack for Melbourne (I played ninety-four games for the Melbourne Football Club in the VFL) . . . gee I'm sorry."

My radiator had obviously burst. Everywhere on the road was broken glass and tell-tale leaking water. Within seconds a tow truck operator appeared from nowhere and wanted my signature on his pink pad! Events were all happening a bit quick for me . . . I still couldn't believe my pride and joy was buried in the rib-cage of this other person's rust-bucket!

The crunch came when I had to ask my dad for the taxi-fare home! He wasn't a happy father. After all, he was the one who told me to be careful if I drove past the corner at the end of our street.

It's obviously not a good idea to drive when you're tired either. Again, I learned the hard way.

After entertaining a large gathering of middle management executives at a Marysville Guest House some two hours from Melbourne, in the middle of winter, I set off into the fog for the warmth and comfort of my own bed.

Visibility must have been limited to no more than 10 metres. I followed the snaking white line as best I could considering the circumstances.

Somewhere along the way, I must have taken a wrong turn, because the big Ford I was driving was sliding around hairpin bends on the muddy surface of a narrow graded road which was beginning to wind its way down the mountainside.

Inside my car the heater was blowing hot air around my feet and the windows were beginning to fog up. I felt warm and comfortable. Then, I must have closed my weary eyes for a brief moment because I woke up with a start only to feel the car sliding off the road into a deep culvert.

It unfortunately came to rest at about forty-five degrees to the shoulder of the road, and at the same time my body lunged forward and thudded into the steering wheel. The impact left very little wind in my lungs – the same sort of feeling as being hit head-on, or shirt-fronted on the football field.

There were only two wheels anywhere near the ground and they were firmly entrenched in the ditch on the passenger's side. The other two were motionless, and muddied, about a metre off the surface of the road.

Gee, what was a bloke going to do now, a million miles from anywhere at 1 a.m. in the morning? Anyway there I was, stranded in the bush for all the animals and birds to laugh at.

Most important though was the fact that I wasn't badly hurt. Sure my car looked out of business but I shudder to think how it might have ended had the car left the road on the right hand side where there was a very steep fall – all I could see through the mist was a wall of gum tree tops.

Isn't it strange? When I needed a tow truck they were nowhere to be seen! I thought of the RACV but the biggest problem was the distinct lack of public telephones on this frontier road.

I've heard of people being able to lift cars with feats of superhuman strength when in trouble . . . well, I was definitely in trouble but do you reckon I could summon that superhuman strength?

Commonsense prevailed and at approximately 3 a.m., after a couple of hours shivering in the cold night air, I decided it was time to stop hoping a car might come by, so it was back into the car to try and sleep.

Sleep didn't come easily. Obviously my wife would be worried to death at my absence – I was expected home at about 2 o'clock.

Morning arrived all too slowly with a beautiful sound of an engine – it was after 8 a.m. I anxiously peered at the pea soup fog waiting for help to appear . . . you little beauty!

It was a farmer and his wife in an old Bedford utility truck. They could have been Dave and Mabel. They stopped as soon as they realised I belonged to the badly parked car and were eager to help. Thank goodness they didn't recognise me!

The rural couple were just fantastic – they hooked up my front bumper bar to their tow-bar, with a rusty old chain. Quick as a flash, my car was back on the muddy road . . . and even though it was extensively damaged on the passenger side, it was still drive able.

The damaged front wheel was a bit wobbly but provided I kept the speed below 30 kmh there was a good chance I would be able to limp home. And that's exactly what I did, ever so slowly.

By the time I reached the Maroondah Highway in Lilydale, the peak hour traffic was still pretty heavy. Cars were banked up behind for kilometres. Horns were honking and talk about glares. I wished, for the time being that I was a jockey, barely able to see out of the windows.

And talking about jockeys, one of my friends was a jockey. A little fella named Peter Bakos. He's only about four foot nothing and if he picks me up to drive to a speaking engagement, he just walks across the bench seat and opens the passenger door for me! The brake and accelerator pedals are specially built up with blocks of wood so he can reach them!

Then when it's my turn to provide the transport I always leave the kids' bucket seat in the back so he can see out of the windows . . . he loves me doing the driving.

Anyway enough about jockeys. I did manage to guide my car home only to be greeted with a barrage of expected questions. You can probably guess the first one! "And where have you been all night?" asked my wife with a not too friendly tone in her voice.

It took a lot of explaining.

So these days I'm much more careful about driving long distances. And fatigue – it's easy to see why it's a killer.

If you're tired don't drive!

Perils of Parking

"PETER BROCK WOULD HAVE BEEN PROUD OF THE CONTROL"

Inner city meter parking in major cities is very much at a premium these days – it's one thing to spot a gap in the kerbside row of cars, but the real problem is winning the race to fill that precious hole with the car you're driving!

Ordinary road users become four-wheeled animals stalking a meter, who'll stop at nothing, and I mean nothing, to get in first. No beg pardons. In fact, the verbal exchanges that result after a "dead heat" can be quite volatile.

Only a couple of months back, I managed to reverse my Ford, á la driving licence test, into an acceptable resting spot in Parliament Place, Melbourne, a short stroll to the heart of the city.

As I listened to the sound of a hungry grey post gobble up four twenty cent pieces and reply with a two hour long, graduated smile, I witnessed a real humdinger of a parking dispute.

Several meters to the rear of my car a spot became vacant. Immediately the previous occupant had driven out, a cruising Jaguar drew alongside the precious rectangle of bitumen and nosed its way a car length forward, with a view to backing in.

At this stage everything was normal – the Jag was ninety percent home – he was definitely first on the scene. That was until a small, not so well loved Mini Minor came down the hill from the opposite direction, spotted the same park and felt lucky.

Talk about cheek – the red Mini, completed a U-turn at a cracking pace. Peter Brock would have been proud of the control.

There, in the rear view mirror it was clear to see . . . the car park went begging. All the power of the polished Jag couldn't have secured the meter.

Out of the mobile shoebox stepped a long legged girl in denim jeans and a T-shirt. A confident young lady to say the least. Well, maybe not a lady . . . but she knew both the potential and limitations of her machine.

She too punctured the flat grey dial of the waiting parking meter with several coins.

As she prepared to smugly walk away from the scene of the crime the unlucky party rolled his classic car to a stop just ahead of the plain old Mini. The Jaguar's tail lights lit up to about the colour of the furious owner's cheeks.

I felt for the occupant as he rolled down the passenger side window, with the push of a button on the console of his air-conditioned chariot.

His first few words were fiery . . . that was clear by the distorted face and shaking fist. I thought this guy's reached boiling point . . . out of control . . . he's gonna dong her on the head with his fist. So I casually walked towards the confrontation.

Sensing an upper hand, the female's reply would have shut most blokes right out of the argument – a beauty! "You've got to be young and smart to be able to do that Grandad!" And with that, flung the pigtail over her shoulder and started to walk away.

The scenario was far from complete. The Jaguar commenced what looked like a three-point turn, backed into a laneway directly opposite the pinched parking meter, and changed gear.

In true *Mad Max* fashion, the V12 engine roared as the accelerator pedal hit the metal. Rubber burned and gravel flew from beneath the spinning tyres. I could have been at Calder Raceway for a dragsters' meet – even a parachute wasn't going to stop the cheated motorist now!

The sound of the expensive Jaguar headlights and grille kissing the Mini's doors caused the girl to spin about face very sharply. She stared . . . frozen in a vacant expression. A state of shock instantly

smothered her cocky attitude. What do I do now . . . why did he do such a terrible thing? I could see the wheels rotating around inside her enquiring head.

If she didn't know the reason why, she was about the find out!

Her angry victim didn't even bother to get out of the car to inspect the crumpled mass of metal and the damaged head lamps. He coolly completed the three-point turn as if going for a driver's licence – bad luck about the other car though!

The driver's window whirred down and his parting, telling shot, went like this: " . . . and you have to be old and rich to be able to do that!"

I continued my casual stroll into town, an innocent spectator. Nevertheless, I couldn't help but wonder whether or not the young girl had an insurance policy. Who would be at fault? He or she!

Was the smart "U-ee", and the sixty cent drop worth the potential thousands of dollars in repairs – not to mention the immobility that any prang involves.

All for the sake of a few extra minutes of surveillance. There never appears enough time for anything these days – only stupidity in the race to plug a meter.

Turning Red at the Sight of Pink

"I ENDED UP DRAFTING WITH AN ALARM CLOCK ON MY DESK"

I don't believe in ghosts, but I'm worried about the effects the "grey ghosts", as we call the parking attendants in Melbourne, are having on fellow motorists. Leave your car unattended for a fleeting moment and they'll slap a pink sticker on your windscreen.

Try and look one in the eye while they're frantically scribbling out the details on their ever-ready pad and you'll be disappointed.

The way in which they go about their job is unbelievable!

On a Test match or football weekend at the MCG when thousands of mums, dads and kids are out enjoying the sporting occasion – the grey ghosts see it as an excuse to work overtime. Honestly, many of these characters give more signatures away than Dean Jones would autographs!

The big difference being Deano gives his neat 'n' tidy signature away free of charge – all you have to do is ask! Our silently lurking friends never wait to be asked and the average cost is about thirty or forty dollars.

Imagine if all their "collections" went to charity? By the way, where does all that loot end up? Certainly not to fit 'em out with new, brighter and easier to spot uniforms. As a group of people, I've never met a more solemn lot.

They gave a serve to a friend of mine who unfortunately happened to have put in a particularly "large" weekend. Yes, my mate had been to a Saturday/Sunday party and after drinking absolute truckloads, he flaked in the back seat of his car. That was late on Sunday night.

By the time he woke up at lunchtime on Tuesday (allowing for a little exaggeration) he couldn't see out of the front window for parking fines.

You'd reckon the attendant might have shown some common-sense after the third ticket and asked a straight-forward question like, "Are you all right mate?" or "How long do you intend staying here? Your meter's expired."

Obviously he needed to accomplish his quota for the day.

Many years ago in Tasmania, my dad had a hot-headed foreman working for him. The project was to replace a jeweller's shop window and fittings which had been broken into by vandals and looted.

The job looked like taking about six or seven hours and it was necessary to park right outside the jewellery shop to save lugging heavy equipment in and out of the shop.

The foreman's name was Brian, and he didn't stop moaning about the amount of damage the vandals had caused to the shop front. The same man was a brilliant craftsman and eventually settled down to the nitty gritty of refurbishing the broken shelves, the shattered windowpanes and the display cases inside the shop. Before he knew it, lunchtime was only minutes away.

Much to Brian's disgust, the sign MEN AT WORK had failed to have much impact. Two parking notices were stuck to the cracked window of his ex-army jeep. Two similar items decorated my old man's windscreen.

The ambitious young parking attendant didn't realise at the time, but by booking these "men at work" he was really playing a dangerous game.

Brian waited and waited for the "smart alec" who booked him to reappear. No such luck! The blood pressure was rising by the minute . . . veins stood out around his temples as the rage inside increased! Finally he cracked!

Without a second thought, he grabbed the hacksaw from the back of his rusty old jeep. Just as a man about to fell a tree would, he sized up exactly where to make the cut.

Booking these men was really playing a dangerous game.

In Brian's case, the line of saw-cut needed to be about six inches (15 cms) below the bright red "expired" sign which now covered the well fed meter's face.

The exercise took him less than five minutes to completely behead the two offending parking meters with his trusty hacksaw blade.

Only a stone's throw away in the middle of busy Elizabeth Street, the Tramways Department were carrying out repairs to their ageing tracks. Deep gashes in the bitumen road's surface exposed the orange clay below. It didn't take long for the two dead meter heads to end up on a big pile of dirt in front of a slowly moving bulldozer. The driver was oblivious to their presence but a curious crowd had grown to watch the blade of the powerful bulldozer bury its two victims.

I'd have loved to check out the expression on the young parking attendant when he did finally arrive on the scene.

Still I guess they're expected to cope with a whole variety of reactions – mostly aggressive.

Apart from football umpires, these parking meter watchdogs must be about the most verbally doused people in town.

When I worked in the city as an architect, I too used to run the daily gauntlet of playing the meters. It meant checking all four tyres every couple of hours for tell-tale yellow chalk marks, identifying exactly how long the car had been parked in the spot.

With experience it was possible to roll the car back or forward to cover the line or remove the marks. Even sandpaper was used.

Needless to say a difficult problem on the drawing board generally cost the price of a parking ticket. I ended up drafting with an alarm clock on my desk.

I'm a great believer in natural justice. Sure enough, one day I saw a parking attendant reach his day of reckoning.

Right before my eyes from the second storey window of an adjacent terrace house, I witnessed the entire contents of a bed pan being emptied over an unsuspecting parking man. One, two, even three tickets the old lady could handle, but not four! That was the one that lit the fuse, and SPLASH! Not a happy ending to that story.

I've noticed motorists prowling around looking for the impossible park, change their tac if a parking attendant was present. They'd wait for the officer of the local council to bend over in order to mark the tyre . . . the driver would speed up level with the car in question, then hoot loudly. That was generally reckoned to be enough to take a few years off the parking attendant's life.

Mates of mine, and I'm not proud of them, have even left a handful of tacks under the back wheel of an unattended motorcycle belonging to a lurking attendant.

I know they're only doing their job but gee, they can be irritating to say the least.

Only a few weeks ago I left my car in a loading zone – I'm on a non-commercial registration – to drop off two pairs of trousers and pick up two jackets at the dry cleaners.

There is no way known I was gone more than four minutes, yet there it was pasted at forty-five degrees on the passenger side window and not a grey ghost in sight – disappeared into thin air.

I don't have to tell you how I felt. My haste sure put up the price of dry cleaning.

It takes all sorts, but it must take an enormous amount of soul searching to finally decide on a career as a parking officer. Whatever the attraction, it can't be for the money. There must be some emotional feedback.

Well, that's done my dash. From now on, I've got no hope in the parking stakes. They'll probably put a tail on me just to get even! I reckon the grey ghosts are well in front already.

CHAPTER SEVEN

Mad Max Caresses a Curb

Victory for the Spirit

"THE ANGEL OF DEATH HAD A TOUGH COMPETITOR ON HIS HANDS HERE . . ."

You don't have to possess a photographic memory to recall that some of the Formula One Grands Prix of recent years have provided numerous unforgettable images of bent machines spinning out of control to an expensive and painful ending. In fact over the years many a Grand Prix driver has sadly been killed – the last being the popular Italian Elio de Angelis.

Then there was the close call early in the 1989 season for Austrian ace Gerhard Berger during the Italian Grand Prix. His red Ferrari malfunctioned, turning his car into a speeding fireball of flame and smoke that looked like it would disintegrate when it pounded into a wall. Fortunately Berger wasn't incinerated. The incident was graphic "live" coverage and one couldn't help but feel a gut-wrenching sickness in the pit of the stomach as the seconds ticked by . . . these were the difference between life and death.

The loud, excitable English commentator, Murray Walker, needed all his forty years of experience at race calling to describe what was happening . . . he did it spontaneously, honestly and sensitively.

Berger owes his life and ability to race again to the medical team that worked as quickly as a pit crew to drag him free of the burning wreck and off to hospital. Like any dedicated sportsman, he couldn't wait to drive back into the fray. Only weeks later Berger was back behind the steering wheel as competitive as ever . . . the only hint of his "charcoal grill" was the few bandages covering burns to his hands.

It was a perfect example of how much technology, in terms of better crash safety, has been developed into F1 cars in recent years. It also shows you how tough and courageous Grand Prix racers are. They understand very clearly that their life is on the line every time they hit the starter button and let loose those 700 horses. Incredibly they don't even have a roof or mudguards to protect them!

These days I don't mind admitting I'm a right regular "petrol head" . . . you name it, if the engine growls and the tyres scream, then I'm into it. I'm not an expert but then how could I hope to be? Unless I get to strap myself behind the microphone when namesake, Murray Walker, gets too worn out to "change the gears". It would definitely be a challenge.

There is much more to Formula One racing than merely what is seen during the race telecasts. The actual race is the end of a cycle of teamwork that begins the moment the previous race finishes . . . it's a bit like TV or any profession – there is no substitute for research, homework and a perfectionist attitude.

One of the many books I have read in recent times was *To Hell and Back* by Grand Prix legend Niki Lauda. The Austrian was champion of the world in 1975 . . . and well on the way to winning back to back titles in '76 against the likes of James Hunt, when in one split second at the Nurburgring in Germany on August 1, it all went awfully wrong.

The familiar red Ferrari jerked right, crashed through the safety catchfencing, slammed into the embankment and then bounced back onto the track. The whole incident must have taken place at about 200 kmh. As the car rebounded back onto the bitumen, the fuel cell broke away and sprayed its potentially deadly contents everywhere as it flew through the air.

What was left of Niki's car was straddling the ideal line when the Surtees of the unsuspecting Brett Lunger came screaming into view . . . and smashed into the Ferrari with such force that it pushed it some 100 metres down the track. Niki's car burst into flames when the leaking petrol was ignited by that dreaded spark – the car was totally engulfed as it finally crunched into the hoarding.

Before the medical team could get to him, he had actually inhaled some of the super hot air and that had seared the inside of his lungs. Because of this injury it was thought that he wasn't getting enough oxygen into his bloodstream to sustain life, even in hospital. Wife Marlene was told that twenty-four hours was about the best she could expect Niki to last.

As the result of that accident, drivers today have a compulsory emergency oxygen supply fitted to their helmets to help them breathe cool air during those few vital minutes – if they are trapped or unconscious – until one of the rescue and medical teams dotted around the circuit can get to them. That safety measure helped save Niki's successor at Ferrari, Gerhard Berger, when he crashed in 1989.

Lauda was very vocal in improving safety in the years after 1976. Today, each Formula One GP has its own doctor, and each track is equipped with a mini-hospital where some urgent life-saving surgical procedures can be undertaken in case there is no time to helicopter an injured driver to the nearest hospital.

During Lauda's accident his head took a terrible mauling in the fire . . . it was swollen out of all proportion. He was taken to hospital with horrific facial burns – his scalp and ears were almost singed away by the enormous heat plus he had shocking burns to his hands.

Twenty-four hours later, in a state of semi-consciousness and enveloped in pain, Niki could see a dark shadow leaning over him – it wasn't the Grim Reaper but a priest who said, "Goodbye my friend." Niki's sub-conscious reaction was, "Hang on! Here's a bloke telling me I was going to die. I want somebody who is going to tell me how to live!" The spirit took control, the heart started to pound and then the adrenalin began to flow.

The Angel of Death had a tough competitor on his hands here . . . in this different sort of contest. Niki was known for his analytical mind and his ability to diagnose motor cars like a neuro-surgeon. Anything to make them travel that hundredth of a second faster. He made a personal commitment lying on that hospital bed – he would race F1 cars again and soon.

No-one really believed it was possible, including many of the Ferrari team. Niki was lucky he couldn't read what was being said about his accident . . . some of the newspaper treatments of the Nurburgring "shunt" were definitely not supportive.

The German newspaper *Bild* shouted in headline, "MY GOD, WHERE IS HIS FACE?" The article began, "Niki Lauda, the world's fastest racing driver, no longer has a face. It is no more than raw flesh with eyes oozing out of it!"

Yet thirty-three days later he was back at work determined as ever not just to be a participant but to be the world's best. He made his incredible comeback . . . it was on my birthday – September 12 – at Monza in the Italian Grand Prix. History tells us that Niki Lauda, clad in a woollen hood like a sock, covering those telltale scars, finished an amazing fourth.

If it's not blatantly obvious . . . then I should explain that I admire so many of the qualities that made Niki Lauda great – a pre-occupation with perfection, mental toughness and an ability to simplify even the most complex issues.

I guess the moral to this story for me was that Niki Lauda had the chance to use the best plastic surgeons in the world to "pretty up" the face again, but his belief was that if you make a mistake in life then you pick up the receipt. You should carry it all the time and don't put it in your back pocket and then forget about it! He chose to wear his "mistake" right up front. Nothing had really changed, only the look of his face. The people around Niki just had to accept him the way he was . . . if they didn't then they probably weren't worth worrying about anyway.

As you can see, I got hooked on this incredible man, his achievements and the sport he loved so much. Ever since then I have followed Formula One. So in 1985 when the inaugural Australian F1

Grand Prix was held at Adelaide and Niki Lauda was making his last race appearance before retiring, I was disappointed to find that there wasn't enough room in the Falcon ute for yours truly. So sadly I had to stay back in Sydney, holding the fort. But chances do come to those who persist . . .

How to Caress a Kerb

"WE MUST HAVE BEEN DOING 180 kmh AND WITH NO ROOM FOR ERROR! I WAS IMPRESSED ALL THE WAY DOWN TO MY JOCKETTES"

DAY 1.   ADELAIDE INTERNATIONAL RACEWAY (AIR):   I arrived high on confidence but low on practice. This was a proper race track forty-five minutes out of town with concrete walls, pits, straights, esses, petrol fumes, incessant noise, high revving, squealing tyres and most importantly of all, with speeding motor cars all going around in the same direction.

This was the countdown to the blast off on Sunday, November 5 1989 . . . the date seemed to have been indelibly etched into my subconscious ever since I accepted the invitation to pilot one of the smart red Nissan EXA's in the Celebrity burn off over five laps at the Adelaide Grand Prix circuit.

My initial contact was a tiny, bald-headed old guy dressed in a spotless white, official-type, three-quarter coat who immediately directed me towards the operations tent (no dressing sheds here) . . . where the full implications of what I was getting into started to sink in. From a distance my racing gear and tailormade overalls looked about as close as I was ever going to get to being an astronaut – all zipped up, covered and protected. Pretty impressive list of safety equipment too – for a car that was hardly faster than my usual daily transport.

The $1500 suits, I was told, were a triple layer, fireproof material that would allow the driver a few minutes protection against direct flame. There was also a fire extinguisher in the vehicle and we were instructed to wear protective gloves and woollen socks – no synthetics.

Yes, this was no lightweight sporty wear. The weight of the suit with my name pinned on it put a hefty strain on the wire coathanger . . . badly drooping shoulders. Once we stepped into our gear it was like five bandaged, invisible men standing there – no feet, no hands, no head – all you could see were five pairs of bulging eyes with possibly a glimpse of fear in some of them . . . in others it was pure excitement in the anticipation of the adventure ahead.

I considered how much Niki Lauda received for advertising signs on his outfit – $150,000 for a tag on the chest, a few million for the helmet. I gave myself a look over – all these patches and logos promoting the sponsors of the celebrity race and I was getting paid nothing! A walking billboard in order to get a free ride . . . and I had to drive myself! And the ride could be very costly if I happened to have a patch of bad luck! Be positive, I thought, there's no way you're gonna crash . . . but what about the rest?

Definitely an unknown quantity.

The helmet was very similar to one Tony Greig wore in the first years of World Series Cricket – a full gloss white crash helmet with the wire cage enclosing the front. I remember one smart comment from Australian wicketkeeper at the time, Rod Marsh, after fast bowler Dennis Lillee hit Greigy flush on the helmet and the ball ricocheted down to fine leg for four byes. The noise was deafening inside Greigy's skull and it sure shook him up. Rod cheekily yelled at him from behind the stumps with a touch of sarcasm: "You don't know where there's a good panel beater do you mate?" I can't repeat the reply!

So with my racing helmet tightly in place and wearing all the necessary safety gear, I was finally ready. I wasn't even scared . . . that is until I parked my bum inside one of the cars. Having driven around the streets of Melbourne for the better part of a decade with two pedals on the floor, driving an automatic, it was a whole different experience inside a little manual Nissan EXA. The 1.8 litre twin cam, free revving, extractor-fitted machines were worth $28,000 and had been equipped with roll cages and safety harnesses fit for racing.

Just to get the feel of the place, we were taken around a couple of times by Jim Murcott and then by Nissan's racing ace, Mark Skaife, and others. I was feeling fine after being shown several tricks of the trade by Jim. Well, that all changed dramatically when I got into the car beside Skaifey!

Talk about a tearaway! Mark was used to driving around tracks at speeds up to 300 kmh in his turbo-charged Nissan Skyline and nothing less – I was more used to Melbourne traffic jams! I almost ripped every spring out of the seat as I swayed around with the G-forces – hanging on for dear life. I tried to play "Joe cool" but it was obvious I was swallowing at a million miles an hour. There was no saliva left and my Adam's apple was bobbing up and down like a yo-yo!

As we careered around the banked oval section onto the main straight, Mark kept saying, "You don't brake, just keep on the accel-erator and let the car slide out to the wall . . . let the car do the work."

Unbelievable! I'm on the side closest to the two metre wall . . . I could see through popping eyes that there was barely a coat of paint between my left elbow and the solid concrete wall. We must have been doing 180 kmh and with no room for error! I was impressed all the way down to my jockettes.

I wanted to say something but I couldn't speak. Our vehicle was the only one on the track – there was nobody racing us! I wondered how bad this must get with cars screeching all around!

We hit absolutely top pace at the bottom of the straight – nothing left in the speeding red bullet. "This," he said, "is where you give it the 'piano player special' . . . use the old heel and toe of the right foot to change down the gears." You have your foot on the brake and at the same time roll the outside edge of your shoe onto the accelerator. Jim Murcott did it like a concert pianist. Mark slipped through the procedure even faster – like a rock 'n' roller at about 30 kmh greater speed than Jim. I don't mind admitting the younger instructor had succeeded in frightening the stuffing out of me in one lap.

The worst part of this whole exercise was that I had no control . . . Mark had the wheel in his hands. Helpless!

At no time did the back wheels follow the front wheels. The com-pact EXA fishtailed everywhere, lap after lap. At one stage Mark nearly lost control in the esses. He warned me that it was a bit slip-pery there – pebbles and dirt were scattered across the edge of the track. He was showing me how to drive the race line correctly – straightening the track out where it twists a little – using all the road. He didn't actually lose it. Nevertheless it had given me a huge adrenalin rush.

During our time together the potential touring car champion didn't bat an eyelid – after all he does this for a living. Like an answering machine, he kept saying . . . "You have got to kiss the kerb out here" – repeatedly during our five laps. Gee, I was glad to climb out of the car. This was only the first day of instruction!

Now it was my turn at the wheel. The moment I had been waiting for! How was baby gorilla, nearly two metres tall, supposed to manoeuvre into the driving seat clad in all this gear. What made the exercise even more difficult was the position of the rollover cage. It took up a lot of additional headroom in an already small car. My head wouldn't go in simultaneously . . . so I tried to hold on to the roof for support and slide my legs and feet in, but then my head wouldn't fit under the doorsill. So it was a matter of poking my bum in first and trying to fold the rest in as best I could. Just as well the sunroof was off too . . . because my helmet was protruding well through the top. One thought that exercised my mind was: if I did happen to roll it, then my head would be in a lot of trouble, wouldn't it? The only answer I could come up with was . . . YES!

Next problem – I couldn't see out of the rear view mirror because the troublesome rollover bar, welded inside the cabin for stability, was right in my line of vision! All that was visible was a thick metal tube. The back of my helmet was pressing firmly against the roll bar . . . Consequently every pebble I drove over registered in vibration through the roof of my brains . . . echoing inside my helmet like a giant attempting to crack the shell on his boiled egg with a spoon. Talk about sound sensitive, it was incredible – acoustically perfect.

The only gear we weren't provided with as part of our driving kit was footwear. Sturdy sandshoes would be fine. So I arrived wearing a brand new pair of the finest adidas Torsion runners money can buy. Bright, iridescent blue and yellow trim – the flashest pair of runners in town. They must have stood out like a ground level, walking neon light. Jim, Mark and the other experts trackside were wearing a kind of slipper – the sole was thin like a piece of tissue paper. Flexible and sensitive were the criteria . . . I guess you learn from experience.

The first time I went for the brake at the end of the main straight, the pimples initially all stuck . . . then jerked clear of the brake pedal and onto the accelerator. Naturally, I endeavoured to come off the accelerator again but my thick, wide rubber sole jammed tight between the two pedals. As a result my car scooted straight off the end of the circuit and sent a row of witches hats spraying in every direction. Embarrassing! Better doing it at AIR than the GP circuit!

DAY TWO: Next morning my top priority, after a refreshing wake-up rinse in the shower, was to hunt out a pair of old faithful sand-shoes – much water stained and particularly smelly after years of pounding the pavements of Melbourne, over many a long agonising kilometre, up hills, into stiff chilly, breezes and driving rain.

Appearance at practice in my 'new wheels' was greeted with a well run rumour that several competitors were giving the fair dinkum students of pedal and pace at least one day's start. Another story "doing plenty of laps" was – John Farnham and manager Glenn Wheatley in a clandestine move had hired two EXAs plus the services of Peter Brock! Peter's brief was to sharpen up their already capable technique for a team assault on the race. "Whispering Jack" was blistering the bitumen in the trials and looking more and more like a Brockie clone every day. Their objective was a form finishing one-two – not that they would ever admit it! But for a mere mortal like myself it seemed unfair! Still we're OK Jack . . . after all, what is fair in sport anymore? Only winning?

John had just returned to the pits looking supremely confident as he jumped out of the car. The brakes were still smouldering as he undid the helmet strap . . . it dangled freely across the advertising patch on his left shoulder. With practice punctuated for the moment, he lit up a celebratory cigar – it quickly glowed bright red as the petrol fumes in the "Voice's" lungs were replaced by pungent cigar smoke . . . one could excuse him for feeling more than just a bit good in this environment.

I shouldn't have been too surprised by this as earlier in the year both the Farnhams and Wheatleys "bribed" their way from Burke to Broome as part of the annual Variety Club fund raising bash . . . a marvellous experience no doubt. But I should mention that their wives showed a clean rear bumper to the vocal duo!

The subtle art of gamesmanship was coming into play within the friendly banter . . . who had done what and how fast. Others like myself merely shut up! After all, I hadn't achieved anything at all in motor sport since qualifying for my driving licence in unspectacular fashion on my seventeenth birthday . . . Yes, the traffic was intense at 4.30 p.m. in Hobart's peak hour "crush". Regularly, three and four cars had to wait for a red light or a roundabout!

Like the rest of the bunch, I was desperately keen to see how fast I was travelling. But the organisers were too shrewd, they kept us in the dark by placing black sticky tape over the speedo screen. Jim's instructions were to drive by the rev counter. "Don't push beyond 6,000 rpm," he repeated every day. Hit 6,000 vibrating, noisy revs and it was time to change gear. "That's how the aces drive," he would say. "Speedos are for wimps!" Nevertheless I had a sneaking suspicion the advice offered was only to make sure the demo cars would finish their torture test in a re-saleable condition.

Anne-Maree then screeched to a halt, barely a car length from my toes . . . out she jumped as if on cue, sporting the most enormous grin – happiness personified! I could feel the pressure gauge inside my head rising like a thermometer . . . how was I going to cope? Somehow I needed to put a few points on the board to back up my presumptuous, competitive smirk.

She then proceeded to crank me up and bruise my faltering ego by mentioning she had been at it for a week, buzzing around the track. "Getting better and better . . . look out, Maxie, here I come!" she threatened.

How did I feel . . . like a Tooheys 2.2.! At this stage I hadn't turned the key in the car . . . so I demanded that Jim spend a few laps on the track beside me. Under my instructor's supervision and without a tractor tread of pimples on my feet to tangle me up, I should do OK . . . but I still hadn't quite adapted to car racing yet. I was no duck to water, in fact I was still far from enjoying the paddling!

Lisa Curry-Kenny completed the first session with eyes wide open – she had "hit the wall" first time out . . . a tumble turn was the last thing she needed to perfect on the Adelaide circuit! We both agreed we were being thrown in at the deep end and were floundering in the early part of the build up.

John Alexander, master of the Brylcreem hairdo, or maybe he had updated to gel since his tennis days, was trying to drive like he served in his heyday. But JA wasn't fooling any one, especially his opponents. Everyone agreed he was footfaulting – his tail-lights illuminated 50 metres earlier than most before the difficult hairpin bend at the end of the straight.

Bill Rule from ABC Radio, Melbourne, connected with the concrete wall during an early reconnaissance lap. Gee these little red cars crumple easily, I thought to myself with alarm! The driver's face flushed a deep shade of red . . . as the blood rushed from his overworked right foot . . . to his embarrassed, vacant head! The result – Billy was out of the race and so was car number 20! Well, no-one was game enough to lend the lovable radio man and avid Geelong Football Club supporter their car – he was bound to bounce a new machine around as well.

I noticed also the desperate, evil-eyed Darren Cahill was causing a buzz in the pits by lapping even quicker than the Farnham-Wheatley combination. He was pleased to be back home in Adelaide after many months overseas. His father Jack had just coached the Port Adelaide football club, the Magpies, to the South Australian National Football League premiership . . . so it was clear as black and white that "Killer" Cahill was keen to win and would let nothing get in his way.

Anyway, by the end of the day I had learned one thing – how to approach a right hand corner, of which most were.

Firstly, as the bend is looming up ahead, you peer over the steering wheel and swear under your breath. Brake, brake hard and finally hit the brake pedal even harder. Change down into whatever gear is nearest with much revving and heeling and toeing across the accelerator and brake. Realise the corner is much tighter than first expected and that you may not make it . . . swear to yourself or blame the car – whatever feels more comfortable. If you have a passenger on board, make sure with a lightening quick glance that you are not endangering their life through a heart attack.

Then get back onto the accelerator hard and steer your way out of trouble with armloads full of opposite lock. Try not to let go of the steering wheel . . . especially if you decide to cover your eyes, then the inevitable WILL happen!! Stick with it and you should make the corner . . . not necessarily on the road, but I promise you will make it!

By Friday afternoon Jim had done the best job possible with a rough but enthusiastic group. He even taught us the relationship between the different coloured flags.

For example a white flag doesn't mean everyone has spat the dummy and surrendered, or that John Platten's mum is on the track looking for her boy to come home for dinner. No, it means that there is a non-competing vehicle on the circuit – it could be a tow truck, ambulance or doctor – or even a slow moving competitor with a mechanical problem.

If the black flag is out, then there is trouble, particularly if the number of a second flag corresponds to the number of the car you are driving – a case of look out buddy and return to the pits immediately for a big smack.

As you would reckon, a red flag means stop racing and slow down drastically and return to the pits because there is a serious problem somewhere on the circuit.

My favourite is the chequered flag . . . the race is not over until the flagman on the finish line runs out and with a flurry waves it furiously at your headlamps like a toreador in a bull fight.

Tuition complete. From here on it was up to the desire of the individual. By Saturday, grid positions were fixed . . . M.H.N. Walker at number 14.

Deservedly Darren Cahill had pole position and half a length back on his right was the diminutive Johnny Platten. John Farnham was on the second row . . . so too was his manager.

Bringing up the rear was the rich and sophisticated Pom, Terence Holmes . . . all the breeding and pound notes were a long way away – just like the finish line!

Saturday was our day of familiarisation around the proper Grand Prix circuit. Full dress rehearsal . . . but first a chauffeured lap of honour with the roof open, a red procession, waving to the crowd, noticing precisely where the TV cameras were set up, and watching comedian Shane Bourne in the car ahead making rude noises and gestures to the masses. This was a gala occasion, but by this stage we had high octane racing fuel in our bloodstream and it was pumping furiously to every extremity of our bodies.

Cut this slow motion crap, I thought impatiently, let's come alive! After all the Confederation of Australian Motorsport racing licences weren't presented to us so that we could be chauffeur driven slowly around a few chosen streets. This piece of paper gave us all access to any race track in the world for twelve months – let's use it!

Eventually we drove four laps of the famous bitumen but at nowhere near full throttle, just to get the feel of the track. It was much more smooth than the abrasive, heavy aggregate and tar at AIR. We couldn't experiment because Jim Murcott took his life in his hands by driving around in front of the pack in a plain white vehicle to show us the right race lines and to think about braking and the correct gear changes. There was no overtaking – Nissan didn't want another used vehicle on the scrap heap.

As we cruised around I thought that this was a pleasant Saturday 'arvo compared with what was coming up tomorrow . . .

No day for Heroes

"THE POTENTIAL WAS FOR PLENTY TO HAPPEN AND ALL OF IT BAD!"

On race morning my eyelids felt like they were stuck to the bottom lashes with adhesive tape. No amount of muscle control was going to pry them apart! Both shoulder blades were nailed to the mattress and my head weighed a ton. This was probably because of the G-forces experienced in my dream at the wheel, negotiating the traffic, moving skilfully up through the field to victory – immaculate, dynamic driving! Like any dreams involving racing, it can only be your own fault if you lose and this rather large dreamer didn't!

Back to reality – I just missed out on getting to the victory dais to spray the champagne – with a tentative peep out of the window . . . rain, rain and more RAIN! What had I done to deserve this – I hadn't killed a spider, other than a daddy long legs, for months.

The storm water drain was choking with the run-off from the cluttered carpark below our bedroom window . . . this was not how I'd dreamt the race would be run – in rain. I've always been a dry weather sailor . . . even playing cricket I liked it fine.

El supremo, devil's advocate and soothsayer, Jim Murcott, had overlooked the possibility of divine intervention. The heavens had certainly opened up with all their fury. Everything our teacher had taught us was out the window, sailing down the overflowing gutter. Jim hadn't given us any technique tips about boat racing – in fact we hadn't witnessed so much as a trickle from a garden hose at practice at AIR all week. History tells us that it had never rained at any of the previous Adelaide Grands Prix, but in 1989 the weather was sure settling the ledger.

At the Grand Prix circuit water was lying in pools everywhere. Even the multi-talented superstars of Formula One weren't keen on putting their very expensive machines – and let's not forget their lives on the line. Conditions were totally disgusting in their view and I agreed!

I sensed it was going to be a tough day from the moment I pulled on my wool-lined jockstrap . . . it didn't feel at all comfortable and began to tickle. I momentarily thought of reaching for my plastic mouthguard . . . still in my kit bag from football days, but it smelled badly of liniment, goanna oil and stale perspiration even after two decades of disuse!

One fact could be stated of my racing uniform – I was definitely going to be warm . . . the zip from my fly travelled all the way up to my Adam's apple, sealing me in for the duration. A nervous "you and me" had to be undertaken now – not during the race.

Inside my blue-quilted, flame-proof jump suit, a sound technician fitted a device that looked and felt a lot like a pace maker . . . it sat snugly in the patch pocket of my cotton T-shirt. About the size of a small hip flask, covered in black leather, it housed the batteries which powered my radio microphone – specially designed to work inside my crash helmet.

Rammed deep into the bowels of my ear was an IFB (Internal Feed Back) . . . this little device was similar to a moulded perspex hearing aid and I had to assure quizzical onlookers that I wasn't turning senile or about to kick the bucket. Then again a quick look at the sheets of water still streaming off the glossy race track, and I wasn't so sure. This scenario activated sobering thoughts of the potential dangers that lay ahead.

The IFB enabled my regular Saturday afternoon co-host of "Wide World of Sports", Ken Sutcliffe, and the director, Geoff Morris, to keep in touch throughout the race . . . a distraction as it turned out that I didn't really need.

This was not the first time I had been wired for sound while actually participating in a sporting event. Two years earlier the replay of the Centenary Test match between England and Australia at the WACA ground in Perth was a prime example. The only sound that could be heard from my microphone during a bowling stint was a fearful imitation of what a heavy breather might sound like . . . it was hard work trying to bowl as fast as yesterday . . . but with today's mature body. Too much sitting and talking – not enough aerobic exercise! Well nothing much had changed in Adelaide other than swapping the cricket flannels for a "space suit" and stack hat. My heart was still trying to leap out of the ribcage as more and more adrenalin was released to the body through pre-race nerves.

One of the reasons for the tension was . . . just before we got serious, I was told by the producer that our race would be beamed around the world to a TV audience of 700 million! Well, you have got no idea what a dramatic effect that small fact had on the metabolism of this racing driver. The anxiety level caused by apprehension and uncertainty, mixed with a huge dose of genuine fear, went straight to the top of my skull.

I had watched Peter Brock and Jim Richards in the touring car race one hour earlier in pouring rain. Their performances were nothing short of awesome – especially when Brockie completed a full 360 degree spinout without crashing into a concrete wall. Momentarily he was totally out of control – the camera operators all took a pace back when he lost it. Nevertheless it was a class act . . . and a top piece of driving.

We had just completed our warm up lap in convoy style . . . hardly an indicator of how the race would unfold. Thirty seconds remained before the green light . . . there was so much activity going on around me and inside my head.

Car number 13 on my left was full of pure muscle and occupied by Irene Nikole . . . she vowed to beat me like all of the four women occupying grid positions ahead of me.

Mounted on my dashboard in a central position was a moving camera the size of a lipstick . . . similar to the ones now used for "stump cam" – housed inside the stump behind the batsman.

I was extremely conscious of this thing continually looking up my nostrils. As well as that distracting cylinder between myself and a very wet windscreen, there was yet another camera fixed to the roll bar above the passenger seat. This one hung and moved like Mr Squiggle – the talking pencil-nosed star of children's TV. As if seeking for my direct line of sight, the miniature lens panned left and right to provide a full view of the car's interior. Honestly, it was like having two robots for passengers, each having a mind of its own!

God help me if I wanted to pick my nose . . . luckily my brilliant red, fire resistant driving gloves and the perspex visor of my helmet made such a feat impossible!

Up went the ten second board to the start – it was now or never. "Don't be a hero," I thought. The countdown was almost complete . . . 9, 8, 7, 6 . . . red light still on, waiting for the green. Jim Murcott's racing school took us to the start line, but what do I or any of us do now!

On the starting grid I was trying to maintain 4,000 rpm, so that I wouldn't stall the start, or roll forward and get penalised a minute like Gerhard Berger did in the 1990 Canadian Grand Prix. It took me back to my driving school days and the handbrake starts on a hill . . . "watch the nose of the Morris 1100 rise, now ever so slowly release the handbrake, ease off the clutch and gently press the accelerator – great!" coached my driving school instructor.

Here I was on the verge of an exciting career as a Formula One driver . . . but why was I so nervous! The large sphincter muscle I was sitting on was now working overtime.

At least I didn't have to put up with Louie in my ear. I had seen my little motor mechanic a couple of bends back during the practice lap with a champagne flute in one hand, a bottle of Moet in the other. He'd bolted for cover at the first sign of rain . . . and was now comfortably rubbing shoulders with all the other "bignoters" in one of the sponsors' tents. Left his mate for dead – again!

Windscreen wipers on, steam rising from a hot engine, rev level rising, red light about to switch any second . . . ready . . . GREEN LIGHT! GO MAXIE, GO!! This race was now on in earnest!

In front of my bumper bar and to my left was a frightening wall of water as front wheels spun and rubber searched for traction, spraying out jets of water from their Goodyear treads. Visibility could only be five metres . . . the noise was deafening, like the symphony of eighteen lawnmowers on a Sunday afternoon . . . all in the one backyard!

I was being filmed and exposed like never before . . . there would be no "take" two or three. This definitely was a one take race. No second chance if I stuffed it up . . . the whole world was going to quite rightly hang it on me then.

In the central commentary studio Ken had with him some astute motor sport commentators – Jim Richards, a professional driver who probably knows more about driving Nissans than anybody else, Bathurst king Peter Brock and two times world 500cc motorcycle champion, Barry Sheene. They had plenty to say on the subject of my talent at the wheel.

"Max, there is a bit of rain around," Ken Sutcliffe opened up with.

I flicked the windscreen wipers up a notch to appear cool and in control before a casual observation: "Normally we cricketers come off the ground when there is a bit of rain around . . . maybe a round of cards or two with Dougie Walters and the boys, which honestly seems the best place to be today!"

While I was talking the wheels were continually spinning and the spray was still going everywhere. There was only a blur of colour up front as the cars frantically headed for the first turn. I reinforced my decision once more, "Maxie, there is no way known you're gonna be a hero here today." In hindsight it was probably the most common-sense I'd shown in a long time!

Within seconds we were moving in excess of 100 kmh and I could still barely see anything but spray. Gosh, I thought, here I am with eighteen other not so experienced drivers. The potential was for plenty to happen and all of it BAD!!

"The last time I had driven in rain like this I was seated in the back of a London cab and I paid for that drive," I told Ken. "I think I might be paying for this ride for the rest of my life!"

At the beginning of this five lap journey I had the wipers on full tempo, briskly pushing the tiny, semi-transparent jewels to one side. Condensation had been steadily building up, rising at the same rate as the rev counter . . . I was very quickly entering the red area. The windows were fogging up with all the activity . . . and the body heat.

"Are you working up a bit of sweat, Maxie?" Bazza Sheene asked with a chuckle down the line.

Obviously the two wheel speed freak with a penchant for practical jokes was in the "know" . . . someone had jammed on my heater before I got into the car. No names . . . BUT . . . ! That's what mates are for, aren't they?

Yes, I was set up beautifully on this one. In fact I had no idea where the heater was on the dashboard . . . and at breakneck speeds in the wet it wasn't a good time to find it. Not a good time to be winding down windows either.

I knew Formula One drivers shed a couple of kilos during two hours in those thick protective suits whilst conducting a super-fast dance routine on the pedals and flashing through hundreds of gearshifts, but I had only been going for forty seconds. But by now the heater had done its worst and I couldn't see through the fogged up front windscreen: you'll keep Bazza, I thought, somewhere, somehow . . . I'll get you!

Then Brockie said, "Beginners always keep two hands on the wheel." But I was trying to fend off the little lipstick camera on the dashboard and the other thing that was still orbiting around my head with gusto. Anyway how many test matches did he play for Australia?

Luckily I fumbled my way beyond the gearstick to instruct the heating to take a rest and allow me to see where I was headed.

The cameras were on me and of course I wanted to look good, so I tried to glue my hands to the quarter to three position . . . adhering to Brockie's advice.

Ken reckoned that I had to become more aggressive. Actually I was very quietly pleased in nudging ahead of car number 13 . . . now for the rest!

It was all very well for my co-pilot on a Saturday afternoon to put tongue in cheek while firing out the instructions. My situation was akin to a "Sale of the Century" contestant seated in the front seat of his or her prize, a motor car travelling at 100 kmh . . . awaiting the last sixty seconds of questions. This definitely was a quiz . . . not a race!

It is difficult enough to walk and talk into a camera lens but try responding to smart alec questions while supposedly concentrating on race strategy and searching simultaneously for the correct gear shift.

The only thing in common that Ken and I had at this moment in time was the four wheels of his chair roughly compared with the four tyres underneath me . . . but he had a "WWOS" blazer and tie, I was very casual; while I had protection for my brains, he had the protection of a script.

Barry Sheene, no doubt with sleeves rolled up, suggested in a serious tone that I look for the brake lights of the car in front and then count to ten before braking. That sounded like good advice until I heard Bazza, Brockie and Jim laughing their heads off in the background.

I couldn't see out of the back window either. I had no idea where I was in the race or how long to go. "You have got Debbie Hutton right up your tail, Maxie," Ken told me.

"That's OK, she's been perving on me all week!" I declared."Plus I have got great tail-lights."

At this stage, Darren Cahill, John Farnham and Glenn Wheatley were in a line at the front, I was told. They were deadly serious! Darren bounced over the kerbs many a time to try and cut the corners. And the plan worked. He squeezed through and passed the other two with very little room for error.

Very competitive people in this race, and they like to be the best at whatever they do. So do I. But I wanted to be around next week to talk about it!

The faster cars at the front (some were definitely faster than others, I should add) had raced off out of sight . . . a clear road ahead . . . and I had streeted the ones behind me. It was just like a Sunday afternoon drive really. That was when Barry Sheene said: "Driving like a vicar on a Sunday afternoon! Aren't we, Maxie?"

Then I knew I must have drifted in the betting from a win to a place. Sarcastic bugger! Let me tell you that Bazza couldn't or shouldn't talk. He had pranged one of Brockie's $150,000 Ford Sierras in a test session only months before. Under my breath I thought . . . out of your depth on four wheels, eh Baz?

Almost one lap complete and in the absence of any competition my mind centred on Anne-Maree. She was wired for sound too and I was wondering what she was saying about me.

I need not have worried . . . I knew her only too well. She was bound to be more concerned whether her lipstick was on straight or if the rain had caused her mascara to weep down onto her cheekbones. Yes, she had plenty to occupy her thoughts as well as the race.

Seriously Anne-Maree's major problem was going to be when the "egg shell" came off the noggin . . . the golden locks would have been flattened down and the hairdresser's symmetry would be lost forever. Tragic really. I'd have bet money that the sun shield flap was down already so she was able to check out the face in the mirror during the race.

Then I heard the news. There was no way the golden girl would be goaded into a chat. Too shrewd . . . our AM had turned down the IFB ;so she couldn't hear the fold back sound and be distracted. She was going to ignore the world for the next ten minutes . . . head down, bum up, grit the teeth and chase the opposition like any self-respecting Collingwood half back flanker. This lady was desperate not just to beat Big Max . . . but to win.

Gee, it was hard not being able to wave to the crowd like yesterday . . . all the windows were fogged up and the roof closed firmly! Also I had both thumbs locked on the inside of the steering wheel, except for the occasional stab at the gearshift.

Nevertheless I was travelling slowly enough to recognise my mates operating the cameras despite their enveloping all-weather gear. It was wrong of me to acknowledge their waves . . . and it didn't help the pace of my race. They were having a tougher time than I because it was so miserably cold and wet. They'd been standing and attending their cameras like lonely sentinels throughout the heavy downpours since early morning!

Dave, Dusty, Warwick, Adam and Drew . . . they all looked like drowned rats but they were the best at their jobs in this country and proud to help make the Australian Grand Prix the finest TV coverage of Formula One in the world. I had my fingers crossed that they'd not only make me look good . . . but also fast!

Gee, it was wet. It brought back memories of driving home from a Sheffield Shield match along the F19 freeway one rainy Sunday night in Melbourne a few years ago. My car slipped after accelerating to overtake and I slid and touched a bloke on the rear end of his "souped up" machine – the sort you love to pass!

I did a Steve McQueen and "spun out". Unfortunately his beloved car was a total right off – the foxtail and the mag wheels were still intact but the engine was on his front seat and glass was everywhere!

I had stalled at right angles to the on-coming traffic . . . a terrifying sight and very little time for reaction. My metallic blue Holden had come to a halt after six spectacular loops . . . 360 degrees . . . around and around I went, out of control, across the wet and slippery medium strip. I attempted everything to get control – braked hard, soft . . . no brakes, accelerated, understeered, oversteered . . . the lot. Absolutely no meaningful response on the steering wheel . . . it was hopeless.

Rrrrrrr . . . rrrrrr . . . rrrr . . . there I was stranded in the middle of the four lane road trying to start the engine and with the traffic barrelling down on me. Finally I drove it back to the correct side of the road and parked it safely.

It was still raining, so I walked sheepishly over to the other car and asked, "Do you want to sit in my car?" I couldn't think of anything else to say other than "sorry", so I offered him the next best thing!

The poor bloke stared at me – there was blood trickling down the side of his face. His white business shirt was ripped. All he was worried about was trying to remove the radio out of his car. The mangled machine was scrap except for the "music box". But it was very difficult to remove because it had one of those anti-theft devices fitted!

This and other bad memories of driving in the wet weather didn't help me in Adelaide! However I knew that I didn't have to drive that well to hold up the honour of the "WWOS" Channel 9 team in this annual event!

The previous year Liz Hayes had gone around in pedestrian pace to record the slowest time in history and finish a long, lost last – she was definitely travelling Australia Post that day. Daryl Eastlake had gone close to winning it that year but then he was well at home with all that noise! Tony Greig had the best record in the race and went on to drive in the Group E production class pretty comfortably.

During lap two it was nice to see Glenn Wheatley in the kitty litter choking his steering wheel, snarling at himself but ever so neatly "parked" off the track – it was no good leaving his best form at practice.

Normally F1 competitors dump their machines in disgust when they spin out or break down, but because of the weather conditions the blond manager remained at the wheel in silence with the wipers waving in front of him . . . what a terrific front seat view he had of the race.

For the statistically-minded Glenn's investment worked out something like this: twenty-five percent of a DNF (did not finish), plus time and effort equals nothing! Still he had another leg lapping well for his stable . . . John Farnham had hit the front!

Actually it was probably best that Glenn didn't finish. If he had beaten John Farnham, Harry M. Miller was waiting in the wings for an excuse to pounce.

Another casualty was John Platten. After the race the marshals just about had to take the roof and the door off to pull him out of the car. He had a nasty bingle with "Spike" Jones.

Spike gave Ann-Maree a bit of a touch up as well. Always in the action, she had a couple of spins. Her excuse was that she was having trouble with a curve. Well, I bet she stopped for a quick look in the mirror before getting back on the track!

Shane Bourne had his fair share of worries too. Not to put too fine a point on it, the guy is a maniac! He said he came down the Brabham Straight at about 180 kmh – I'm not sure how he knew that with the speedo covered up. But it's pretty fast to be travelling in one of these little Nissan EXAs.

At the end of the Brabham Straight, there is a hairpin bend . . . well, bad luck about the turn. Shane went straight through and ended up in about the same place as Nelson Piquet did later in the afternoon during the main event . . . but at half the pace of Shane!

Jim Murcott had explained to us all that when (not if) you do come off the track and you're going to crack the concrete, what you do is jump on everything – the brakes, the clutch, the lot! "My mind went into reverse," Shane recalled. "I came off the clutch, came off the brake, came off the accelerator, pulled the half full ashtray out . . . turned the wireless off, grabbed the keys and was about to get out of the car. Then I thought, 'Gee I'm still in this race!' So I hopped back in and away we went."

The studio "chat" warned me that there had been a couple of incidents up ahead. "Maybe I'm going to pass a few people?" Just the thought of it excited me.

"We would like to see you pass a few cars . . . move up a couple of places," Bazza called back. There was money on me, I was told, but I was still unaware if it was for finishing FIRST or LAST!

My race was just drifing along. I was still unsure of how fast I should push my car or how many revs to use . . . if I wound up above 6,000 revs the on-board camera would be a bigger giveaway than marks on the collar. There was a mark on the wall towards the end of the main straight indicating braking distance. That was at about 150 m. But I started braking halfway down the straight!

I was trying to remember all the things Jim Murcott had told me over the three days. But it was sort of washed away as I burned down the straight. I remembered the chat about kissing the curb . . . not just kissing, I was bloody slobbering all over them . . . it was so slippery.

The lessons had been all about turning late, brushing the kerbs, squeezing the brakes, using all of the available road, holding the pedal flat down and trusting the brake distance markers to brake as late as possible before the corners – even when you think it's not possible to stop in time.

Jim had taught us most of the tricks of the trade, the proper technique and now it was all going down the drain with every drop of rain. He gave us a folder full of information to refer to. I had it in the glovebox but there was not enough time to get the right sheet out of the folder!

There was also a sheet to remind us about the warning flags that are waved by the officials at each corner. But there was no flag warning me that there were dirty big puddles on the main straight!

The news from the radio was that about six had bitten the dust. "Well, that was bad luck for them," I grinned.

"A few more incidents and you might win this, Maxie!" Ken laughed.

So I started to fix my lines and caress the kerbs just like Alain Prost would. Finally I could see the bloke in the bright yellow coat holding the tablecloth on a stick! Yes, this was the best part – seeing the chequered flag.

This was what I was waiting for . . . the big moment. Accelerator flat, sprint to the line to get the flag waved over the bonnet!

A win? Well, it felt like it, but in reality it was twelfth after starting fourteenth. My finishing time was 11 secs behind the winner, Darren Cahill. That might sound a lot but it was just a little more than Flo-Jo took to win the 100 m at the Seoul Olympics!

Lisa Curry, who should have been right in her element with so many pools of water around, was one who summed up the race fairly well. She said that swimming and car racing are exactly the same. The starter's gun goes off . . . you go as fast as you possibly can against the clock, and your opposition – but in swimming you can't get killed!!

For me it was a terrific experience to actually go out and learn a bit about racing motor cars. Because I had taken part in the celebrity race, I had my endorsed racing licence. Technically, I'm told, I could make my way into Formula One and race anywhere in the world!

The cruel thing was that I was too big to fit in a Formula One motor car. They are built for speed and lightness and so are the little jockey-sized drivers. They tell me the taller, bigger blokes really have a hard time in F1 with cramps in the legs – there is hardly enough room for pressing the pedals. In fact Ferrari have done away with a clutch entirely and now have an electronic gearchange behind the spokes of the steering wheel!

Anyway, I could sit back, relax and watch the Formula One drivers and see if they could do any better! The atmosphere before the Grand Prix was thick and that wasn't just because of the rain. Defending champion Ayrton Senna reckoned the last few races had been rigged by the F1 rule makers to stop him winning another title.

His opponents, including team-mate Alain Prost reckoned he was playing it pretty rough out on the track. Those blokes should have watched the celebrity race more closely – then they would have seen some real desperates!

This was going to be a do or die effort by Senna. He had to win here and then win the other race in the courtroom against fines and penalties if he was to keep the title away from champion-elect Prost.

It was pretty tense stuff, especially when Prost and some of the other drivers weren't too keen to race, saying it was too wet and too dangerous. What had I been doing for five laps! Nobody had come up to me and said, "Maxie, it's too wet for you to race. We don't want you to get hurt!" Let's not forget that aerodynamically designed F1 cars don't have a roof . . . and the drivers don't carry umbrellas with them. Come to think of it, there isn't even a boot.

It was enough for me to put my life on the line, with a little, short wheelbase car on skinny tyres in the wet – but not for some of the skilful, professional Grand Prix drivers like Alain Prost who are paid millions of dollars to drive on those fat wheels! But then as I watched Williams-Renault driver, Thierry Boutsen, take a surprise win in the main event, I had to concede that I didn't realise my dream to become world champion at Adelaide in 1989 . . . maybe if the weather had been better.

CHAPTER EIGHT

No Pain, no Gain

Attack of the Mower

"I'D HAVE TO HANG ONTO IT
LIKE A RODEO RIDER"

Let me say categorically that am not at all mechanically minded. As for being a home handy man – no way! And in the garden? Merely a stranger in paradise. Now that I've come clean, I feel a lot better!

For a car to go anywhere it needs petrol, water and oil. The key also needs to be in the ignition and the accelerator pedal longs to be trodden on by a large right foot. Beyond that I get easily confused.

My first flat tyre was quite an experience. Amazingly it came nearly seven years after my licence was granted! I was stranded on the side of the freeway between Melbourne and Ballarat staring at a flat driver's side rear tyre. My destination was a speaking engagement in Dimboola, three or more hours further down the bitumen.

With huge roadtrains passing barely a metre away, I set out to discover the mystery behind changing a tyre. Out of the glove box came the Ford manual with relatively simple instructions on how to elevate the car, etc. This was all brand new to me . . . and easier said than done!

I'm sure I looked and felt a long way from being comfortable . . . dressed in my attire for the evening – a light grey, pinstripe suit, standing with the boot ajar, trying to fathom out exactly how each piece of equipment fitted together. One can't help but admire the skill used by the mechanics at the Australian Grand Prix who can change a tyre in a seven and a half second pitstop. It took me fifteen minutes to get my hands very dirty – which I hate – and to complete the wheel swap. Thank goodness I haven't had to repeat the effort too many times lately.

Inside the house, my form is not much better. I've spent many sleepless nights listening to the maddening sound of a dripping tap, only to get up in a grumpy mood, call a plumber, stand by and watch him replace a fifty cent washer in no time at all! The resultant silence helps you comprehend the megabuck bill that usually has to be paid in seven days.

I know I'll never be a Mr Fixit. I'm very aware of my limitations . . . and they're plenty! You really have to be so very careful. Danger lurks at the end of every spanner and behind every blade of grass – especially if I'm anywhere to be found.

So, I thought my decision not to tackle any gardening tasks more difficult than trimming the standard front and back lawn, was a good one. Until, I decided to buy a handmower. These days my only regular exercise seems to be climbing staircases or chasing aeroplanes. So, I thought pushing a handmower across the hallowed turf of the Walker backyard would be good for the heart and limbs, and therapeutic for the soul. But let me tell you, there are traps for novices like myself!

Prior to this burst of fitness fanaticism, I used to be the proud owner of a screaming motor mower. A real beast of a machine. The chassis was bright orange, it had mag wheels – a real "GT Super Sloop" if ever you've seen one. Talk about power . . . I'd have to hang onto it like a rodeo rider on a prize bucking bull. All that high octane energy was just bursting to get out.

Some days it was easier to start than others. Mind you, it would have helped if you had forearms like Arnold Schwartzeneggar! The number of times I've pulled my shoulder out of the socket yanking that temperamental *#;!*&@;! It makes me swear every time I think about it!

On those deafening afternoons when lady luck smiled on my backyard, the rotor blades used to spin savagely in a whirlwind of power. Woe to any self-respecting daisy, weed or harmless blade of grass that dared to grow any higher than 25 mm. Whoosh! Cut off at the knees. But unfortunately the screech of this macho machine would scar the peaceful tranquility of a weekend at home and has long since gone by the by. Now I have a more modest and obedient apparatus – the handmower!

My first little outing with this upgraded unit was decidedly unforgettable, despite being wonderfully quiet and rhythmic. No engine to curse, no tantrums. I was taking to my new machine like a duck to water . . . click-clack-click-clack. Even the smell of freshly cut grass instead of the petrol fumes was wonderfully refreshing. I couldn't help but smile! Close to nature. Environmentally friendly!

Suddenly the unexpected happened and it came to an abrupt halt. No, not a little garden gnome jumping out from behind a rock, and the neighbour hadn't popped in for a chat . . . Just a clunk and everything stopped dead. The wheels locked and the blades jammed.

Thanks to some fancy footwork by one of my feathered friends searching for worms – a stray piece of tan bark had caused the problem.

How do I remove this troublesome hunk of wood? Commonsense should have prevailed but somehow my fingers were quicker to react than my brain. One decent ol' stab with the thumb and index finger did the trick . . . away flicked the stubborn bark! What I didn't realise was that by dislodging the obstruction I freed up the cylinder of shiny metal blades – the cutters!

They rotated firmly enough to work like a guillotine on the longest finger on my left hand. The blade was swift and effective and it didn't take long for the severed nerve endings to ricochet the pain signal off the inside of my cranium. I'm not telling you what I said, but it was something like: *@#*;*#*0!

Now, without doubt the best place for my throbbing finger was in my mouth. Well, until I tasted the blood – lots of it too! There I stood with barely a quarter of the back lawn mown and half my finger was missing. "Nice old mess this is!"

A few minutes later when the shock slowly receded, I inspected the damage. Miraculously, the end of my finger was not completely sliced off. Actually the cut was wonderfully symmetrical, about halfway down the nail. The fingernail possibly saved me from being ringbarked, and fumbling through the rest of my life with a very unique fingerprint.

Who was going to help me? Alone in my backyard with only the doves, sparrows and starlings as witnesses to my stupidity. By gee, it was starting to hurt. Words really can't explain the pain. After all pain is definitely a personal thing – one deep! Within a couple of minutes my clenched fist was full of pedigree Walker blood, despite one of my ancestors enjoying the drafty hospitality of the penal settlement at Port Arthur in Tasmania. It wasn't my fault he made the trip out from the mother country below deck! I've never been game to ask what his punishment was for!

I don't know about you, but I'm a real wimp at the sight of blood. A long time ago my boxer dog, Paddy, cut his bum on a large spiked cactus while playing a little over enthusiastically. Can you believe it! I fainted in the veterinary surgeon's rooms, while poor old Paddy was getting a dozen or so much needed stitches. The patient was fine. As for myself – nothing but a wobbly mess!

Nothing's changed and having recently moved house, my "local" doctor was now more than half an hour, and fifteen suburbs, away. Forget him! I needed help from much closer and quickly.

Somewhere deep inside there was a necessity to tell someone what had happened . . . maybe it might ease the pain! One thing was for certain, a phone call wasn't going to stop the blood! I used a white handtowel. Perhaps a coloured one may have been less dramatic.

The first call I made was naturally to Kerry . . . I needed some sympathy badly, but before I could explain to Julie – the receptionist at Kerry's office – she had recognised my voice and put me straight through . . . Bad luck, Kerry already had the phone in her hand . . . nothing but engaged signals. Wait, wait, wait! Not even the tedious "waiting" music to soothe my nerves and ease the pain! Only Telecom beeps.

By this stage, yours truly was starting to feel a bit woosy and dizzy. No choice but to hang up. What happens if I faint? Well, nobody was going to be around to slap my face like the vet many years ago and bring me around. I tried to remember what you should do in this situation. Should I lie down first or put my head between my knees? I opted for the horizontal version with a tightly wrapped, crimson-stained towel clutched to my pounding ribcage. Beads of perspiration were trickling down the chooks feet creases that stem from the outer edge of the eyes of most forty-year-olds. C'mon, you know what I'm talking about . . . even make-up won't hide them. But a face lift might fix 'em.

After five minutes of hovering in and out of consciousness, like an early morning dreamer, I thought, "Let's have another crack at that phone. After all, I've only taken the end off one finger. I haven't got paralysis of the hand."

Before punching the digits on the phone with my good hand I deliberated for a second or two . . . who else should I ring? Maybe Garry Sparke, my publisher, is cruising around nearby with his car phone handy – certainly would save a drive. So I gave him a bell . . . not in the car, switched through to his office. All lines were occupied. The music was like a funeral parlor – *Greensleeves* I think. The sympathy wasn't too forthcoming when I finally did get his ear.

"How can a grown man get his finger caught in a handmower?" he asked sarcastically. "Maybe a motor mower but definitely not a bloody push mower!" Before I could explain, " . . . is it your writing hand . . . or the other one?" he butted in.

"No! it's my left hand" I said.

He didn't know whether or not I was sending him up as I usually do, so he quickly replied in the comfort of knowing my right hand and fingers were all in mint condition, " . . . take a couple of Panadol and get back to the drawing board – we've got a deadline to meet with this book!"

Next, I thought I'd try Channel 9. "Channel 9, one moment please . . ."

It seemed like an eternity of piped music. Maybe it was radio 3AK. Finally, I managed to talk to Robyn at reception who informed me that the station used a doctor in Burnley, just around the corner from GTV 9.

"Let's go," I said. Robyn made the necessary phone call and I was set.

One more try for Kerry. This time, straight through. She said I sounded a bit vague. Very intuitive – the big bloke was fading fast.

Without dramatising the scenario too much I told her I'd cut the end off my finger, was bleeding to death, felt very faint and had to get to a doctor immediately. Oh, and the good news for her too was that . . . I didn't let any blood drip on the new leather lounge suite when I put my body down to rest. She was very pleased with my thoughtfulness under extreme duress . . . Let's just forget the white towel for the moment.

Basically she was about a thirty minute drive away, so she wanted to meet me at the Medical Centre to save time. Her support was great and just what I needed.

Into the car, I discovered that power steering is an absolute must for one handed lawnmower enthusiasts!

Gee, I must have looked a bit shifty, pale faced and sweaty . . . with my left hand and its blood-stained covering taking on a butler's pose. I couldn't blame the guy in the adjacent car stopped at one red light, for wondering if I might have been a wounded bank robber making a getaway. My towel could have been concealing a bullet hole or worse – a loaded gun.

I was extremely lucky! The doctor was waiting – and ushered me straight into a dark, sombre consultation room – no time to gaze around checking out the decor, with a view to referring it to the editor of *Vogue Living*. . . . Don't think it would have made the pre-selection cut anyway. For the first thirty seconds it was an eye ball to eye ball encounter, then the doctor's eye-line dropped to where my aching hand was supported on his typical doctor's antique desk. My attention span was failing . . . all over the shop, a real jumble of thoughts.

I couldn't help thinking of the yarn about the teenage boy seated in the reclining dentist chair with the drill getting very close. "Open wide son," the dentist said. The youngster sat bolt upright, quick as a flash slipped his hand under the white dentist's coat, and grabbed him firmly by the testicles in what Lou Richards, my co-host on "Wide World of Sports", would called the "squirrel grip". "Now, we're not going to hurt each other Doc, are we?" Very descriptive images!

Maybe it was just my warped sense of humour but I was hoping like hell the Doc wasn't going to inflict too much pain on me. I unveiled the damaged hand in the manner befitting a jeweller examining a precious diamond. In my view those long, lean fingers are priceless. Without them, it's very difficult to pick up the small change off the counter, isn't it?

Unfortunately, he wanted a much closer look! That's when the pain began. First he placed his stainless steel kidney-shaped bowl full of hot water onto the desk. The steam made me feel dizzy. Two gentle dabs on my "onkaparinga" and that was enough! I sheepishly requested to lie down – the lights were spinning out of control.

You wouldn't think a solitary finger could cause so much pain and subsequent loss of balance! Did you hear about off-spinner Fred Titmus, the English Test cricketer, who lost his big toe in a nasty water skiing accident in the Caribbean? It upset his balance quite substantially and as well it made his foot look very funny in a pair of dirty ol' cricket socks. In my case . . . just the end off a finger and all 6'4" of me is immobilised! This was ridiculous! What would people say if they ever found out? At this stage I didn't really care!

As the Doc continued his meticulous cleaning . . . the cottonwool balls felt like sandpaper being dragged over bare flesh. I answered his cricket questions to try and ignore what was going on. Then he explained that stitches were not possible (boy, what a relief) – unless he took the nail completely off first! Not over my dead body was I going to let him have a crack at that! Well, not while I was conscious. The thought of jabbing a painkilling injection straight up the centre of that open ended finger didn't thrill either.

No, I was very happy with the doctor's other solution . . . a firmly taped up wound. This technique was quite creative – tape from underneath to the top of the split nail, same wrap around on both sides and then a loop or two over the last joint to keep it firm. Now all we could do was to keep our fingers crossed and let nature do its deed.

I suppose it would have been a bit much to hope to escape without some real pain. The tetanus injection felt like a three inch nail going in!

"See me in two days' time and we'll have another look . . . and keep it dry!" he said.

Gee, it was fantastic to be greeted by a great big, yet concerned smile, and a comforting hug in the waiting room – Kerry was there. It was nice to have a shoulder to lean on and a caring ear to pour out the silly deeds of the afternoon . . . and not feel too bad about it. Home we drove – and it was the one handed bandit at it again, as we were in separate cars!

Keeping that finger dry was quite a feat in itself. A bath was the obvious way but I have bad memories of taking a tub one morning in England before playing cricket. Never again . . . it's abnormal to try to bowl fast after a hot bath at 8.30 a.m.

I clad my left hand in a dry cleaner's plastic wrap, with an elastic band around the wrist, to keep it watertight. Have you ever tried soaping up your right armpit with your right hand? I know there's a touch of gorilla in all of us but this is very much mission impossible. It required an extra dose of spray-on deodorant on that side for a few days.

Soon both finger and nail were fit enough again for a manicure . . . and to mow the lawn. It is a bit like a car accident . . . you've got to get back out in the traffic before you lose your nerve.

Initially my timing was astray. Like an ageing fast bowler I tried the acceleration technique, hoping the long run up would send the blades scuttling across the defiant couch. Speed was essential as the lawn had grown a bit during the four weeks I was on the sidelines!

That tactic didn't work. Couldn't get a clean run at all. Take a deep breath and slow down, I tell myself. Don't let it beat you. You can't go flying over the edge and into the tomatoes or sailing into mid air with the long handles on full throttle, like a bikie. Now, same as the old days . . . line and length. Up, down, up, down, up and away. Forwards and backwards. Roll the mower forwards, pull it back . . . aah! Very therapeutic.

Life is always full of learning experiences. This one has taught me to keep my fingers out of places I know they shouldn't be! Click, clack, click, clack . . .

Facing the Wardrobe like a Man

"THE MORE WE GET, THE MORE WE WANT"

Isn't it amazing how many problems go away when the junk in your life disappears. Once something is eliminated, its capacity to clutter and mess up your day or your home, or most importantly your life, is gone, I only wish I'd realised that painful truth years ago.

I don't mind owning up to the fact that I grew up in a family that always believed in hanging on to all kinds of junk, just in case it might come in handy for something in the future.

Keeping stuff still seemed reasonable as I grew older. When my drawers, shelves and cupboards were filled, I followed the example of other people and got more drawers. I built more shelves and even elevated my bed so that I could hide and store more good junk underneath it.

No doubt I'm not the only one though. I know people who have used the services of an architect to design elaborate storage spaces, in the form of a "house extension" for the sole purpose of housing excess possessions.

I suppose most people are the same – we set out to attain the pleasures, places and things that we want, when and where we want them. Most of us do just that: attain, accumulate, collect. Enough is never enough. The more we get; the more we want.

The big crunch comes when we realise what all that comfort, convenience and "stuff" costs. We have to pay for it, keep track of it, protect it, clean it, store it, insure it and worry about it.

There doesn't appear to be enough time left to have some good old fashioned fun and a laugh or two . . .

If we're not careful, not only will our houses, drawers, cupboards and motor cars become so crowded that it's difficult to breathe, but minds, emotions and personal relationships will buckle at the weight of all of our junk with the result being – dull, boring and stagnant people too preoccupied with possession mania.

Sometimes I sit back in my chair and look at a desk piled with clutter – bills, letters, assignments, newspapers, research and filing material etc. and think "What am I doing this for? I should be trying to master a 3-iron on the golf course."

Anyway I decided things must change – I felt exhilarated and keen to get on with the job of dejunking. But where would I begin?

I decided on the wardrobe – there must have been a small fortune invested on the various shaped coathangers that caused the hanging rail to sag badly under the weight.

The fashions ranged through flared trousers, stove-pipes, sloppy joes and wide-lapelled suits. Somehow I'd gathered all these clothes (some were twenty years old) packed them tighter and tighter into the limited space with never any chance of wearing them out. I suppose being fashion conscious is an even greater waste than greed is.

I still even had a dinner suit, shirt and bow-tie I purchased at a bargain basement sale the first year I arrived in Melbourne as a skinny adolescent lad in 1967 . . . needless to say, I couldn't get near them today. I've blossomed into a big boy just as my dad suggested I would.

So out they went – trousers, suits, jackets and shirts – even some that I'd worn to the ground on the day I'd taken heaps of wickets or made a few runs – lucky or not, I just had to let go. I almost cried as I stuffed a couple of my well-worn beauties into the green, plastic garbage bag – but it was time to go!

My theory used to be that if I wore a certain shirt on a particular day to a sporting event, then I'd be successful. Amazingly, nine times out of ten it seemed to work. Actually instead of telling myself to be a winner in the true mode of all positive thinkers, I used to wear my lucky shirts. But since I wasn't going to be playing Test cricket any-more and they wouldn't fit me anyway, it was "bye bye" to some trea-sured Alan Solley shirts.

Next to go were the squadrons of shoes – platform soles, chisel toes, worn-out runners, football boots, buckled cricket boots, thongs, etc. – you name it, I probably had at least two pairs of each to discard.

By this time I was into the third plastic bag . . . all destined for one of the St Vincent de Paul opportunity shops in Melbourne. How does that adage go? "One man's junk is another man's treasure."

Wherever they ended up didn't really matter, as long as they didn't lob back in my wardrobe.

I shouldn't forget to mention the ties – literally hundreds of 'em; skinny ones, wide ones, loud ones and plain ones; I was never going to tie the knot in these ghastly accessories, so, like a big bag of small multi-colored off-cuts, out the door they went.

Along with the ties went twenty-three single socks – without mates or holes. I've got no idea where the other half of each pair disappeared to . . . odd socks seem to be a universal problem!

So there's the challenge, face up to your wardrobe like a man or a woman should, with doors wide open, lights at full bore, and say to yourself, "Why should I keep it?"

You'll probably end up with two piles after leaving all the clothes that you wear regularly and feel good in.

Pile one is the lot that needs to be mended – at least there's some practical reason for not wearing an item. Pile two – out of style, won't fit or you just plain don't want to know about this lot anymore.

Possibly after a second look at the first pile of clobber, you'll end up with a few of these pieces in pile two as well.

When you think about it, junk really is everywhere – open up your wallet and a great wad of mostly useless business cards fall out with numerous other bits of paper.

Open the boot of your car and the odds are it's a beaut space for extra rims, hub caps, jacks, gravel-dented, old, insect-splattered number plates and cardboard boxes.

And inside the car – well that's no better – a filing cabinet for old parking stickers and unpaid fines, antique gas bill receipts, peanut shells, drink cans, crushed fast food containers, tissue boxes, sweet wrappers, directions to last month's party, single-lensed sunglasses, dried out first-aid kits and a bottle opener.

Yes, it would be fair to say that some of the finest clutter collections in the world are hoarded in the confines of our cars.

And how embarrassing it is to have so much clutter, clobber, trash or whatever that you don't even remember where it all is. Having extra vacuum cleaner bags, fuses, candles, tape measures or scales, are of no use when you can't find them!

When I don't know where something is, I'll dig like a hungry dog for a bone trying to unearth it and tear up every storage space in the whole house to get it.

My study used to be a real mess . . . in fact it was quite intimidating to walk into the room. Piles of magazines, newspapers, folders, letters and boxes of stationery enclosed the work space, desperate for a home, or even just to be acknowledged. Everyone keeps old magazines and newspapers but what about all those less obvious stray bits of paper?

Have you ever noticed how people must keep expired life insurance policies? Just in case re-incarnation might occur in reverse. We paid too much for it. It looks so legal. We'd better keep it!

The other old faithful piece of paper that's never thrown out is the raffle ticket. The fact that we keep it, though it was drawn in 1973, I suppose indicates that human hope never dies (as long as we keep junk around to remind us).

How much unopened junk mail, how many outdated catalogues and newsletters, obsolete timetables, old lists, worn out slogan stickers, wrinkled posters and old Christmas cards and calendars, half-filled out questionnaires, old competition entry forms and magazine subscription offers, outdated reports, box tops, expired coupons and unidentifiable envelopes of "stuff" do you have stashed away somewhere? In my case they're all based under and on top of a bench in my study.

Yes, I've even kept unused 1985/86/87/88/89 diaries that might come in handy – when? Also there's ancient address books . . . I know I'll never use them.

Now, let me see, where will I start?

Carry on Doctor

"TOO MUCH SITTING DOWN AND TAKING. NOT ENOUGH EXERCISE AND DOING"

It's often been said that a person's body is merely a vehicle to travel from birth to death in!

It's our own choice whether or not we make that journey, in an aerodynamically designed machine, similar to a Formula One racing car, or maybe we're just happy to get along on a daily basis in a beat-up old jalopy that doesn't take too much looking after!

And just like all motor cars, no matter how old or how new, our bodies also need constant attention and sometimes a major overhaul.

Well, I had a look at my calendar and realised it had been about three years since I had my last full-scale doctor's check-up. And judging by the speedometer that continually whirs inside my head, I could sense my visit to the Shepherd Foundation Health Testing Clinic, in colourful Fitzroy Street, St Kilda, was long overdue.

For example, during the summer, Channel 9 cricket commentators clock up almost 50,000 km each in air-travel between capital

city match venues and towards the end of the season, we all need another aeroplane ride like a hole in the head!

A phone call confirmed the appointment. The whole exercise takes about two hours. But the strict discipline and dieting procedures expected prior to arrival at the centre are similar to what super coach Kevin Sheedy would expect of his high flying Essendon Bombers, the night before a big match! Difficult for a man like myself in the twilight of his sporting career.

"Please avoid any excessive alcohol consumption." That was only the beginning!

It is necessary that you fast for eight to sixteen hours before eating a "special meal" which must be commenced exactly one hour, forty-five minutes prior to your appointment time.

As my appointment was scheduled for 10 a.m., I was told to commence my last normal meal at 7.00 p.m. on the previous night, and then to have no further food or drink until 8.30 a.m. the next morning. I can tell you it was a very dry old night – thinking about what I couldn't have made me even thirstier!

Then the last line of the instructions: "You may satisfy your thirst with water before eating the special meal." Generous mob aren't they?

In fact, I needed a couple of extra glasses of water, to allow myself to swallow the special meal of two slices of dry toast plus banana and a glass of lemonade. Very exotic stuff and bland too!

Now after drinking all that water and lemonade I almost overlooked another requirement – a painful one too! "Do not pass urine for at least two hours before your appointment."

That's easier said than done, especially with a bladder full of water. In fact, there are very few sensations in the world that will go even close to passing water when you're really under pressure.

All for a good cause and in the end I arrived there fairly relaxed and on time.

The aim of the health testing is directed towards a wide range of medical conditions. Scientific analysis of the test results then helps your doctor evaluate your health and develop a health correction plan if necessary.

I'm not a huge rap for seeing blood at the best of times, so with the blood sample programmed first up, it was just a matter of "Hello, Sister?" Then, tightly clenching my teeth to give me strength. I hate pain, especially from needles so thick in diameter! There was no escape. A sharp turn of my head away from the white-clad woman, quickly labelled me a coward.

"Just a small prick and it'll be all over!" she said with a knowing smile – I'm certain she's hurt many a man before me by puncturing his veins and his ego!

Next was the urine sample. I waited for so long I had almost forgotten how. But not just an ordinary urine sample – no, this one had to be "mid-stream". A cute little term isn't it?

"Start. Stop. Collect. And start again" . . . talk about a circus, after a two hour wait.

Then the idea was to discreetly plant my warm little amber-coloured container on the appropriate tray with all the other successful attempts at "mid-streaming" – embarrassing to say the least! Gee it's moments like this that make me realise how lucky I am to have large concealing hands.

On the other hand it also makes one wonder how the world's best athletes get on after competing in a big international event and then being asked to give a compulsory urine sample for drug tests. I'm told many have stood and addressed the plastic containers for up to three hours before "winning" the struggle against their body to come forward with a trickle.

Next it was time to clear the wax from my ears with the "audiometry" or hearing test. Too bad if you don't like being locked up. Into the old-fashioned fridge-like booth I went. Through the glass window I could see my attractive medical technician attending the appropriate gauges necessary to test each patient at six different frequencies of the acoustic spectrum. I'm certain she tried to trick me a couple of times too! But what the nurse didn't realise is that I used to be able to hear a batsman get the faintest of edges – off my own bowling of course – and even when the wind was blowing a gale down the wicket so that the umpire couldn't pick it up! I've lost count of the number of times I've been unlucky and watched the offending batsman given NOT OUT.

Judging by my career batting averages and several indifferent attempts to score a cluster of runs, it would be fair to say I couldn't bat, and probably had problems with my eyes.

Well, I couldn't wait to receive the results of my eyesight test back. I might have scored full marks there. If so, maybe I ought to be an umpire rather than a commentator. On second thoughts, with the slow motion replays it could be a bad move.

Even a few pounds heavier than my playing weight, I was ready for the "physical". Time to take my gear off! But into what sort of garment was I going to step?

As it turned out, a very flimsy blue paper robe. It was hardly a 46 extra long – my size! In fact, the length finished a long way above the knees.

I must have looked outrageous! Heaven help me if someone recognises me. And that's exactly what did happen. Here I was having a chat with a fit looking fifty-year-old who had just completed some time on the treadmill and another big guy who looked like a moving picture show he had that many tattoos on his body. All of us were conscious of how silly we looked – all three bodies were nothing short of polar bear white.

My height measurement showed up the fact that I had shrunk almost half an inch since I played football, or maybe as an architecture student my hair was much longer?

Weight needs to be lost! Enough said about that. Too much sitting down and talking. Not enough exercise and doing!

These two basic items led me into a breathing exercise – a respiratory test to measure the capacity of my lungs. After one practice run it was fair dinkum stuff. Whilst blocking my nose with my left hand, I had to blow as hard as I could into what looked like an empty toilet roll holder connected to a flexible plastic hose. By the time I'd run out of breath my percentage of lung capacity steadied at ninety-four percent. So it's obvious I've lost some wind from the good old days of shouting: "Owzat ump?" Although there are a few people who would argue I'm still all wind!

Now for the big one – vital sign tests! Blood pressure was taken and recorded both lying down and standing up!

Television is the sort of industry where blood pressure and tempers are always high on the scale – I'll be interested in the result.

Then while lying down I was prepared for an ECG or what is commonly known as a standard electro-cardiogram. The nurse had me wired for sound, so to speak, and that meant fixing special rubber suction cups onto my ankles, wrists and chest. These were then connected to the machine recording the electrical characteristics of my heart's performance on a graph paper printout.

The sight of tangled wires and suction cups dissecting my motionless body brought some humour from the nurse: "Now you know what it's like making love to an octopus," she said.

I couldn't help but smile and replied: "I bet you're into bondage in your spare time?" There was a deathly silence from the woman in white but her assistant giggled and offered her two bob's worth with, "I dare you to answer that?"

The banter was all good fun and made the two hours fly and it took my mind off the man next in line, a shivering Chinese patient, who had trouble understanding anything the girls said. I tried not to offend him by laughing, but in the end I couldn't help myself. Some of the situations were straight out of "Carry on Doctor."

The sensation of cold glass against my rib cage for the standard chest X-ray brought a different look to my face . . . it was difficult to stand perfectly still because, like my Chinese friend, I was shivering as well, even my teeth were chattering. Who knows, I could be out of focus when the X-rays come back, but one thing is for sure, the pictures will be in black and white!

To finish off the tests we had to answer a wide range of computerised questions about past health conditions and current symptoms in the privacy of a booth and the comfort of a "cuppa tea and bickies". They went down very well at the time because it had been about seventen hours – apart from the toast and banana "special" – between meals.

I'd like to think my body is a Ferrari but I know it's not! But as I get older I do know it's the only one I've got and the only one I'm going to get!

So from here on in I'm going to make sure it gets the best possible treatment.

Why don't you do the same for yours!

In Fright of the Drill

"IT WAS TOO LATE, THE CAVITIES WERE THERE"

Dentists may occupy one of the highest paid professions in the community, but to the average person in the street, I am pretty sure they are still looked upon as the "fang snatcher" – a professional with the ability to inflict unforgettable pain at will!

Then, after reducing the helpless patient to a frightened and crumpled shadow, they'll explain with a toothy smile, that the ordeal was necessary for your own good – a piercingly painful penalty for not looking after your teeth.

Of course, my pain threshold is somewhere around my ankles when it comes to the dentist . . . I can withstand a fair amount of pain (like any self-respecting man should) in broken noses, bruises, cuts and the like, but the intensely focused shrill that ricochets off the inside of one's skull and rebounds into the extremities, reduces me to the stature of a "Mr Puniverse" if a nerve is touched.

When I look back on an erratic career of visiting these white-coated gentlemen, many things have changed . . . yet the same old pain occurs when they tweak a nerve!

My first visit to the dentist was as a small boy in Hobart. Ether was used to put me to sleep – I can still feel my head beginning to blow up like a football bladder and the glare of the lights above the antique barber's chair spinning around frantically like a Ferris wheel at night!

A couple of years later chloroform was used instead of ether . . . this was much better, but when the bad teeth had been extracted, the clotted blood and the gaping hole were still a constant source of attention for my probing tongue! How big was that tooth?

In those days the chairs had arms, but not any more. During my last visit to the dentist, I discovered the hard way that they were missing – maybe he got sick of paying for repairs to the regularly dismembered chair!

I was fascinated by my dentist's new poster on the ceiling, strategically placed directly above the head-rest on the reclining chair – something different to occupy my mind this appointment!

As usual the large protective bib was placed around my neck, while I nervously fumbled for somewhere comfortable to support my awkward arms. I opted for the folded arms and clenched fist position and braced myself ready for the systematic "scraping of the teeth" ritual.

Dentists tell you not to clean or pick your teeth with sharp metal objects. So what do they do? Probe every little crack and crevice with a miniature stainless-steel spike.

How do they know where the cavity is? They judge by the height their patient jumps off his chair as the exposed nerve is prodded. Sometimes that exploration into the plaque is more hurtful than the drilling and filling.

Next stage a nurse in uniform appears and some friendly three-way chatter occurs . . . maybe an X-ray is necessary?

Then comes the CRUNCH . . . how many fillings, and where?

In my case it was two – perhaps I'd been drinking too much Coca Cola. Anyway it was too late, the cavities were there.

My worst fears came true when he suggested a needle! I tried to shut my eyes before he produced the painkilling injection . . . but I failed!

There it was a dirty big syringe with thumb cocked on the plunger ready to squirt its contents deep into my jaw bone – the fine metal needle on the end looked about 75 mm long and even a bit blunt! My anxiety level trebled as the plastic cylinder hovered above my head like a sputnik in space.

"It might hurt a bit . . . and it might make your eyes water," the dentist suggested.

He should have said, "It's going to hurt and it'll certainly make your eyes water!"

Into the flesh went the needle – first to the left of my two upper front teeth, then direct hits above each of those and finally a fourth jab to the upper jaw.

I could have sworn the second plunge of pain-killer was buried deep enough to touch my sinuses . . . simultaneously a pair of huge elephant-sized tears rolled off the assembly line in each tear duct.

Slowly my upper lip, plus my moustache, appeared to float right off my face . . . yes, the painkiller was definitely working.

I know it's easier if you're relaxed, but somehow my whole body seemed tensed up and my tightly clenched fists had "white knuckle fever".

Now for the drilling! Ready, aim . . . contact! I search for the expected pain but none is forthcoming. Maybe, just maybe, it won't hurt.

What feels like huge boulders of broken tooth drop into the saliva that has been secreted into the region beneath my tongue . . . then the watchful nurse puts her stainless steel-tipped sucker hose to work. Like an underwater vacuum cleaner, the by-products of drilling soon disappear into the hose.

Once the decay has been removed only a gaping hole remains!
"Rinse!" says the dentist.

I nervously pick up the glass of pale pink liquid and attempt to swirl it around inside my mouth without spilling a drop, but as we all know, that's almost impossible when you haven't got an upper lip. Like a baby, dribble runs rapidly and embarrassingly from each corner of my mouth.

Next task is to spit the remaining rinse into what looks like a miniature bidet – the smell reminds me of formalin and the city morgue!

Back to the reclining position . . . the nurse is mixing the filler paste somewhere away from my eye line . . . the dentist rams the first wad of filler hard into the man-made cavity.

Next, a plastic wedge to hold it in place. My mouth cannot possibly open wider without tearing at the edges!

Then when least expected, my dentist asks my opinion about an architectural problem of his . . . it really is very difficult to speak in depth on any subject when somebody else has filled your mouth with about eight fingers and various other items of dental equipment. I grunt but the questions keep on flowing through the cotton mask covering his mouth.

More pushing, more probing, an extra finger, two more plastic dividing strips and another mix of filler, yet, still no pain . . . I can't believe it!

My fear of dentists can be pinpointed to a bad experience during my early teens in Tasmania.

It wasn't until I came to Victoria to play VFL football with Melbourne that I regained some confidence in these "madmen with electronic drills". I'm still not super comfortable about visiting them even though mine's a good one.

I had no alternative. I needed a mouth-guard to protect my teeth while playing football. Only a dentist could supply one personally fitted! Especially to wrap around a set of munchers like mine.

Have you ever tried to keep your mouth shut for five minutes while completely full of a sloppy mix of plaster of Paris? The other problem is to try not to swallow any. The taste is terrible and time passes so slowly. When your nose has been broken several times it's very difficult to breath with a zipper on your mouth!!

I don't know why I worried about getting the mouth-guard, because with a nose as large as mine – the first item on my face that was going to get into trouble was always my nose (five times broken) . . . and I must admit I'm not getting any better looking!

Anyway . . . drilling is almost completed. My lip feels fatter than ever. The time is 11.30 a.m. – will there be any feeling there by 6 p.m.? Because I am supposed to read the Sports News on Channel 9?

The plastic separating strips are painlessly removed from between my teeth and a file or similar tool is used to shape the filling flush with the original tooth surface.

The water drill has worked, unlike the painful machines of old.

Gee, it must have been bad in the early days of colonisation, when decaying teeth were wrenched from terrified patients with a pair of pliers – sometimes a knee to the throat helped the dentist get more leverage on his patient's jaw!

I believe the first drills were pedal-powered and they provided an awful "slow grind" and the constant smell of burning teeth.

So much for the past!

The only ordeal remaining for me was a high powered polish!

Still no pain . . . I can't believe it . . . a quick rinse into the miniature water closet, and I'll be okay. Sure, there was some blood but I could handle the blood. You little beauty, it's almost over!

Another dribbling session on to my bib, and I'll be away . . . I sat up and stretched my arms which had been locked tightly around my ribs for the previous hour.

In six months time there will be another check-up, but this time I won't be so frightened!

Thanks, Doc!

Getting into Piles of Trouble

"IT WAS BAD ENOUGH WEARING THE JOCKSTRAP BACK TO FRONT"

Ever had a pain in the rear end? I mean the real thing – haemorrhoids. Anybody who has been alerted by that stain on the toilet paper knows that it brings to you a whole lot more than heartburn!

It was confirmed I was suffering from the condition when I arrived at work, during the period when I was employed as a secondary draftsman. As a "trainee" architect with the Research and Development Group of the Public Works Department in Melbourne, I spent much of my time on my derriere, deep in thought, bent or buckled over a drawing board. So the bottom end was pretty important and needed to be comfortable in order to produce creative work.

place my bum on the drafting stool. Fair and square! I quickly came to the conclusion . . . that I had a nasty problem. What do you do when you've got a problem? You almost never try to fix it yourself . . . you always look to mum or dad or a doctor. Now I was pretty sure the doctor would do the trick. Little did I know . . .

In fact it was the first time I had suffered from haemorrhoids. The previous night I discovered the colourful truth. I thought I was bleeding to death, but then my father, Big Max, assured me the ailment was merely another form of varicose vein and a doctor with the aid of a hypodermic needle could puncture it! The whole exercise wouldn't be too painful and my problem would be over quickly.

As soon as I arrived at the doctor's practice he gave me a thorough check over . . . and said he'd never seen anything like it. I thought he was sarcastically referring to the shape of my bum – not the grapes. Even wearing one of those clingy, rubber, hygienic gloves there was no way the GP was going to touch 'em. A real case of stage-fright – he didn't want to accept the responsibility. He was adamant I needed to see a specialist.

Maybe two hours later on the same morning I was back to where I'd left, on the footpath at Parliament Place – opposite the office where I worked. The specialist's rooms were across the road . . . I could have saved myself a trip to the suburbs. Within no time I was flicking through two-year-old copies of the *Australasian Post* in the waiting room, sitting very uncomfortably on my pile of trouble.

My turn arrived before I had had too much time to think about what might happen. Well, as you would expect with an examination like this, a quick chat and . . . off came the trousers, up on the examination table. I was told to bring my knees up to my chest and face the wall . . . which was by the way a pretty ordinary beige colour, didn't even have a print or a painting to analyze. I definitely needed a distraction.

You have always got to look over your shoulder . . . particularly when you play games like Australian Rules football, to see what's coming! I could see what was coming alright! He whipped a glove on – my troubles were beginning – it was one of those clear clingy variety definitely a lot better looking and feeling than those diabolical pink and green ones we all use for washing up. And the Doc definitely wasn't gonna be doing the washing up!

This was the first time I had ever had an internal inspection. It wasn't the nicest happening. Actually the whole episode was pretty painful – unforgettable!

The expert quickly came to the point – my condition was chronic, as the GP hinted. By 2 p.m. that afternoon I was sitting up in a bed at the Masonic Hospital in Melbourne, looking out the windows at the gardens beyond, reading the first edition of the *Herald* and contemplating an operation early the next day. Hospitals are fairly nice places to be, providing they haven't planned something terrible to happen to you! Like undergo the knife.

One of the most humiliating experiences I had to face up to prior to the operation concerned the visit to my ward of an ethnic charac-

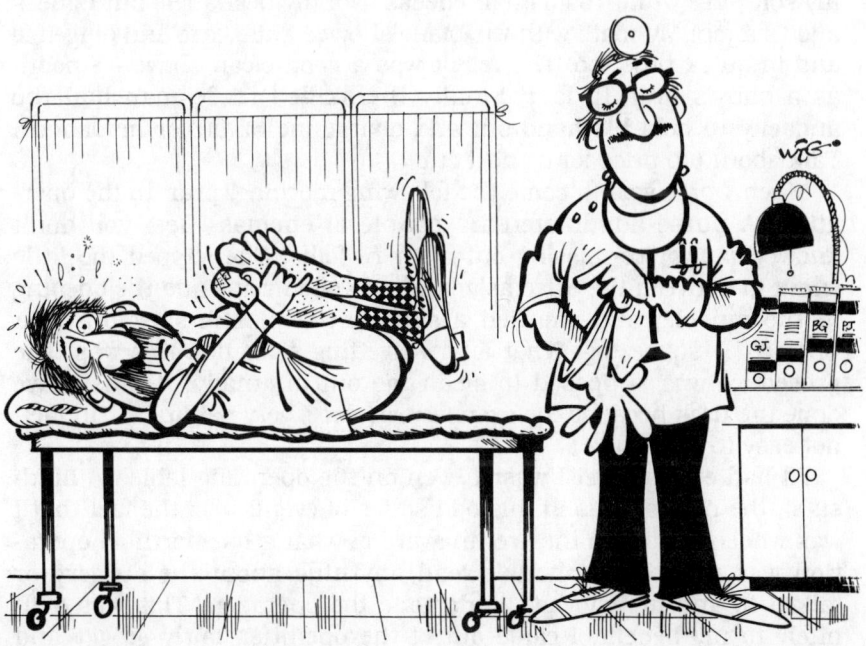

ter. He was wearing a very dark 5 o'clock shadow below his high angular cheek bones. I suppose you could call him a barber. The man's assignment was to clean up and make ready the area which needed to be operated on. Can you imagine yours truly on hands and knees, head buried in the pillow, pyjama trousers draped around my knee caps . . . waiting in anticipation. Now the guy with the accent hadn't stood too close to the razor himself yet he was preparing to shave every hair off each very sensitive cheek.

He used the old fashioned method – a squirrel-hair brush and a quick slap and tickle . . . but didn't use hot water. So there he was having a ball lathering up the soap, slip, slap, slip, slap . . . across the fleshy part of my buttocks, the cold water was trickling irritatingly down the back of each hamstring. He didn't care. I wanted to wipe them dry! But I couldn't move.

"Don't squint, don't squint!" he commanded as I peered over my right shoulder. I observed a huge razor with a plastic handle in his grasp. My friend held the instrument poised to strike as in an old-fashioned slapstick comedy movie. It didn't take too much imagination to picture him standing in between a pair of those red spiral striped posts that adorn every real barber's shop doorway. Have you ever tried not to "squint" when a cold blade of super sharp steel makes contact with your backside! Goose bumps sprang up all over – like a signal to "come to attention"!

Nevertheless onward ever onward! I pleaded for him not to nick my soft pure white Tasmanian cheeks. Not my best angle but I guess a job's a job! My mate with the blade showed skill, care and diligence and in quick time too. The result was a good clean shave – smooth as a baby's bum in fact! Finally the skilled tradesman had the audacity to hold his hand out and charge me $5.00 for his labour. Talk about top price for a short cut.

Much worse was to come the following morning, prior to the operation. A nurse administered a couple of enemas. Gee, you don't know what you're missing out on here folks. She slipped the little snout in between the extremely tender swollen veins and the opening in the muscle, and emptied a substantial plastic sack of water "inside" by squeezing. What a . . . rivetting sensation this was! The procedure was supposed to clean me out internally. It must have done the trick because the exercise was very, very painful . . . in fact, not easy to describe.

I'd had enough, yet I wasn't even on the operating table. In hindsight, the biggest plus in this odd series of events was the fact that I was wheeled into the theatre unaware of what a haemorrhoid operation was all about. I hadn't read anything about the surgery or talked to anyone who had undergone the operation. This was definitely to my benefit. I came out of the operation fairly groggy and feeling pretty wrung out, not knowing what to expect next. Ignorance was bliss.

What a sight . . . there I was wearing only a white singlet, white cover cloth, and a jockstrap on back to front supporting a woman's napkin. I felt bad enough wearing the jockstrap back to front, because it offered absolutely no support up front at all. But then I had to have a napkin tucked down the back. Well, I must say that it was very embarrassing because all the nurses were girls, of course, and being a fairly humble, easily humiliated sort of guy and a private person as well, the inspection four times a day was a bit harrowing.

Successes in actually going to the toilet were very few and far between. In fact, I was told that it would be about four days before I looked like being in a frame of mind to attempt number twos.

When I did try number ones, I strained, grunted and groaned as I hovered over the porcelain bowl. Not even a drop. A frustrated man, I had to go back to bed. Eats were very soft, so when in fact the day of reckoning did arrive, the end product was always going to be a soft mess!

Finally when day four did eventuate, the occasion proved one of my life's great endurance tests. The medical staff explained how it was time to see whether everything worked. To get me up and firing the sister in charge dispenses me a quantity of Agarol and a couple of lethal little pellets. She promised, "Inside ten minutes you will be seated on the toilet seat."

"Oh yeah," I thought. "Where are the laxettes? Nowhere in sight!"

Like a good boy I did as I was told . . . the perfect patient! I swallowed those harmless looking pills and drank the milky liquid. Sure enough, I was out of the blocks at precisely the seven and a half minute mark without the starter's gun.

Away I went, at a million miles an hour, screaming in the direction of the ablution area adjacent to my bed. The same W.C. was also accessible from the ward down the corridor a few metres further on . . . and if another patient had beaten me to it . . . *engaged*, I can honestly say I would have been in heaps of trouble and without trouser legs to conceal my predicament.

Fortunately the cubicle was vacant! Now without becoming rude, crude and totally unattractive, I lifted up the shirt around my hips, released the all important jockstrap to the safety of the tiled floor and became beautifully positioned on the white plastic seat. Everything was white . . . I could have been in heaven. But I wasn't

The pain was excruciating . . . difficult to put into words. Unbelievable! My eyes fixed on the highly polished sloping handrails on either side of the toilet. I had wondered in the past about their purpose. Well it didn't take long to find out! I reckon I pulled the two walls of that tiny room at least another 10 cm closer together. The motion felt like ripping a twenty-four barbed spear "backwards" out the wrong way . . . slowly!

Having completed the mission, I then believed I was going to bleed to death. So I pressed the small red button. I figured this had to be the panic button! Correct. A very efficient nurse promptly answered the call.

Not the nicest way in the world to greet someone! At this stage I was up on my feet, and there was a fair bit of blood around. "I'm gonna bleed to death," I said.

"No sunshine, there's no way you're going to bleed to death," she smirked. "I don't know what you're whingeing about. This happens to us every month!" Much tongue in cheek and a roll of the eyes.

I mused to myself, "I've got a comedian here." Not that I was in much of a mood for laughter – it was my blood on the floor.

Whilst I was feeling sorry for myself, she filled up the bath. It was like an attack scene from the movie *Jaws* when I hopped in. You have never seen anybody splash around so much in your life, like a big, white sperm whale . . . the old cheeks twinged and tweaked plenty in the stinging hot water!

After that eye watering experience, whenever nature called in the near future . . . I remembered the operation! I definitely didn't want to go through all that pain again – never!

The only problem since the op occurred at home. I was standing at the bottom of the staircase during the moment of truth, not knowing whether to attack the ground floor toilet near the laundry or dash for the one at the top of the stairs near the bedroom. Big decision up or down? I'm embarrassed to say . . . but I never successfully made it to either! A case of bye bye to another pair of perfectly good underpants! Only worn a couple of times!

Thank goodness it was a successful operation because I haven't had a hassle since – touch wood!

But, there was one minor yet memorable incident. The doc wanted yours truly back on the very same examination table for a final inspection before giving me the all clear.

This time the doctor produced an instrument called a stainless steel "horse". It was like a telescope, had a telescopic eye and a tiny light inside. Before the specialist inserted it, he instructed, "When I do this I don't want you to cough!" He shouldn't have mentioned that, because the moment he suggested it . . . up came a tickle in the throat.

Lying on my side, knees up on the throat, desperate for a cough, almost choking and he continued to comment on his work, "Beautiful. Lovely. Oh, clean. That's a good job." I could feel the probing piece of stainless steel in line with my bottom rib, then the second rib and finally right up near my breast plate. "Gosh," I imagined. "I must be made of rubber inside. It is physically impossible for this to be happening to me!"

The examination was all over quickly. Well, so I thought. "Just one more tiny thing before we conclude," the doctor requested. "We'll just clean it up a little."

I was of the opinion that the learned man turned away for a tube of ointment or the like . . . whatever they would put on, to fix it up. But when he turned around he had a scalpel in one hand and a pair of tweezers in the other! "Just a tiny piece of skin that needs tidying up," he grinned. I could see he enjoyed inflicting pain.

In one rapid but educated slash the doctor sliced off about half a millimetre of rough skin. Wow, do you reckon that didn't sting! Golly! Put down the glasses! I could've crashed straight through the wall and out onto the street!

I suggested firmly to the Specialist that he had better have finished because he was definitely not going to get a second shot. "Beautiful . . . complete . . . all we need is a bandaid now," he smiled. He placed a bandaid on the wound but the rough textured cotton felt like grade ten sandpaper every time I took a step.

In summary, this was the most painful experience of my sporting life, but at the end of the day, I can now sit down in comfort . . . and wait for my chance to bat.

Footnotes to a Sporting Life

"FAINTED AND FELL FACE FIRST TOWARDS THE FLOOR"

For anyone who has attempted success, fame and fortune through sport, the common denominator would have to be pain. It would be fair to say pain is a constant companion to the committed sportsperson.

The greatest fast bowler the game of cricket has ever produced, Dennis Lillee, once said: "If you're fit enough to walk through the gates, then you're fit enough to play!"

But, what if you can't stand up, can't walk or just plain can't make it?

Every time I received a setback whether a knee, back, neck or arm injury, I reckoned that that particular ailing limb or joint was the most important part of my body. This was possibly because all the pain had localised and my thoughts were dominated by this one negative aspect of my body.

How then did I treat little things like blisters and in-grown toe nails? If I answer honestly, I would have to say gingerly.

I often managed to end up with an ingrown toe nail or two. I think the first time I suffered was a direct result of my biting my toe nails. Can you imagine that? Don't try! In those days I was a very supple, long-legged kid.

Imagine had I studied and even practised yoga! Maybe my action might have been much smoother, instead of bowling right arm over left earhole, with my legs crossed in the delivery stride? Still, it's difficult to be both good looking and pretty on your feet!

I matured slowly and by the ripe old age of nineteen, when finally learning to shave (although I didn't need to), I was taking my sport very seriously, especially my football!

Perhaps I was guilty of neglecting my feet at the expense of the fluff on my face. The result was an in-grown toe nail. Precisely what I didn't need at the beginning of the 1967 VFL season with so much fitness work and kicking of the football to do.

Yes, it did hurt to kick! My big toe hurt a lot. It even hurt to put my street shoes on . . . thongs were more the order of the day!

Consequently I fronted up to practice one cold and wet Tuesday night in April hoping not to have to train. I walked into the medical room only metres past the numbered, grey metal lockers in the Melbourne Football Club's dressing room at the Melbourne Cricket Ground.

The first person I ran into was our medico, Bob Ashbey, who took one look and referred me immediately to our physiotherapist at the time. The Demons used to go through them like half-back flankers!

After asking the educated man if it was possible to give me a couple of pills to fix up my badly festered toe, he said, "The medical profession has come a long way but unfortunately for you – not that far!"

He confirmed my worst thoughts – there was no pill in the world capable of fixing an inflamed and badly infected in-grown toe nail!

This made me reflect on how it happened . . . I really don't know! I'm sure I regularly cut the little "v" in the middle of the nail. Maybe I hadn't cut the toe-nail square on the end of that ugly hammer-head toe. Even if I did everything a young footballer ought to do. All these beliefs weren't going to fix my toe.

Confront the problem like a man, I kept telling myself, unfortunately the club doctor didn't appear at training that evening. This meant I had all night to contemplate what the Doc might have to consider to cure my condition. A warped imagination didn't help me sleep.

My confrontation with Dr Colin Galbraith, the MFC club doctor, turned out to be pretty horrific. After exchanging the normal pleasantries in the consulting rooms at the rear of his house, we settled down to the business of a remedy.

Soon I was sitting on a very low stool, exposing my right foot for him to inspect. Expecting the worst, I was naturally on edge, And when he grabbed my big toe in his right hand it was like levitation – I rose about half a metre vertically off the stool in response to the acute pain!

Doctors sometimes suggest they have to be cruel to be kind – well they're not wrong! When he let go of my foot, the doctor said in a jovial manner: "I've got just the thing to fix this up my boy!"

He walked away to the antique, roll-top desk. All I could hear and see was what appeared to be re-arranging of papers. When Doc finally turned around, there before my eyes was . . . this huge needle about 15 centimetres long!

Before I could prevent my cold-hearted friend from grabbing my toe again, he had it in a vice-like grip. Then with a great deal of conviction, almost pleasure, the silver haired, bespectacled doctor plunged the shiny silver needle deep into the heart of my much throbbing toe – the pain was excruciating to say the least and this was supposed to be a pain-killing injection. I wanted to shout, but no sound came forth . . . like a goldfish.

Next he opted for a second dash at the action. This time he drove the pain killer into the top of the rather red big toe. At this stage, not only was a yellow looking liquid seeping from the edge of the toe-nail, but my eyes were also beginning to well with moisture.

I almost blacked out when the third and final jab scored a direct hit below the toe.

It seemed like eternity before the toe "deadened". Now for the real heavy stuff! The doctor began to cut out the offending piece of jagged nail from deep in the edge of my big toe. I was still conscious . . . surgical scissors performing their task – a precise cut was made parallel to the edge of my toe. Then a change of instrument – a pair of right angled scissors were produced. Blood was freely flowing from the wound, despite the lack of feeling, I didn't like it!

The good doctor continued the "operation" with a right angled cut – this was too much! I fainted and fell face first towards the floor.

Quickly I was helped to a nearby couch. I remember feeling very groggy when I came to. I know all we're talking about is an in-grown toe-nail but the pain was unbearable. "Never again!" I said to myself as I limped out of the surgery.

Quite incredibly the same nail and toe became infected again . . . and we did it all over again a week or two later – and believe me the procedure wasn't easier the second time around.

My big toe kept me out of action for three weeks – we don't appreciate how important our feet are! Do we?

So if you bite your toe-nails be careful!!

CHAPTER NINE

The Serious Business of Having Fun

The One that Got Away

"THE FINE NYLON CORD CUT LIKE A KNIFE THROUGH MY INDEX FINGER"

The 55 kg breaking strain nylon fishing line snapped as the tiny loop around the small metal bollard fastened tightly. Whatever had momentarily taken the bait on the end of my rapidly diminishing handline, treated the fine, almost invisible thread, like a piece of cotton!

It was difficult for a relatively non sea-loving person like myself to gauge the power and dimensions of the creature lurking beneath the sparkling blue-green tropical waters. Not to mention the potential danger!

The action of my leather-gloved companion in yanking against the drag of the tackle, then gaining sufficient slack to loop it around the chrome-plated fixture on the boat's handrail, certainly saved me from getting wet, maybe even losing the bottom half of my right leg. True to form, I had tangled most of the line in a huge mess beneath my feet. No wonder my nickname's Tanglefoot!

This little saga had begun by pulling in what I thought was about 3 or 4 kilos of fish, but some monster of a fish had other ideas and must have followed my catch on its painful journey to the surface.

Then, without warning, my hand-line whistled through helpless fingers at a frantic pace, back into the depths below. The fine nylon cord cut like a knife through the index finger of my right hand. Blood streamed freely from the widening wound . . . a burning sensation followed and I immediately let go of the line.

My bare feet thrashed up and down like a piston in an attempt to keep clear of the snaking fishing line as it disappeared over the edge.

Directions were being shouted at me from everyone, but too late. I was desperately in trouble with my footwork – the pale green fishing line was pulling taut against my right leg, just above the ankle . . . three or more coils tightened. Blood started to dribble slowly down my leg . . .

Even worse was that I was being dragged overboard . . . by the leg! Yes, the huge fish, or whatever, was winning this tug of war, and I couldn't get my hand near the razor sharp line! Not that it would have done much good without a glove!

My host, Gary, realised the seriousness of my predicament before my head crashed against the aluminium bottom of the twin-hulled shark cat. What a sight – a six foot four human scarecrow striking a rather inelegant pose with legs pointing skyward.

His experience quickly showed as he grabbed my line, and as they say . . . the rest is history. A classic case of the one that got away. He would have been a beauty! But . . . just as well that line snapped, eh?

My predicament was purely a laughing matter for my mate, Dougie Walters, but I shudder to think what might have happened had I splashed overboard and into the ocean.

Mind you, there was no shortage of sarcastic suggestions for about fifteen minutes . . . "See, Tangles you could have ended up like that guy who tried to harpoon Moby Dick and you didn't even throw a dart . . . !" or "Gee, Tang, you might have drowned."

My mates on board continued to take the mickey out of my painful, unfortunate incident as I patched up my wounds. A bandaid sufficed on my index finger but my white leg looked like a pillar from an old fashioned barber's shop. And the salt water in my cuts didn't help much either.

The accident taught me a couple of hard lessons.

Firstly, never wear thongs in a boat while you're fishing, and definitely don't wrap the hand-line around your fingers when fishing in deep waters – you may lose 'em! Still one learns by experience. But what an experience – and the action didn't stop there!

The secret location where our guides stopped to wet the lines was called "The Chasm" – about an hour off the coast of Groote Eylandt in the Gulf of Carpentaria, east of Darwin.

We were taken to the spot by two off-duty Northern Territory policemen, who turned out to be magnificent hosts. They also mentioned to us that it would be merely a matter of dropping down anchor, and the fish would literally jump into the boat . . . and strangely it turned out to be exactly that way, except in my case, I almost ended up in the drink!

Everything was just beginning to quieten down again . . . including the mocking laughter, when I was asked to have a look over the side of the boat, opposite to where I was fishing. It was still only 7 a.m. with the sun barely in the sky.

I could see by the expression on Dougie's face I really ought to take a peep! No cheeky grin, his eyes narrowed and what little colour he had in his cheeks disappeared. In front of me was the biggest fish I've ever seen!! There it was, a huge, charcoal grey shadow gently nudging our craft, only an arm's length away from where I stood, speechless.

I could tell the fish was a shark because I'd sat through Jaws 1, 2 and 3 with extreme discomfort. And I know a shark fin when I see one.

This fella must have been almost 8 metres long . . . like a baby submarine. One of the policemen suggested we shoot it . . . in fact he even took aim with his hand gun.

But judging by its size, I reckon the bullet would have merely ricocheted off the shark's sinister skin – this may have been the beauty I missed, and just as well too! Because with him on tow I know who would be taking who for a ride.

Once the blood from my wound stopped and the giant shark disappeared from the scene, we got on with the job of serious fishing.

In all, our catch consisted of a variety of fish – about fifty-five of 'em! And as predicted the fishing had been just a matter of putting bait on the hook and dropping it in the ocean. I soon regained my confidence to land a 20 kilo jew fish . . . Dougie's best effort was a miniature 3 or 4 kilo catch.

All this happened after I'd completed reading the script for a new television commercial . . . yours truly was cast in the role, unfairly, as the world's worst fisherman.

Who do you think my partner in the dinghy was to be? My mate and former cricketing great Dougie Walters. We were both happy to be drinking the product – Tooheys 2.2 light beer.

The shoot turned out to be very funny for all involved except Dougie. Our dinghy was the most unstable vessel I have ever been asked to go fishing in – 1.5 metres of round-bottomed aluminium with two baby oars.

The concept was for both "heroes" to end up overboard after successfully delivering our scripted lines. But nobody had mentioned this to Doug. In all we had seven identical pairs of shorts and tee-shirts . . . in case we didn't get our words right first up. Yes, we were going to get very wet and more than once . . . just so the cameraman could get his act together. The other fact that Dashing Doug failed to mention was that he couldn't swim . . . minor detail but nevertheless important 50 metres from shore.

Well, sure enough, the first time I rock the boat and upend Doug in the process . . . I knee him on the back of the head as we fall into the sea.

The boy from Dungog in New South Wales bobbed up about 5 metres from me shouting, "Help, Tangles, help!!"

Now what would you do if one of the great practical jokers of the world asks for help . . . you just let him sink back under for a second dip.

As he surfaced again . . . looking and sounding in real stress I must admit I thought twice . . . "Help, help, help . . .!" The cries became more frantic but I still thought he was having a lend of me. So under the water went his head again.

Finally, as he surfaced for the *third* time I could see he'd swallowed copious quantities of sea water and was in real trouble.

This is where my *Herald* Learn to Swim Certificate came in handy. I cupped my hand under his chin and instructed him not to struggle or I'd knock him out completely.

Slowly but surely the pair of us progressed towards the beach to the waiting gathering of anxious onlookers.

There were two options. One was to press on his ribcage then extend his arms to work his lungs. The other was not a nice alternative . . . mouth-to-mouth resuscitation with a bloke who smokes eighty cigarettes, on a good day.

I whispered in Doug's ear that I thought the world of him but not enough to suck lips with him, so pressure on the ribs it was.

Most importantly, I had to drag his bum out of the water as I stretched the water-logged Aussie legend onto the wet sand . . . because had it remained even in two or three inches I would have siphoned half the ocean . . . in one end and out the other.

As it was he coughed up plenty . . . and I doubt if he'd ever felt that crook even after a long innings on the Tooheys.

White Man Down a Hole

"I REACHED THE SAFETY OF A FARAWAY TUNNEL WITH SEVENTY-THREE SECONDS TO SPARE"

I've played cricket in almost every cricketing country in the world. Some of the Test match venues have had a beautiful lush green covering of turf, combed in a geometric pattern similar to the equally well prepared centre wicket area, at Lord's in England.

Other grounds such as Port of Spain in Trinidad, used to make diving in the outfield feel a bit like diving on razor blades – the wicket itself was not unlike grade nine sandpaper, a very abrasive surface indeed – hard baked mud with grass showings sprinkled on to hold the pitch together.

But never have I seen anything quite like the football-cum-cricket ground at Coober Pedy.

It even has a racetrack around the perimeter, if you could call it that! I'm sure the scant metal pipe fencing is only to stop the cheeky little jockeys from taking a short cut across the playing area. Many people have said to me, "It's different in the centre", and they're not wrong. Wonderfully different!

For many years I have been very keen to travel to the red centre of this great country of ours. I've seen too many first class hotels and major cricket grounds in Australia's populated cities around the coastline. "What is the real Australia like?" That's the question a "little fella" inside of me has been continually asking.

Well, now I know first hand and believe me I'm not disappointed. Incredible!

It has been said that the only way to achieve anything in life is to make it happen yourself. Well, make it happen I did. With the help of my good friend Graham Charlton from radio station 5RM Berri in South Australia, a speaking engagement was arranged for me in Coober Pedy. Coober Pedy is an Aboriginal name for "white man in a hole". It seemed a fairly apt description after seeing some of the dwellings of the residents.

Driving from Adelaide, as we approached this unique town, the horizon appeared much like a purple moonscape. The setting sun brought down the curtain on a fabulous day, rich in red dust and brilliant blue skies. Everywhere we looked were huge ant-hills or mullock heaps – piles of waste rock and earth collected neatly on the barren surface.

My reason for being there was to entertain the locals at a sports-man's night. I wondered how many people would turn up to see me perform at the Opal Inn. In fact how many of the townspeople even knew who Max Walker was?

The answer could not have been more pleasant – especially as it was a Saturday night and we were competing with the re-opening of Porky's night club just down the road.

The night was mixed for gals and guys – standing room only. There was, of course, the odd rowdy element and local comedian in the audience but it all added to a very good night. The hospitality of the community was as good as I've ever received.

I was standing at the bar after I had spoken, when Terry and Peter made themselves known . . . I'm not sure, but it must have been well after midnight.

They were a couple of genuine guys – opal miners, who, by the way, had already had a pretty terrific night. So it seemed crazy at this hour to be making serious plans to go below the earth's surface at 7 o'clock in the morning in search of that rare and wondrous gem – the opal.

I thought: "Why not – you're dead a long time, and I'll never get another opportunity to mine opals." I just wasn't quite sure what to expect.

Nevertheless shortly before 8 a.m. I found myself sitting on a piece of scantling timber about 50 x 24 mm in section, fitted crudely to a steel wire pulley system to form a lowering apparatus. That was to be my ride down into the depths of the mine – a bit hard on the bum and not the same secure feeling of the Myers elevator. Anyway, worse was still to come.

I had to fit down a one metre wide access shaft which was about twenty metres deep. My two mates had disappeared below the surface with just the steel cable for support and a plastic stack hat on their heads in case a rock fell down on top of them – nice thought, and very possible too!

Only a corrugated iron tank, with the top and bottom missing, prevented the surface edge of the hole caving in. A very flimsy looking rusty ladder hung from a casually resting 50 mm steel pipe on one side of the small opening, just in case any trouble was encountered.

My first problem was the length of my leg from the seat of my pants to the point of my knee cap. It was looking as if I might have to go down standing up and not sitting down – what was I doing here?

Well, I did make it to the bottom, but not without collecting every second rung of that metal ladder with my awkwardly folded knees, as I rotated anti-clockwise to the bottom. Housemaid's knees had nothing on this! – both of mine felt like they had St Peter's church bells ringing inside them. I suppose being that far underground coupled with my precarious surroundings didn't raise my pain tolerance one little bit either!

Surprisingly, the space below was like a well defined cave with drives or tunnels shooting off in seven or eight directions.

We were told that geologically, Australia is the world's oldest land, with some of its rock being formed as long ago as three billion years, and that ninety-five percent of the world's opals are mined in Australia.

Millions of years ago, non-crystalline silica gel seeped into crevices and cracks in the sedimentary strata. Gradually over eons, the gel hardened, capturing within it darting, glowing colours that dance and leap as different angles of light bring them to the surface. Opals have a life and inner fire all of their own.

Black opal is the most sought-after . . . in fact more valuable than diamonds. It is extremely rare and considered to be the ultimate in gem beauty – a bit like holding a little bit of outer space in your hand – filled with stars of brilliant colours.

Time was of the essence, and it didn't take the bearded Peter long to get down to business. He quickly set about making up nine explosives. To him it was like making up a paper bag full of lollies. I said, "What happens if one of those things goes off?" His reply was simple: "I wouldn't worry too much – if it does go up you're not going to know much about it anyway!" A nice comforting thought, eh?

Each of the long, slender, brown paper bags, approximately 50 mm in diameter, was gently filled with tiny grains of Nitro-Pril. I didn't bother to ask Peter what Nitro-Pril was but I had a fair idea! One by one they were placed almost lovingly on the rough textured sandstone floor.

Idle, nervous chatter continued until all the explosives were knotted and positioned inside the sinister little bags. When all nine were completed, wicks intact, the tiny, lethal detonators were taped to each stick – just like in the movies!

Now the morning was beginning to get interesting. I quickly scraped the sleep and dust from the corner of each eye . . . the wheels inside my head were really turning . . . what about the small print in my insurance policy? Too late to read it now I guess! My heartbeat increased three-fold.

With just a small filament globe for light, all four of us, including the stockily built Terry, moved to the end of a nearby drive. This was to be the face to blast. Any debris or rock from the previous blasting was removed with the help of a very powerful vacuum pump connected to a generator above ground . . . gives some perspective to a tarantula being sucked up by a vacuum cleaner at home!

The last time I had a brace 'n' bit in my hands must have been during my years as a student of architecture. But never one which measured two metres long and 50 or 60 mm in diameter. It was double hernia material just to pick this one up. When I pressed the trigger, all the meat balls, pies, sandwiches and saveloys from the previous night came perilously close to the top.

Terry would have made a great orchardist. The symmetry of the freshly drilled nine holes in the stark rock face was excellent. Just like a lovely row of apple trees back in Tassie!

Terry and Peter said I could have the dubious honour of lighting the first wick. Eighty seconds was all the time we had from the lighting of wick number one to wick number nine. By the 80 second mark the first big bang was guaranteed.

The tomcat's tail (or wick) dangling at my right hand side got my approval. Ideally I would light the fuse creating a spark and puff of smoke and pose for a picture at the same time. "Let's be bloody quick then and no second takes, okay!" was my firm answer.

With a mini-gas flame thrower in my hand, I gingerly crouched in position . . . cameras, aim, action! Just as a fierce orange and yellow flame extended from my small oxy-acetylene-type lighter, Peter, who placed himself directly behind me, pressed the trigger of the industrial jack-hammer he was leaning on. "Bzzzzzt ttbzztt!" I'm glad my trousers were tucked in – because scared was not the word!

I successfully lit the fuse. The small igniting device now took on the proportion of a relay runner's baton. A perfect change-over was effected from my right hand to a smirking Terry. The seconds were rapidly passing by . . . eventually all nine fuses were alight. Pace was never one of my greatest attributes, but I reached the safety of a far-away tunnel with seventy-three seconds to spare. I was totally, absolutely and comprehensively terrified!

Some forty seconds later the two "pros" appeared in the tunnel looking very calm about proceedings. Fellow visitor Brian and I were told to put our earplugs in and brace ourselves for the explosion – Terry and Peter used only their index fingers, seeing that we had their plugs.

Boooom, boom, boom, boom, boom, boooooom . . . the two visitors plus the effervescent Terry could only count eight bangs! "What now my friend"? It was a big question.

The percussion from the blasting had sent quite a substantial vibration from my toes to the top of my skull . . . it was an exceptionally unnerving experience.

Silence reigned supreme. Just moments later a thick wall of brown dust caused by the explosion engulfed our bodies on its journey to the extremities of each tunnel or shaft. It took quite a while for the dust to settle and the colour to return to our faces.

Still, the problem remained – what happened to number nine? Did two go off simultaneously – one bang – or is there still one "live bugger" left?

I wasn't about to volunteer going back into that rabbit warren full of rock and dust. Brian's eyes had "NO" fully imprinted across the face of them . . . his eyebrows heavy with the burden of freshly landed red and white dust plus the urgency of the problem.

Terry, with the words, "I dig it mate", stretched across his T-shirt, decided everything was okay and ventured back into the silence of the doubtful tunnel.

He left with a poker face but returned with a flashing grin like the entry to Luna Park. "I don't know what you blokes were worried about, no problems, looking good!" he stated.

Brian and myself still weren't convinced, but we didn't want to look too much like squibs. Mind you, we could just as easily have been dead heroes!

I laugh now but it was deadly serious at the time. Many old timers have died in similar circumstances . . .

Ten minutes later all the fallen rock had been sucked to the surface and we were ready to dig opal. You bloody beauty!

I think at that precise moment I was bitten by the bug. The possibility of finding a rare specimen of opalised fossil, or similar, felt like a big chance. Adrenalin started to pump as my eyes bounced up and down the rockface . . .

After investigating the newly exposed wall, Peter began to dig with the deafening jackhammer. Next my turn came, and I discovered how energy-sapping it could be. Nevertheless, if I were to find a fossilised opal the size of a scallop shell, I'm sure I'd find a second wind.

Well, I didn't find one and my shoulder was soon beginning to feel like a toothache. The boys were laughing – I was supposed to be fit.

The hand pick took on the weight of a toothpick by comparison, as I eased flakes of "potch"from sedimentary layers above my head, not knowing what the next swing would prise away.

I became more and more excited wondering, if I found an opal, how to get it out of the mine without them knowing!

Well, the problem didn't eventuate, and back at Peter's dug-out, bags and bottles of cut and uncut opals were produced, along with the scales. I really couldn't go home empty-handed could I, and when a couple of beauties caught my eye, the trouser pocket lightened its load. A couple of the gems caught my eye and I made a purchase or two. I only hope I have more luck than I've had with my diamond and gold trading.

Mixing with the Underworld

"SOME CANDLE, IT WAS A STICK OF GELIGNITE"

It was barely 8 a.m. when the security guard on duty at the Olympic Dam Project site lifted the boom gate to allow the red Falcon entry. My passengers Graham Charlton and Brian Tolhurst were pretty excited at the prospect of exploring the largest uranium ore deposit in the world.

The mere mention of the name Roxby Downs can bring forth an incredibly wide range of reactions from friends and strangers alike. Uranium is a very emotional and political subject – group it with South African and religion and you've got the trifecta!

Not many people are given the privilege of a guided tour of the mine – so Graham, Brian and myself jumped at the chance. I might add that the closer we were to actually entering the earth's depths, the more apprehensive we became. In fact it would be fair to say we were pretty scared – and in Graham's case very frightened! He claimed he was both terrified of heights and suffered from claustrophobia – that's no prerequisite for a day in the mines, eh?

Jim Perkins, the man responsible for my visit to the development site, made sure we were well organised and pointed in the right direction – down.

It was a gutsy effort because not only did Jim set up and attend my speaking engagement – he worked night shift right through the early hours and was still with us when we came out of the mine shaft, four hours later. I like the man's stamina. He'd have made a good medium pacer!

We checked in at the administration block a short distance from the mine shaft. By just reading a few of the signs fixed to the walls of the temporary building, it was easy to see we were in a restricted area: "Private Property" and "Trespassers Will Be Prosecuted" notices everywhere. I briefly thought about the potential for my mates and myself becoming radioactive. Uranium has that effect on you! We'd glow at night, eh? No need to turn the lights on at the MCG for night cricket now!

The procedure for checking in was a bit like entering jail, not that I've been in the lock-up thank goodness.

First we signed a book, handed in our valuables, and were told to strip to our underpants. I said to the others, "I hope they are not going to do a body search as well, it could be a bit embarrassing, eh?" They sheepishly agreed, trying to quickly camouflage their polar bear white bodies. Three better tans you wouldn't find on three Eskimos!

Dressed in our green all-in-ones and oversize gum boots, we reported to the front desk again. Immediately we were issued with a stack hat complete with battery-operated miner's light – high and low beam too! . . . a very heavy, bright blue belt fitted with a battery pack for the floodlight and a safety respirator.

Being naturally inquisitive I asked what it was for. "That's in case something goes wrong down there!" was the reply. "Don't want to get carbon monoxide poisoning, do you?" We all agreed with a simultaneous shake of our heads. Last of all, the bright orange ear-muffs and a brief instruction on how to use the equipment if bad luck and a lot of rock fell on us. Nasty thought, that. The closer we got to the mine shaft and lift, the more prevalent these thoughts became.

Seven of us stood like sardines in yellow raincoats, jammed in a rusty-looking steel bucket. They referred to it as a lift but we hadn't even left the surface and it already felt very unstable. I looked above me to see several metal ropes disappear over the large guide wheels at the top of the scaffold-like construction tower. The lift was controlled manually from a room some 30 metres away. Here two men are responsible for getting all personnel in and out of the mine as well as getting the copper, gold and uranium ore to the surface.

The ride down was of very poor quality – far inferior to any office block elevator. On the way down it became obvious why we had our raincoats on and our cameras in a plastic bag. Artesian waters spilled down the sides of the crudely cut shaft and onto our colourful helmets. The spillage of water from my stack hat almost drowned the fellas adjacent during the 480 metre journey.

It seemed like eternity getting down and there was no light either – it was impossible for anyone to lift an arm to turn on the floodlights attached to each stack hat.

The steel cable stretched some one and a half metres, I reckon, as we pulled up short of our exit level in the pitch-black, hot mine shaft – we began to bob up and down like a yo-yo. Frightening stuff. Several expletives were uttered to relieve the nervous tension.

We filed out of the lift like the seven dwarfs strolling after Snow White, Indian file. Now for the action.

To my amazement it was just like a mini township carved out of the earth, between 300 and 500 metres below the ground. It was mentioned that the mineral deposits present extend to some twenty-six square miles or the size of a city like Adelaide. Mining was being carried out on three levels within the rich deposit range.

The speed limit along any tunnel was 8 kmh – forwards or backwards. Some of the vehicular machinery was enormous. Fifty tonne pickup trucks with wheels the size of a man and with flashing blue lights were a common sight.

Most of the larger tunnel walls and ceilings had been sprayed white to reflect the light from fluorescent fixtures which disappeared into tiny white spots along the direction of each excavation. Everywhere safety signs confronted us as a sure indication of the serious and dangerous mode of operations carried out. The movement of air fascinated me. Large canvas, fan-driven socks were slung from wall fixtures along with the power and water tubing. It was possible to move the air from its intake position to 600 metres into each level.

The relative levels of each shaft were clearly marked on the rock face in large bold black numbers. Each level had been accurately plotted with the use of a laser beam.

Three hours below ground seemed like half an hour, I couldn't get enough of the place. The weight of my emergency power pack and safety respirator became almost non-existent as I continually aimed my camera at a new and different aspect of the mining process.

There were about 300 personnel on the site keeping the mine operational around the clock.

We travelled the length and breadth of the developed mine in a filthy white jeep, sending out a wake of mud. It was like being in the movie *Indiana Jones and The Temple of Doom*. You drive around almost oblivious to what's happening just around the corner, because of the continual sound of the mine. Every now and then a 50 tonne loader approached and it would threaten and intimidate the uninitiated in such a confined space – which was just the width of the pick-up trucks in many cases.

On the way to a drilling site, I sat on something on the car seat which felt a bit similar to a candle. Some candle! It was a stick of gelignite without the detonator! My heartbeat increased twofold especially after being warned not to take photographs of the explosive stores because the heat of the flashlight might send the entire area up in smoke. Needless to say I was very careful where I aimed my camera.

The driller is a skilled man. We talked to Steve and his understudy, or apprentice, Joe. Once an ore deposit is established, the driller prepares the drive face for the powder monkey to come in and set the explosives. The skill of these men is evident when watching the precision used to position about seventy holes to accept the sticks of gelignite.

Apparently the technique is to plan the drilling chart in parallel lines and diagonals, with a couple of extra sticks in the middle so that the fractures focus towards the middle of the explosion, bringing the rock face down. The machinery used to make these holes is a bit like a multi-armed dentist's drill, on wheels. My teeth ached just looking at it.

Then the powder monkeys come in behind the drillers, clear the area, and set the explosives in position. A count-down and then "Boooooomm!" Even though we were some 70 metres from the blasting, the vibration in the ribcage was unreal. So too was the sound and movement of air.

Now I know what it must feel like to be a fish in the river when some crazy person decides to use dynamite instead of a bent nail.

Generally an explosion of that dimension will increase the tunnel or shaft by removing 400 tonnes of rock. That is in volume six metres wide, about 4.5 metres high and up to 3.8 metres in depth. Some blast, eh?

Then along come the team of extractors and their heavy mobilised machinery to transport the rock to an area called the open hole. With the use of a large vibrating machine, the ore is collected ready for relay to daylight. The capacity of each bucket lifted to the surface is about six tonnes, and the trip up takes on average 100 seconds.

In all a fascinating and eye-opening experience. Time was against us as we had to be in other parts of South Australia that night. But we couldn't leave without eating at the "Hard Rock Cafe", also underground.

A cup of coffee took the dusty coating from my tongue and I could even bring myself to tackle the meat pies from the micro-wave oven.

I'd taken my hard hat off to drink, placed it on the table and forgotten about it. On the word "go" I immediately jumped to my feet ready to catch our ride upstairs, forgot about my helmet, which was attached to my battery pack, comfortably supported by my buttocks. The result was a runaway helmet on the table top and tangled lead around my feet. Sugar, sauce and tupperware containers, followed me to the floor. It is a good thing I'm not a miner.

Well, I'd done it again!

Real Cricket in the Red Dust

"A WICKETKEEPER HAD BROKEN HIS HAND TRYING TO REMOVE THE BAILS"

The day was March 13, 1985. I'm not superstitious but . . . I woke up with a start as my head bounced off the passenger door window. Coming straight at our car at 120 kmh, was a yellow and black, diamond-shaped sign post saying: FLOODWAY.

In that split second of opening my eyes it was terrifyingly obvious that the car in which I was a passenger was not on the black bitumen stuff where it ought to have been!

There was no question and no escape – we were definitely going to crash into the post. In fact we hit it dead centre and it buckled like a tooth-pick. The next few seconds were horrific to say the least.

The metal sign crashed into the windscreen right in front of my eyes. Splinters of glass flew everywhere as the window crazed like a spider's web.

My door began to open but I pulled against it. The potentially lethal sign somehow didn't get through the window but ricocheted over the bonnet as the car began to spin.

I momentarily felt like Steve McQueen filming *Bullit* but what a waste – there were no cameras.

Finally, the car came to a standstill after completing about eight loop-the-loops over the red dust and short-tufted scrub grass. My arm was aching from holding the passenger's door shut against the force of gravity. At this stage I had stopped screaming expletives!

Lionel, the driver, looked ashen. The colour returned, except for the knuckles of his fingers tightly gripping the steering wheel. A deathly silence prevailed.

Yes, we were very lucky to be alive after leaving the road at such a speed and not rolling the vehicle.

We were on our way to a speaking engagement at Leigh Creek football and cricket clubs, some five hours driving north of Adelaide.

As I looked back to the road, I could see the mangled signpost about 100 metres away pointing to the sky like a scorpion's tale.

I also noticed a two-metre wide concrete culvert or waterway only ten metres from where the car had stopping spinning . . . again I recounted all the possibilities. We sure were lucky!

Within minutes a big blue Range Rover came to an abrupt halt in a cloud of dust and two guys, Dave and Leon, rushed over to see what had happened.

As I found out later, this occasion wasn't the first time these two blokes had stopped to lend a helping hand. "Anyone hurt?" they shouted, scampering quickly towards Lionel and myself.

All four of us did a complete lap of honor, inspecting the white, late model Ford Falcon. By the time we had completed the enlightening walk, I noticed Leon staring at me.

He thought he'd seen me somewhere before but the penny didn't drop quickly for him. Then again, I guess he thought, "What's Dennis Lillee or maybe Max Walker doing in the region of the iron triangle? No, it couldn't be him!!" After all, we were a long way from the hallowed turf of the MCG.

I felt a pain in my left hand, blood was dripping from my fingertips. Lionel said: "Max, are you all right?" then Leon, the short, yet enormously wide man, smiled with recognition.

He must have weighed twenty-three stone (convert that to metric if you can), dressed for the journey in blue singlet and shorts, topped off with a very much unpressed khaki shirt.

His thin mate Dave's trousers told the story of his trade, such was the amount of grease on them. In many ways together they appeared like the original Laurel and Hardy team – Leon providing the laughs while Dave was the straight man.

Boy, were we glad to see them as we stood in front of the crumpled bonnet and watched the tell-tale spiral of steam escape from our badly damaged radiator.

All efforts to prise open the bonnet failed until a crowbar was produced. Watching Lionel perspiring profusely as he worked, any hope of the car being driveable was quickly diminishing.

Then, the sound of air brakes punctuated the outback silence. We looked up and saw a magnificent road train pull up, chrome shining. In circumstances like these you reflect on the world and there really are some tremendous people around. The first two vehicles to come our way had stopped and couldn't do enough for us.

The two-way radio inside the cabin was of great assistance in calling the local Ford dealer in Quovis. Lionel stayed with his car on the roadside and waited while everyone agreed I should continue on to Leigh Creek.

As luck would have it, Dave and Leon were going to Leigh Creek to send several pieces of heavy earthmoving equipment on the train to Port Augusta.

Some 100 kilometres down the road the reason became clear why Lionel wanted to stay with his stationary car. My new friends described many an incident of cars being stripped whilst the owner went for petrol or the car had been left after a crash.

Dave had learnt the lesson in an unusual way. He'd completed jacking up his car to change a flat tyre, while his mate looked on from his own car parked in front. A late model sports car pulled up behind both of them. A guy in trendy gear jumped out, raced over to Dave and said: "Let's not be greedy, eh? You take the back tyres and I'll take the front two!" Dave couldn't believe his ears as he shouted, "It's my bloody car!"

His reaction saw the shifty character hightail his car off into the distance at extremely high speed.

When we finally arrived at our destination, words didn't seem to be enough to express how grateful I was for Dave and Leon's help. Maybe one day I will be able to reciprocate.

After a quick shower, my room at the canteen soon became the venue for some cricket stories. This time I was listening . . . fascinated by some real red dust Australian tales of bat and ball.

The match was an annual event played for the fourth time between Wilpoorinna, a team provided by wealthy station owners, the Litchfield family, and of course the Leigh Creek boys, selected from those still standing and available.

I hadn't heard of the Wilpoorinna Sporting Complex before – this apparently was where the game was played.

An early disappointment was the fact that "Two Step Terry" the president of LCFC would be unavailable due to poisoning – it's not known what sort but I doubt if you'd need a medical degree to guess.

The wicket itself was a four feet wide concrete test strip laid by an inexperienced local. From end-to-end there was no less than a six-inch fall – talk about the ridge at Lords!

A boundary line was achieved by dragging around a fallen log behind a horse about sixty-five yards from the concrete pitch, thus forming a groove. The outfield consisted of Leigh Creek "mulch" or basically a lot of rocks and no grass – no curator needed at this ground.

The main pavilion was two horse drays and a canvas secured only by logs – this provided limited shade considering temperatures regularly hit forty-five degrees Celsius in this part of Australia. In the outer I'm told were a couple of EH Holdens with their own tent outhouses and well-stocked coolers.

The stumps fascinated me – firmly set in concrete and made from one piece of flat metal – and the metal bails were welded on! This had been a contentious point because in an earlier game a wicketkeeper had broken his hand trying to remove the bails! There was even talk of removing the bails with a hack saw blade!

Beside each of the fieldsman's feet it is not unusual to spot a stubby marking his position. The general idea with these "markers" is to break your mate's stubby with a rock before he can drink it.

Three cork cricket balls are used per innings because of wear and tear caused by the rocky surroundings. Fieldsmen obviously don't dive in these games because the possibility of the ball ricocheting into your face from the rocks is very real. As they say in Leigh Creek, you can either be a dead hero or a squib.

Because of the type of balls used, the bats themselves are covered with black polypipe melted by oxy-torches and shrunk around the face of the bat – most bats weigh around 4 pounds. You'd need forearms like Rod Marsh to lift one, eh?

Casualties were a common occurrence, the worst being "Kempie" who had only just returned to Wilpoorinna. He was on ten looking for a second run after a particularly fast single, when he ran smack bang into George Menangitus, a new school teacher in the town. The final outcome was ten stitches in the chin. And he'd just driven 600 kilometres from Mt Barker to play. Then he drove eighty km to hospital and desperately drove the return eighty km to the club only to find the beer off and the club shut! You can't beat bad luck.

One interesting dismissal entered into the score sheet on the back of a piece of cardboard was: "Thommo" caught Tort (wicketkeeper) bowled Bouncie (swing bowler). Score – not many.

I should mention that Leigh Creek won this 1985 encounter for the first time in four years after scoring 124 in twenty overs. The contest raised $1500 for the Isolated Children's and Parents' Association and a great day was had by all.

That's what I call real cricket – no coloured gear, flash $5 million lighting and white balls.

Death of the President's Dog

"LILLEE RETURNED BRUSHING DOWN HIS JUMPER AND COMPLAINING ABOUT THE BLOODSTAINS"

A series of events during the 1973 Australian tour of the West Indies had us in stitches of laughter . . . even if they did cause some of the locals a slight embarrassment. This story really should be known as the "tale of the President's dog", and not surprisingly centres around that irrepressible character D.K. Lillee.

Although that tour was not a happy one for Dennis – he suffered a severe back injury which put him out of cricket for more than a year – he certainly did his bit to give the boys some comic relief off the field.

Lillee had developed a stunt which involved scaring the daylights out of the drivers who ferried us around in the team bus.

The buses we used had wooden slatted seats and no windows. In fact, very tinny conveyances all round.

One day our driver had been manoeuvring to squeeze the bus through a pair of large gate pillars, with plenty of encouragement from the lads.

Dennis leaned out of the window and nearly belted a hole in the red metal panelling with his fist. The sound was like a bomb exploding, and someone yelled "You've hit the bloody post you stupid fool!"

The poor driver slammed on the brakes, stalled the bus and was quickly out of the seat and around to inspect the damage, looking as if he was to face an execution squad for his folly. Of course he couldn't understand why there was still a good six inches of clearance between the bus and the post when he had clearly heard a crash.

Eventually he began to get the message, and even saw the funny side.

On another occasion when we were on a shopping expedition, Lillee and the same bus driver cooked up a bit of a stunt between them.

A very old jalopy was parked in the spot where the bus driver was supposed to be, so Lillee persuaded the driver to drive as fast as possible at the old wreck, pull up with a squeal of the motor and scream of tyres.

As he did so, Lillee and a couple of the others were out of the bus peering at the "damage" to the jalopy and of course berating our driver for his "carelessness".

This display caused the driver to laugh until the tears ran down his cheeks and he was laughing all the harder when out of the jalopy stepped two nuns in full regalia.

Suddenly the humour of the affair had disappeared for our man Lillee – and we saw no more of his favourite trick for quite a while.

One night however he decided it was about time for a comeback.

We were attending another of those tedious official functions that cricketers around the world have to endure. I can't even remember which island we were on, but I'm sure it was the President who threw this particular cocktail party. I know the team arrived after a long hot day's cricket and we didn't have time to have a meal beforehand.

Cricketers, like most sportsmen on tour, get a bit blasé about these functions. They are rather like hotels – once through the door you could be anywhere in the world.

But the setting for this party was extraordinary. We drove in through an enormous, white ornate gateway and along a driveway that seemed to stretch for a mile.

The house – more like a palace – was fronted with Corinthian columns and a huge flight of white marble steps led up to a doorway even more ornate than the gates.

Inside, there were vaulted ceilings towering twenty feet above us and the function was held in a ballroom that might well have featured in a Hollywood musical extravaganza.

As usual there were servants moving among the guests with paper-thin sardine sandwiches curled up at the edges and the drink was flowing like the Amazon.

But we were hungry and a group of us – team manager Bill Jacobs, Dennis Lillee, Greg Chappell, Kerry O'Keefe, and myself decided to take up an invitation from the Australian Trade Commissioner for a few drinks and some good Aussie pies and sauce at his residence.

Our transport that night happened to be a company operating under the name of Taboo Taxis.

We woke the driver from his slumber and gave him directions to the Trade Commissioner's house. As we approached the two white stone pillars of the gateway D.K. Lillee made his play.

He put his arm out of the window and gave the outside of the door a very heavy thump. Then he turned poker-faced and told the startled driver, "Look what you've done – you've run over the President's dog."

Quickly the fast bowler was out bending over the front wheel yowling for all the world like a dying dog. The noises were realistically blood-curdling. Lillee, shielded by the darkness kept up the mimickry. Then he carried the "body" over to the culvert as the "dog" gave its last gasp.

Lillee returned brushing down his jumper and complaining about the bloodstains. Greg Chappell intervened with his voice very serious too. "You'll have to go back and tell the President what you've done to his dog."

"I can't do that man," the driver wailed. "I've got a wife and six kids."

He had gone Persil white under his sun-tan.

"Then let's get the hell out of here," Lillee suggested.

We shot out on to the main road which must have been all of twenty feet wide and were making good time when Lillee struck again.

"Watch out for that dog!" he shouted.

There was a wild screech of brakes, the cab slewed sideways and the driver sat there quivering. "Hey, man, I didn't see nothing," he moaned.

"You didn't?" Lillee sounded incredulous. "It was a big black one. He ran right across the road in front of you. You only missed him by an inch."

Twice more in the next couple of miles there was a re-enactment of the scene. Lillee yelling, car slewing, driver perspiring and near to the point of collapse.

After the third incident we proceeded at a much more cautious pace and as luck would have it, the first lamp post we came to had a black and white spotted dog sitting at its base.

About 200 yards from the lonely post the driver dropped right through the gears back to first and crawled along at about half a mile an hour, all the time watching the dog for all he was worth.

Once past, he accelerated like a rocket into the night. The problem now was we had driven the driver into such a state of shock he was thoroughly lost. We had no idea of where we should be heading. We talked him into stopping at a run-down shanty shop to seek directions.

As we slowed down, a very old grey-haired fellow was alighting from an equally old push bike. The old bloke propped it up on the kerb as our cab pulled in close behind.

Lillee gave the outside of the door a further clout and low and behold the bike fell over of its own accord!

Dennis was immediately out of the car pretending to push the rear wheel of the bike back into shape watched by the old gentleman whose eyes were standing out like light globes.

Inside the cab the driver was getting a real bawling out, "You've hit the bloke's bike. It'll cost a fortune to fix. Are you drivers all blind?"

At that moment another car arrived on the scene. By sheer coincidence it was the Trade Commissioner. He stopped abruptly with puzzlement all over his face.

Bill Jacobs was quickly over to the other car explaining our little game to the Trade Commissioner.

He immediately entered into the spirit of the affair. He strode around to the front of the cab peered into the window and said: "I want to see your licence, driver."

The driver was in an absolute panic. He turned out his pockets, emptied the glove box . . . but no licence.

All the while he was telling the commissioner how poor he was, and how he had to support twelve children (amazing how the number doubled in half an hour!) Not to mention what a law abiding citizen he was.

The commissioner began to lecture the poor fellow on the seriousness of knocking down bicycles, but presumably he was getting as peckish as we were, because he brought the show to an end by instructing our driver to follow his car to the "station" where the matter would be more fully investigated.

He then led the way to his palatial home on a hill overlooking the city. Anything less like a West Indies police station would be difficult to imagine. There the driver received another lecture and the commissioner mentioned that another matter had come to his attention – that of the President's dog.

This brought forth a torrent of apologies from the hapless driver and a promise that nothing like it would ever happen again.

The poor fellow was then sent on his way but his ordeal was not over yet because the house was in a narrow dead-end street, and the cab had to go to the end, do a three-point turn and then come back past us.

Never one to let any opportunity slip by, Dennis grabbed hold of a lemon from a nearby tree and as the cab drew level, he let fly scoring a direct hit on the front mudguard.

For a fraction of a second the brakes were applied, then the driver stepped on the accelerator and the cab vanished in a whirl of blue smoke.

I don't remember much about the beer and pies, but I'll never forget that cab driver. And I have a suspicion that he'll never forget us!